Dear Reader,

Writing *My Baby, Your Child* was a truly heartening experience for me. Tackling the difficult subject of adoption, I was able to explore the many facets of love we experience in our lives.

For Tess, the painful choice of giving her baby up for adoption is made out of love. And years later, when that child's adoptive parents ask for her help in saving his life, again she responds out of love.

For Will, loving Tess could mean the loss of the only family he has. But his love for her is as strong and sure as her love for him. Together they find the peace and happiness they have always deserved, and together they bring a measure of peace and happiness to all those they love, as well.

I hope you enjoy reading *My Baby, Your Child* as much as I enjoyed writing it.

Nikki Benjamin

Heading to the Hitchin' Post

1. *Unforgettable Bride* by Annette Broadrick
2. *Precious Pretender* by Stella Bagwell
3. *Mail-Order Brood* by Arlene James
4. *A Willful Marriage* by Peggy Moreland
5. *Her Kind of Man* by Barbara McCauley
6. *Storming Paradise* by Mary McBride

He's a Cowboy!

7. *Christmas Kisses for a Dollar* by Laurie Paige
8. *Lone Wolf's Lady* by Beverly Barton
9. *Love, Honor and a Pregnant Bride* by Karen Rose Smith
10. *Some Kind of Hero* by Sandy Steen
11. *The Cowboy Takes a Lady* by Cindy Gerard
12. *The Outlaw and the City Slicker* by Debbi Rawlins

Lone Star Lullabies

13. *Texas Baby* by Joan Elliott Pickart
14. *Like Father, Like Son* by Elizabeth August
15. *Mike's Baby* by Mary Lynn Baxter
16. *Long Lost Husband* by Joleen Daniels
17. *Cowboy Cootchie-Coo* by Tina Leonard
18. *Daddy Was a Cowboy* by Jodi O'Donnell

Texas Tycoons

19. *The Water Baby* by Roz Denny Fox
20. *Too Many Bosses* by Jan Freed
21. *Two Brothers and a Bride* by Elizabeth Harbison
22. *Call Me* by Alison Kent
23. *One Ticket to Texas* by Jan Hudson
24. *His-and-Hers Family* by Bonnie K. Winn

Feisty Fillies

25. *A Girl's Best Friend* by Marie Ferrarella
26. *Bedded Bliss* by Heather MacAllister
27. *The Guardian's Bride* by Laurie Paige
28. *Millie and the Fugitive* by Liz Ireland
29. *My Baby, Your Child* by Nikki Benjamin
30. *Hannah's Hunks* by Bonnie Tucker

Trouble in Texas

31. *Guilty as Sin* by Cathy Gillen Thacker
32. *Family Ties* by Joanna Wayne
33. *Familiar Heart* by Caroline Burnes
34. *Double Vision* by Sheryl Lynn
35. *The Loner and the Lady* by Eileen Wilks
36. *Wild Innocence* by Ann Major

Men Most Wanted

37. *Lawman* by Laurie Grant
38. *Texas Lawman* by Ginger Chambers
39. *It Happened in Texas* by Darlene Graham
40. *Satan's Angel* by Kristin James
41. *The Lone Ranger* by Sharon De Vita
42. *Hide in Plain Sight* by Sara Orwig

Cuddlin' Kin

43. *West Texas Weddings* by Ginger Chambers
44. *A Mother for Jeffrey* by Patricia Kay
45. *Desperate* by Kay David
46. *Father in the Middle* by Phyllis Halldorson
47. *The Texas Touch* by Kate Thomas
48. *Child of Her Heart* by Arlene James

MY BABY, YOUR CHILD

Nikki Benjamin

Feisty Fillies

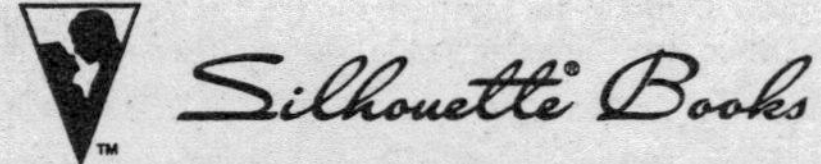

Published by Silhouette Books
America's Publisher of Contemporary Romance

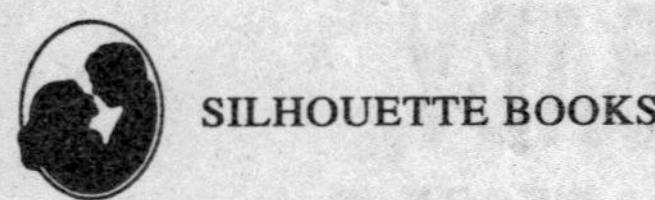

ISBN 0-373-65243-7

MY BABY, YOUR CHILD

This edition published by arrangement with Harlequin Books S.A.

Visit Silhouette at www.eHarlequin.com

Printed in U.S.A.

NIKKI BENJAMIN

was born and raised in the Midwest, but after years in the Houston area, she considers herself a true Texan. Nikki says she's always been an avid reader. (Her earliest literary heroines were Nancy Drew, Trixie Belden and Beany Malone.) Her writing experience was limited, however, until a friend started penning a novel and encouraged Nikki to do the same. One scene led to another, and soon she was hooked.

Books by Nikki Benjamin

Silhouette Special Edition

Emily's House #539
On the Whispering Wind #663
The Best Medicine #716
It Must Have Been the Mistletoe #782
My Baby, Your Child #880
Only St. Nick Knew #928
The Surprise Baby #1189
The Major and the Librarian #1228
Expectant Bride-To-Be #1368
Rookie Cop #1444
Loving Leah #1526

Silhouette Desire

More to Love #1372

Silhouette Intimate Moments

A Man To Believe In #359
Restless Wind #519
The Wedding Venture #645
The Lady and Alex Payton #729
Daddy by Default #789

For my very dear friend and mentor, Sandra Canfield,
with thanks for believing in me long before
I believed in myself, and for continuing to keep the faith.

Special thanks to Linda Joullian, R.N.,
for answering all my questions,
and to Dawn Mulholland for *Walking on Alligators.*

Prologue

"I think I've found her, Julie." William Landon paced the length of his sister's elegantly appointed living room, paused in front of the bay window and tucked his hands in the back pockets of his jeans. As he eyed the quiet, tree-lined street beyond the wide expanse of manicured lawn, he weighed the possible consequences of what he'd done. Maybe he should have left well enough alone.

Then he thought of his nephew, his dying nephew, and knew that he'd had no choice. Saving the boy's life was all that really mattered right now. "I think I've found Jonathan's birth mother," he continued as he turned and met his sister's wary gaze.

"Oh, Will..." she murmured, her soft voice wavering. Running her fingers through her shaggy auburn curls, she sank onto the plush rose-and-cream-striped sofa. "But...how...?" Hands clasped in her lap, she stared at him, a glimmer of hope edging away the apprehension in her bright blue eyes.

"Someone from the Amberton Home, a Mrs. Gruen, called Philip just after he arrived at his office this morning. Apparently she talked to Dr. Wells yesterday, and he managed to convince her that you and Phillip had a valid reason for requesting information about Jonathan's birth mother. Unfortunately Mrs. Gruen didn't have much to offer except the woman's name. She left the home two days after Jonathan was born and didn't leave a forwarding address. There was no mention of a next of kin anywhere in her records, either."

"Philip talked to Mrs. Gruen today?" Julie frowned and shook her head as if unable to comprehend what he was saying.

"And she gave him the name of Jonathan's birth mother," Will repeated patiently.

"But he...he didn't mention it when I talked to him earlier this afternoon."

"He knew the odds of finding her weren't good." Crossing to the sofa, Will sat down beside his sister. Reaching out, he smoothed a wisp of hair away from her face. "He didn't want you to get your hopes up. At least not until we had more than a name to offer."

"We"?

"Philip called me after he finished talking to Mrs. Gruen and asked if I could recommend a good private investigator. Instead, I offered to try to find the woman myself. I figured I'd have as good a chance as anyone of tracking her down," he admitted as he slipped an arm around her shoulders and drew her close. "Especially after twelve years on the Houston police force and a couple of years working as an investigator for the Harris County district attorney's office."

Without hesitation Julie leaned against him and uttered a weary sigh. As he had all too often over the past few weeks, Will wished he could ease the anguish that had been eating at her since she'd been advised that her adopted son had less than six months to live. But there was nothing he could say or do to change the fact that an incurable virus was slowly but surely destroying the boy's liver.

Without an organ transplant Jonathan would be lucky to make it through the summer. And regrettably Dr. Wells had warned the Drakes that finding a suitable donor before the boy became too ill to survive the surgery would be all but impossible. Their son was one of several hundred children around the country already awaiting a liver transplant.

Of course, if someone stepped forward, offered to serve as a living donor for the boy and proved to be a suitable match, the odds in his favor would increase immeasurably. Taking part of a healthy liver, especially from a parent or sibling, and using it to replace a damaged or diseased liver had proved to be quite successful over the past few years.

Both Julie and Philip, as well as Will, had volunteered to be tested, but unfortunately none of them had the same rare blood type as the boy. Dr. Wells had then suggested that they try to locate Jonathan's birth parents, since one of them could very well be a suitable donor. Philip hadn't wasted any time contacting the Amberton Home, but no one there had been willing to open records—sealed almost ten years ago—and give him the information he needed. At least not until Dr. Wells had convinced Mrs. Gruen of just how serious the boy's condition had become.

With nothing more than a single name to go on, Will had been afraid that finding the woman would take days, maybe weeks. But with the help of a buddy at HPD, he'd tapped into the department's computers. One bit of information had led to another, then another, until he was almost positive that the woman he'd traced to San Antonio was the same woman named in the adoption agency's records as his nephew's birth mother.

Now, if only she had the same blood type as the boy, agreed to be tested and was found to be a suitable donor, then consented to have the necessary surgery—

"And you did, didn't you?" Julie prodded insistently, interrupting his reverie. "You found Jonathan's birth mother."

"I *think* I've found her," Will cautioned.

As she tipped her head back and met his gaze, Will couldn't help but see the faint shadow of fear that had begun to war with the hope in his sister's eyes. She'd always been afraid that one day Jonathan's birth mother would demand to have the boy back, and her fears were not totally unfounded. It seemed lately that the news was filled with stories of women regaining rights to children they'd given up for adoption. And now, faced with the fact that her son's only hope for survival could very well lie with the woman who'd given birth to him almost ten years ago, the one woman she'd never wanted to meet, Julie suddenly seemed to realize that her nightmare might become reality.

However, Will couldn't see that they had any choice but to approach the woman and ask for her help. From what he'd found out about her, odds were in their favor that she was an honest, upright individual. Still, considering all that they'd be asking of her, and human nature being what it was, Will had no doubt she'd want something in return for her time and trouble. Luckily Philip Drake was a very wealthy man. He could afford to compensate her well, and he would. As long as she agreed to stay away from Jonathan.

Which she'd more than likely do in any case. She obviously hadn't wanted the child ten years ago. And again, from what he'd found out about her, there was no reason to believe she'd want him any more now.

"What's her…her name?" Julie asked at last.

"Mary Theresa McGuire," he replied, offering what he hoped was a reassuring smile.

"Where does she…live?"

"San Antonio."

"Do you know anything else about her?"

"She's twenty-eight years old, she teaches history at St. Scholastica, a small women's college in San Antonio, she bought a house near the campus about a year ago, she drives an old Volvo and pays all her bills on time. Also, as far as I could determine, she's never been married, at least not in the state of Texas."

"So…" Julie hesitated a moment, her eyes searching his, then bent her head. "I…I guess Philip and I should go to…to San Antonio and talk to her," she murmured, twisting her fingers together in her lap. "Shouldn't we?"

"Philip and I agreed that it would be wiser if you let me approach her instead. Jonathan needs both of you here with him now," Will advised. "And while I'd like to believe that

Ms. McGuire is a fairly decent kind of person, there's always a possibility she's not. If that turns out to be the case, I don't want her to be in any position to give you grief.''

''You'd do that for us, Will?'' She met his gaze, tears shimmering in her eyes.

''What do you think?'' he chided softly as he gave her a quick hug.

''I think you're a very special man, Will Landon, and I'm really glad you're my brother,'' she admitted, offering him a watery smile.

''You're the one who's special. Not many sixteen-year-old girls would have made room in their lives for an eight-year-old boy the way you did for me after Mom died and Dad went a little crazy. You were always there for me, Julie, *always.*'' He paused for a moment, recalling all she'd given up for him over the years, and knew that he'd do anything for her, anything at all to make her happy. ''Vetting Mary Theresa McGuire for you is no big deal compared to what you've done for me,'' he added.

''When do you plan to go and see her?''

''I'm scheduled to testify at a trial tomorrow afternoon, but if all goes as planned, I should be able to drive over to San Antonio on Friday. According to the registrar at St. Scholastica, graduation is scheduled for Saturday night and the faculty are required to be in attendance, so I shouldn't have any problem catching up with her.''

''And if she agrees to be tested?''

''I'll try to get her to drive back to Houston with me on Sunday. All right?''

Julie hesitated for several seconds, then nodded reluctantly. ''All right,'' she agreed. Easing away from him, she rose from the sofa, slipped her hand into the side pocket of her denim skirt and pulled out a set of keys. ''Want to take my car?''

''What do you think?'' Grinning, he stood, too, and took the keys from her, then glanced at his watch. ''What time are you planning to go back to the hospital?''

Worried about his wife, Philip had sent her home to rest

earlier in the afternoon, but Will knew that she wouldn't stay away more than a few hours.

"As soon as you give me your car keys."

"Why don't I drive you over there myself?"

"Sounds good to me."

"Then let's do it."

Taking Julie's hand in his, Will tugged her toward the foyer, more happy than he could say to see her smiling, *really* smiling once again.

Chapter One

"Good news, ladies," Tess McGuire announced, aiming a teasing smile at her graduate assistants as she reached for the last stack of papers sitting on her desk. "All we have left to grade are the essay questions on the World History exams and we're finished."

"The bad news is you had almost seventy students in that class last semester," Mary Lewis muttered.

"And you couldn't be satisfied with the usual one or two essay questions. You just *had* to include three," Amanda Hart added, making no effort to hide her disapproval.

"Now, now," Tess admonished softly, even though she was as eager as her assistants to be done grading papers. With her long-awaited trip to Ireland less than two weeks away and her preparations barely begun, she had some very busy days ahead of her. But first...

"The questions are reasonably simple, and since I asked everyone to keep their answers as short as possible, it shouldn't take you long to read through them."

"How many points are they worth?" Mary asked.

"A maximum of ten each." Stepping over the empty pizza boxes that were all that remained of the late lunch they'd shared, Tess crossed to where the young women sat Indian style on the floor of her small office. "Concentrate on content, but pay attention to grammar and spelling, too. If you end up giving a student less than twenty points total, set the paper aside so I can take a look at it myself," she added as she handed each of them an equal share of the test papers.

Holding the ones she'd kept for herself, Tess headed back to her desk. She hadn't taken more than a few steps when a flicker of movement outside her office doorway caught her attention. Pausing, she turned and saw a man standing in the hallway watching her.

At first she thought he might be a parent who had come to discuss a student's progress. But then, upon closer scrutiny, she thought not. Though she could be mistaken, he simply didn't appear to be old enough to have a daughter in her late teens or early twenties.

She was also fairly sure that he wasn't a member of the St. Scholastica staff. Although she rarely dealt with anyone outside the history department one-on-one, she would have remembered if she'd seen *him* at any of the de rigueur all-faculty functions held occasionally throughout the school year.

Though he wore a well-tailored dark gray suit, starched white shirt, burgundy-striped silk tie and elegant black leather loafers, he wasn't a dazzlingly handsome man. Yet she found him attractive in a rangy, rugged kind of way. He was at least six feet tall, broad shouldered but lean, with features that could only be called rough-hewn. His nose had probably been broken at least once in his lifetime; his shaggy auburn hair needed a good trim, and while he'd more than likely shaved that morning, his dark beard had already begun to five-o'clock-shadow the long line of his jaw and the edge of his strong, square chin.

Dressed in worn jeans, a black T-shirt and a pair of old boots, he'd certainly give the Marlboro man a run for his money, she mused. And if he asked, she had a feeling she'd be more than tempted to ride off into the sunset with—

Suddenly aware of the wayward trail her thoughts were taking, Tess gave herself a firm mental shake. What in the world was wrong with her? She'd learned the difference between fantasy and reality a long time ago, and since then she'd rarely gotten one confused with the other, especially where men were concerned.

And the man loitering outside her office doorway, eyeing her so…so assessingly, was a stranger. He could be anyone up to just about anything, including no good, she reminded herself rather grimly. In the moments that had passed since she'd first noticed him standing in the hallway, he certainly hadn't been what she'd call forthcoming about his presence there.

Maybe she ought to call campus security. But what had he done except stand and stare at her? Just as she'd stood and stared at him… She didn't want to embarrass him unnecessarily, especially if he needed nothing more than pointing in the right direction.

She hesitated a few seconds longer. Then, taking a deep breath, she squared her shoulders and crossed to her office doorway.

"May I help you?" she asked politely, pausing just inside the threshold as she met his calm, steady gaze.

"I'm looking for Professor McGuire. Mary Theresa McGuire," he replied, his voice deep and oddly…alluring.

So he did have a good reason for being there. He'd come to see *her*. But…why? Tess imagined she'd find out soon enough once she told him who she was. Yet she hesitated once again.

That he knew her name didn't automatically guarantee he had her best interests at heart. Maybe a little prevarication on her part would be wise. But she had a feeling that eventually he'd catch up with her again. He'd known where to find her during her working hours, so obviously there was a good chance he'd also know where to find her at other times of the day…or night.

Better to deal with him here and now, with Mary and Amanda nearby, rather than on her own at home, she decided. Even if his reason for wanting to see her turned out to be totally innocuous, she'd rather not be alone with him. Because she really did find him much too attractive for her own good. No matter how she'd like to convince herself otherwise.

"I'm Professor McGuire, but everyone calls me Tess."

His gaze unwavering, he nodded as if he'd already come to that conclusion on his own. But how could he have done so when she was positive that she'd never seen him before in her life?

"And you are...?" she prodded, her uneasiness growing with each moment that passed.

There was nothing lewd or lascivious about the way he was looking at her, yet Tess found his almost blatant interest unsettling. There was more than a hint of appreciation in his bright blue eyes as his gaze swept over her. Appreciation and...approval. Not only did he seem to like what he'd seen, but Tess had the strangest feeling that, in a completely unintentional way, she'd lived up to some sort of standard he'd set for her.

All of which pleased her much more than it should have. Especially since she still had no idea who he was or what he wanted. And he definitely wanted something. Even though he appeared to be in no hurry to let her know what it was.

Maybe she *should* call campus security after all, she thought, tightening her hold on the papers she clutched to her chest as she began to back away from him.

"My name's Landon, Will Landon." As if aware of her need for reassurance, he smiled slightly but made no move to close the distance she'd put between them. "I'm an investigator for the Harris County district attorney's office," he added as he took what appeared to be a black leather card case from an inner pocket, opened it and extended it toward her.

Frowning, Tess eyed the photo ID and gold shield he displayed. Although there was no way she could know for sure, both appeared to be official. And he was wearing a handgun. She'd seen the straps of his shoulder holster when he'd reached for his ID.

He could be attempting some sort of elaborate ruse, impersonating an officer or whatever. Yet she couldn't think of any reason why he'd go to that kind of trouble just to see her. More than likely, he was legit. Which still didn't give her any idea why he was looking for her.

"Harris County?" she questioned, making no effort at all to hide her confusion.

"Houston," he amended as he put his ID away.

"I see..." Actually she didn't. But she wasn't sure what else to say, and she desperately needed time to think.

It had been over a year since her last trip to Houston, and then all she'd done was take part in a symposium on the Norman invasion of Ireland at Rice University. She'd driven there and back without a mishap of any kind, and she'd paid her hotel and restaurant bills in full. She certainly hadn't consorted with any criminals, at least not to her knowledge. She'd spent most of her time meeting with fellow history professors from around the country. And other than that, she'd kept to herself.

So why would an investigator with the Harris County district attorney's office want to talk to her? She couldn't recall having been involved in any kind of wrongdoing in Houston, or anywhere else, for that matter. However, confronted by an officer of the law, she couldn't help but feel she must be guilty of something. But...*what?*

"Am I in some sort of trouble?" she asked, mentally bracing herself for the worst, whatever that might be....

"Not at all," he replied with a smile he probably intended to be reassuring.

Not at all.

Tess stared at him for several seconds, not the least bit heartened. She wasn't in any trouble at all. Okay, fine, she could accept that. But...

"Then why are you looking for me?" she demanded, making no attempt to hide her exasperation.

"I have something personal I'd like to discuss with you."

"Something personal?" Maybe he had her confused with someone else. "With *me?*"

Meeting her gaze, he nodded slowly.

"Are you sure?" she asked, though she already knew what his answer would be.

"Absolutely."

His certainty sent a quiver of unease edging along her spine. No matter who the man standing before her claimed to be, Tess knew better than to think of him as anything other than a stranger. A stranger who not only wanted to invade her privacy, but could quite possibly have something very unpleasant in store for her.

"So, Mr. Landon, what exactly is it you want to discuss with me?" she prodded, more anxious than ever to hear what he had to say to her.

"As I said, the matter's personal, and you're obviously busy right now."

Reminded that she hadn't been alone when she'd caught her first glimpse of Will Landon, Tess glanced over her shoulder. Mary and Amanda sat quietly just a few feet away from her. They eyed her avidly for several seconds, then ducked their heads and began to shuffle through the papers in their laps.

Frowning once again, Tess turned away from the young women. Though she trusted them to be discreet, she felt they'd heard more than enough already.

"There's a diner just a few blocks from here. I could meet you there in a couple of hours," she suggested.

"I think it would be better if I came to your house. What I have to discuss with you could take a while, and I'd really like to do it where we won't be interrupted." He paused for a moment to pull a business card from his jacket pocket, then offered it to her. "I know I'm asking a lot of you, considering you don't know me from Adam, but the D.A. will vouch for me. His number's on the card."

So...the man wanted to come to her house. Why hadn't she guessed as much already? From the first, he'd been pussyfooting around about his reason for wanting to talk to her. He'd given her just enough information to hook her, and now he was reeling her in as he'd probably planned to do all along.

If she weren't so damned curious about what he wanted from her, she'd tell him to take a flying leap. Not that she really believed it would do her any good. There was a kind of quiet determination about him, coupled with a won't-take-no-for-an-answer attitude that had begun to intimidate the hell out of her.

With or without her agreement, he'd show up at her house and make her listen to whatever he had to say. She knew it as well as she knew her own name.

"What time shall I expect you?" she asked, resigning herself to what she deemed inevitable as she took the card from him.

He glanced at his watch, then met her gaze once again. To her surprise, there was no flash of triumph in his eyes, but rather a shadow of…uncertainty. He'd gotten what he wanted, yet suddenly he seemed to be having second thoughts. Only for a moment, though. Apparently no mere twinge of conscience was about to keep him from his goal.

"How about six o'clock?" he suggested quietly.

"I'll see you then."

Turning away dismissively, Tess tucked his card in the back pocket of her jeans, walked back to her desk and sat in her chair. She hesitated for several seconds, then directed a glance toward her office doorway. Much to her relief, he was no longer standing in the hallway.

With a barely audible sigh, Tess shifted her gaze to Mary and Amanda. Once again she caught the young women watching her with wide-eyed interest.

"Sorry about the interruption." She set aside the test papers she'd been holding. Then, not wanting to answer any questions they might choose to ask, she continued as nonchalantly as she could. "Guess we'd better get busy now or we'll never get out of here."

As the young women murmured their agreement, Tess took one of the papers from the stack in front of her, opened it to the essay page and forced herself to focus on the questions and answers written there. She could worry about Will Landon and what he wanted once she'd finished with the task at hand. For now, however, she had papers to grade. Lots and lots of papers that required nothing less than her undivided attention.

Sometime around four o'clock Mary and Amanda handed Tess the last of the papers they'd been grading. After many thanks for all their help and a promise to keep in touch over the summer, Tess finally said goodbye to them. She knew she'd miss seeing the young women over the next few months. But both of them would be back in September, when she'd once again be lucky enough to have them as her graduate assistants.

After they'd gone, Tess gathered together the paperwork she planned to do that evening and quickly loaded her briefcase. Then she pulled Will Landon's card from her pocket and called the D.A.'s office.

The man she spoke to gladly verified Landon's identity. However, he wasn't able to answer any of her other questions. At least not to her satisfaction. More confused than ever, she cradled the receiver, locked her office and headed for her car.

Not quite ten minutes later she walked into her cool, quiet little house, set her briefcase on the hall table and glanced at the clock on the wall. She still had forty-five minutes until he was due to arrive. Forty-five minutes to wait and wonder, just as she'd been waiting and wondering for almost three hours now.

She'd sat at her desk and tried to concentrate, knowing all along she was fighting a losing battle. Despite her best intentions, she'd allowed her mind to wander more than she should have. Quite a bit more… Which meant that she'd have to regrade the papers she'd worked on earlier or live with the knowledge that she hadn't been as fair to her students as she'd always sworn she'd be.

Her nerves more on edge with each moment that passed, Tess strode into the living room. She moved to the front windows and opened the blinds, allowing as much of the late-afternoon sunlight as possible to filter through. Then, although the room was just as neat and tidy as she'd left it that morning, she flitted from one end to the other, plumping a sofa cushion here, straightening a stack of magazines there, even adjusting the angle of the framed print hanging over the fireplace.

Finally, after several minutes of what could only be called frenetic activity, Tess realized she was doing nothing more than increasing her anxiety. With a muttered curse, she crossed to her favorite wing-back chair, sat down and folded her hands in her lap. Taking a deep breath, then another and another, she willed herself to calm down. She had no intention of making herself crazy. Nor was she about to give in to the feeling of helplessness that threatened to overwhelm her.

She'd spent the past ten years not only gaining, but maintaining control of her life. Allowing herself to fall apart because an investigator from the Harris County district attorney's office wanted to talk to her about a personal matter was simply... ludicrous.

She'd worked two, sometimes three jobs while she'd gone to school. Against all odds, she'd earned a Ph.D., and at a time when many colleges and universities were cutting back on staff, she'd won a full professorship at St. Scholastica. All so she'd never be at anyone's mercy again in her life.

Not that she was at Will Landon's mercy. Not by any stretch of the imagination. Still, she could think of a lot of other things she'd rather be doing than waiting for him. Of course, there was no law saying she *had* to stay there. But if she didn't, she'd only be putting off what she'd already determined would be ultimately inescapable.

He was an investigator for the Harris County D.A.'s office, or so she'd been told when she called the number he'd given her. And, since he hadn't asked for directions to her house, he apparently knew where to find her. Which she had no doubt he'd do eventually, one way or another. Better to be done with him once and for all. Especially since she'd found him so damned...attractive.

Obviously she'd been buried in the halls of academia much too long. Otherwise, she'd never have been so smitten by a total stranger.

Obviously, too, it was past time to deepen her relationship with Richard, if only to dull the primitive yearning that had been eating at her all afternoon. He'd been her mentor, then her friend. And they *were* traveling to Ireland together, albeit as...companions. Still, lately he'd begun to hint that he'd like to be her lover. And she'd only put him off because she hadn't felt as if she was ready for that kind of commitment.

"But Will Landon certainly made you feel ready, didn't he?" she muttered as she pushed herself out of her chair and crossed to the front windows once again.

It was probably nature's way of letting her know she'd been celibate way too long.

Still, in all the years she'd known Richard Bering, she'd never been drawn to him in quite the same way she'd been drawn to Will Landon the instant she'd seen him standing outside her office doorway.

Which meant that no matter what he had to say to her, she'd be wise to see to it that he said it as quickly as possible. The less time she spent with him, the better. At least then she wouldn't be tempted to do something stupid like...fall in love.

Considering her track record, that *would* be a stupid thing to do. She'd cared deeply about only two men in her lifetime; first her father and then Bryan had abandoned her when she'd needed them most. And she certainly wasn't foolish enough to let herself be hurt that badly again. Not by anyone...anyone at all.

With a rueful shake of her head, Tess turned away from the window. What in the world was wrong with her? Will Landon wanted nothing more than to talk to her, and here she had him breaking her heart. She really did need to get a grip.

She glanced at her watch again, then headed toward the kitchen. Twenty-eight minutes and counting. Time enough to brew a fresh pitcher of iced tea. Common decency dictated that she offer him something to drink, but that was as sociable as she intended to be. She wanted him to say whatever it was he had to say and be on his way, hopefully no later than six-thirty.

Then maybe she'd call Richard and ask him if he'd like to drive down from Austin and have dinner with her. Maybe...

Braking at the four-way stop on the tree-lined street in the quiet neighborhood near St. Scholastica where Tess McGuire lived, Will glanced at the digital clock on the dashboard of his sister's BMW. He'd taken his time driving the short distance from downtown San Antonio, yet he still had another ten minutes to go until six o'clock.

She probably wouldn't mind if he arrived a bit early. He knew that if their roles had been reversed, if *he* had been the one left hanging for the balance of the afternoon, he'd be crawling out of his skin right about now. But he wasn't quite ready to confront her yet. At least not as ready as he ought to be, he admitted as he drove through the intersection, pulled to the curb and parked in the shade of a shaggy old oak.

He'd come to San Antonio with a series of goals in mind, but first and foremost among them had been finding Mary Theresa McGuire. Then and only then could he determine whether or not she was Jonathan's birth mother. When he'd arrived in the city just after noon, he'd stopped to buy a street map, taken a look at it, then headed straight to her house. But, of course, she hadn't been home.

Aware that she could very well be somewhere on campus and intent on at least catching a glimpse of her, he'd driven the short distance to the college. Parking in the visitors' lot, he'd walked to the administration building, where he'd gotten directions to her office without any trouble at all.

He hadn't actually planned to talk to her there. Considering the extremely personal nature of his business, he wouldn't have done that anywhere but at her home, just to be sure he didn't cause her any embarrassment. But then she'd caught him lurking in the hallway. Caught him in more ways than one.

He'd had no idea what his initial response to her would be. Though he'd always found it hard to understand how a woman could give away her baby, he'd come to San Antonio with what he hoped was an open mind. He'd realized that sometimes circumstances were such that a woman felt she had no other choice. And he'd wanted to believe that had been the case with Mary Theresa McGuire.

He'd had to remember, too, that in putting her child up for adoption, she'd given his sister and brother-in-law a very special gift. She'd given them the child they'd wanted more than anything but had begun to believe they'd never have. For that reason, if for no other, he'd hoped that he wouldn't feel any animosity toward her.

Never in a million years would he have anticipated the strange sense of wonder that had stirred somewhere deep in his soul when she'd turned to face him. One look at her and he'd known without a doubt that he'd found his nephew's birth mother. The angle of her cheekbones and the elegant arch of her eyebrows, the dark hair curling softly around her face and the slight smile tugging at the corners of her mouth had all fit together in a most familiar way.

Her eyes, however, had been the real clincher. They were pale gray rimmed with black. Just like Jonathan's…

He should have been elated. But as she'd stared at him with those lovely eyes, those ghost eyes, he'd seen something startling in their shadowy depths. Longing…the same longing that had begun to thrum through him the first moment she'd met his gaze.

In the space of a heartbeat she'd become more to him than a name he'd jotted down on a piece of paper…much more. Instinctively he'd known that she was a good person. He'd dealt with enough of the other kind to tell the difference. And though she'd stood her ground, eyeing him watchfully, he'd also realized just how vulnerable she was. He had gotten the feeling not only that she'd been hurt before, but that she fully expected to be hurt again…perhaps by him. And suddenly, much to his chagrin, he'd wanted to put his arms around her, hold her close and assure her everything would be all right.

Which wouldn't have necessarily been true, considering why he was there. With a few well-chosen words he was going to disrupt her nice, quiet life in a way that most people would find impossible to forgive. He was going to remind her of a time in her life she'd probably just as soon forget. Then he was going to ask her to risk not only her health, but her emotional well-being for a child she'd given away at birth. Her child, yet not really… Not since she'd given up her right to him almost ten years ago.

Frowning, Will glanced at the clock on the dashboard again. Seeing that it was almost six o'clock, he shifted into gear and pulled away from the curb. Much as he'd like to let her be, he knew that under the circumstances, it just wasn't possible. He had to think of Jonathan first. And he had to remember that no matter how he felt about Professor McGuire, he didn't owe her the kind of allegiance he owed his sister and brother-in-law. They were his family, the only family he'd had in a long time, while she was simply the means to what he hoped would be a happy ending for them.

Not that he intended to go out of his way to cause her any grief. One question and he'd know whether or not she had the same blood type as her son. If she didn't, there would be no reason for him to say anything to her about the boy. He'd find a way to convince her that he'd made a mistake, then get out of there as fast as he could.

But if she was AB negative...

He'd be as straightforward as possible about what he wanted, then do his damnedest to convince her to return to Houston with him Sunday afternoon.

At the end of the block, he eased the car over to the curb again, parked on the street in front of her house and switched off the engine. As he'd done the first time he'd been there, he sat back in his seat and admired the small, Spanish-style, white stucco house complete with red tile roof. Though the place had to be at least thirty years old, it had obviously been very well-maintained. The front yard, too, had been lovingly tended. The grass was neatly mowed, while a wide variety of brightly-colored flowers overflowed the beds clustered under the front windows and tumbled out of an odd assortment of clay pots set along the brick walkway.

As he had off and on for most of the afternoon, Will wondered if she lived there alone. Not that it really mattered to him one way or another, he thought as he straightened his tie, then climbed out of the car and started toward her front door. He'd made sure she understood that what he had to say to her was personal. He could only hope she'd taken him at his word. Because he certainly didn't relish talking to her while some overly protective type lurked in the background, ready to do battle on her behalf. Of course, he could deal with that eventuality if it arose. But for more reasons than he liked to admit, he'd really rather not.

He rang her doorbell, then stood quietly, waiting for her to come to the door. After several long moments, he began to wonder if she'd changed her mind about seeing him. Her car was in the driveway, but that didn't mean *she* was there. Maybe she'd gone off with someone.

With a muttered curse, he reached out to ring the bell again, but just as he was about to press the button, the door swung open.

She stood just inside the entryway, still dressed in the faded jeans, sleeveless white cotton shirt and leather loafers she'd been wearing earlier, her long, dark hair curling around her face just as it had then, too. Volunteering no word of greeting, she squared her slender shoulders and tipped her chin up as she eyed him with obvious distrust.

Hoping to put her at ease, Will smiled tentatively as he lowered his hand to his side, but she didn't smile back. She simply stood and stared at him as if he was the last person on earth she wanted standing on her doorstep.

"Thank you for agreeing to see me," he said at last. He knew he didn't deserve a warmer welcome, and obviously he wasn't going to get one. Yet he had no choice but to forge ahead.

"By all means," she murmured. "Please, do come in." Lowering her gaze, she moved to one side so that he could walk past her, then gestured graciously toward the living room. "We can talk in there if you'd like."

Though her words were politely spoken, Will couldn't help but hear the irony in her voice. In her own subtle way she was letting him know that although he'd wrangled his way into her home, she didn't like it. Not one bit. Still, she hadn't shut him out. At least not yet. Which meant that he'd probably have one chance, and only one chance, to gain her cooperation.

Willing himself to mind his manners, he ambled through the archway leading into her living room as she closed and locked the front door. Though sparsely furnished, the cool, quiet room was unexpectedly inviting.

A Chinese carpet in shades of rose and cream and blue covered part of the gleaming hardwood floor. An old-fashioned blue-and-cream-patterned camel-back sofa sat against one wall. A single wing-back chair, richly upholstered in teal blue, had been angled off to one side to complete the seating arrangement. The mahogany end table sporting a brass candlestick lamp and the matching coffee table covered with magazines were obviously antiques. Both pieces had been lovingly restored, as had the oak wardrobe tucked into a far corner.

Apparently the nice lady liked nice things, the kind of nice things a struggling single mother probably wouldn't have been able to afford. Grimly Will eyed the simple wood-block print of a crumbling castle set high atop a craggy cliff that she'd hung above the fireplace. Then, more than vaguely aware that he was judging her unfairly, mostly for his own benefit, he reined in his wandering thoughts.

Though he didn't know all that much about her, especially about her past, she certainly hadn't struck him as being either self-centered or irresponsible. And to be honest, he had absolutely no idea what her life had been like before her baby was born. Nor had he any idea what she'd gone through since then to get to where she was. Granted, having a good reason to dislike her would have made it easier for him to disrupt her life. But trying to manufacture one only made him feel like even more of a crud than he already did.

Talk about being caught between a rock and a hard place...

Shifting uncomfortably from one foot to the other, Will turned toward the entryway again and saw that she hadn't taken more than a couple of steps into the living room. Hands tucked in the side pockets of her jeans, she stood quietly, eyeing him as if he were a snake slithering across her carpet. He wanted to assure her that he really wasn't that bad a person, but figured he'd only be wasting his breath.

"I assume you called the D.A.'s office to check on me," he said, though he was already sure that she had. Otherwise, he doubted she'd have opened her door to him.

"I did," she admitted. "Unfortunately no one there had any idea why you wanted to see me. Something *was* said about your taking the day off, though." She hesitated a moment, gazing at him thoughtfully, then continued. "Which means you aren't here in any *official* capacity, are you?"

"No..."

"So why are you wearing a gun, Mr. Landon? Are you

afraid I might be...dangerous?'' she asked, her tone laced with the faintest hint of laughter.

She was dangerous, all right. Dangerous to his peace of mind. Especially with the corners of her mouth tipped up half-teasingly.

Yet the wariness in her eyes hadn't eased a bit. She knew he wanted something from her, and until she found out what it was, she obviously intended to keep her distance, physically and emotionally. Which meant she was one smart lady.

''Not at all,'' he replied, trying another smile on her without much success. ''It's just that I like to have it with me all the time.''

In reality, he usually kept his weapon in the glove box when he wasn't actually on duty. Why he'd worn it today, he wasn't really sure. Perhaps to remind him to keep his mind on business. He certainly hadn't meant to intimidate her. He'd never been a bully and he never would be. That simply wasn't his style.

''And I thought I was paranoid,'' she murmured.

''Comes with the territory,'' he admitted.

''If you say so.'' Giving him a wide berth, she crossed to the wing-back chair, then turned to face him again.

''You sound...skeptical.''

''Trust has never been my long suit, Mr. Landon.''

''Well, then, I'll consider myself forewarned.''

''An excellent idea.'' For one long moment, a smile played around the corners of her mouth. Then, tilting her chin challengingly, she gestured toward the sofa. ''Would you like to sit down?''

''Yes, thank you.'' After a moment's consideration, Will settled into the corner of the sofa closest to her chair.

''Can I get you something to drink? I have iced tea and soft drinks in the refrigerator. Or I could make a pot of coffee.''

''Iced tea will be fine.''

''Lemon and sugar?''

''Just lemon.''

''Make yourself comfortable, then. I'll just be a moment.''

As she turned and walked through the archway leading into

the kitchen, Will leaned back against the sofa cushions. However, he knew better than to relax. He'd been in her home approximately five minutes, and she'd been more gracious than he'd anticipated. But he had yet to reveal his reasons for being there. Once she understood what he wanted of her...

Eyeing the heavy brass lamp on the end table, he wondered if she was strong enough to heave it at him. Probably not, but he'd better be ready to move out of the way just in case.

"Iced tea with lemon, Mr. Landon."

Accepting the tall, frosty glass she held out to him, Will murmured a word of thanks. He took a long swallow of the refreshing drink. Then, aware that there was little else left to do but speak his piece, he set the glass aside.

As she sat in the chair across from him, he turned to face her. But when she met his gaze, her pale eyes filled with trepidation, he couldn't seem to find the right words to begin.

In the end, after several long moments of silence, she drew in a deep breath and asked the question he'd been expecting since he'd walked through her front door.

"So, Mr. Landon, what do you want?"

Chapter Two

"That depends, Professor McGuire."

As she had when he'd first walked into her house, Tess once again sensed Will Landon's hesitation. Whatever he'd come to discuss with her, he wasn't finding it easy. Yet he seemed unable or unwilling to let it go. As if he was honor bound to see something through, something that gave him...pause. He'd say what he had to say eventually, but in the meantime, he was holding back, perhaps for her sake.

She appreciated his thoughtfulness. Really, she *did.* Just as she acknowledged his basic decency. He obviously didn't want to upset her. But her patience was definitely beginning to wear a bit thin. Especially since she'd managed to convince herself that he really *had* mistaken her for someone else.

"On what?" she prodded.

She was more anxious than ever to get rid of him, now that she'd admitted liking more than his looks. Finding him physically attractive was one thing. But allowing herself to be lured by his kindness and consideration would be downright foolish—

"Your blood type," he stated simply.

"My...*blood type?*" Momentarily taken aback, Tess stared at him, a frown tugging at the corners of her mouth. What difference could her blood type make?

Unless he *wasn't* certain he'd found the Mary Theresa McGuire he was looking for. In which case it could make all the difference in the world. Blood type was often used as an identifying factor, wasn't it? And since she'd been told that hers was relatively rare...

"It's AB negative," she said, sure that she'd be accepting his apologies and sending him on his way within a matter of minutes.

Much to her surprise, however, he didn't seem to be put off by her admission. In fact, he looked almost...relieved. Yet Tess also saw a glimmer of regret in his azure eyes. And suddenly she was not only confused, but frightened. Very frightened indeed.

She could no longer believe that Will Landon had mistaken her for someone else. And instinctively she knew that whatever he had to say next, she wasn't going to like. Yet she didn't seem to have any choice but to hear him out. Especially since he was still sitting on her sofa, eyeing her more intently than ever.

"Please, Mr. Landon..." she began, her voice barely above a whisper as she twisted her hands together in her lap. "Just...just tell me what you want."

"Believe me, Professor McGuire, it's not my intention to upset you, but..." He hesitated, his gaze wavering for a moment. Then, drawing in a deep breath, he continued quietly. "Ten years ago a woman by the name of Mary Theresa McGuire gave birth to a baby boy on August 17 at the Amberton Home in Dallas, Texas. From what I've been able to determine, you're that woman. Aren't you, Professor?"

Tess couldn't have been more astonished if he'd accused her of being an alien from another planet. For several moments she sat and stared at him in stunned silence, barely able to think, much less speak. Surely she must have heard him wrong. *Surely...*

How could he possibly know something so…so intimate about her? She'd told no one about the child she'd given up for adoption the summer after her eighteenth birthday. Not even the close friends she'd made over the years. And the people at the Amberton Home had assured her that her records would be sealed.

Not that she was ashamed of what she'd done. Contrary to the accusations Bryan Harper's parents had made, her pregnancy had been an accident. She'd loved Bryan and she'd believed that he loved her. Trapping him had never been a part of her agenda. She'd hoped that he would stand by her. But, of course, he hadn't….

She'd been left with no one to turn to but her abusive, alcoholic mother, and nowhere to go but a tumbledown house that had been more of a hell than a haven since her father had abandoned them. Then she'd heard about the Amberton Home.

She hadn't wanted to give up her child for adoption. But at the time, she'd truly believed she had no other choice. So she'd packed a few of her clothes and as many of her books as she could manage and she'd taken the bus to Dallas, sure that she was doing the best she could for her baby.

Signing the adoption papers only hours after her son's birth had been a devastating experience. Remembering the moment when she'd no longer had a right to claim him as *her* child had been hard enough over the years. Actually discussing it with anyone had been totally out of the question.

Which brought her back to Will Landon, sitting quietly across from her, a wary look in his eyes. He'd already admitted that he wasn't there as an investigator for the Harris County district attorney's office. Yet he'd obviously done enough digging to know that she'd given birth to a child ten years ago. More important, he wanted her to know that he knew. But why? What exactly was he after?

Considering all the hedging he'd done since she'd first spotted him standing outside her office doorway, Tess wasn't sure she really wanted to know. But she'd never been any good at lying and she could think of no other way to forestall him.

"You're right, Mr. Landon. I'm the Mary Theresa McGuire

who gave birth to a baby boy at the Amberton Home almost ten years ago,'' she admitted, then continued quietly. ''I was told that a Houston couple had been chosen as his adoptive parents. However, since adoptions at Amberton are closed, I never actually met—''

A Houston couple...

Meeting Will Landon's gaze, she frowned thoughtfully. And then, quite suddenly, everything seemed to click into place.

''You're my son's adoptive father, aren't you?'' she asked, her voice wavering slightly.

''Actually he's my nephew,'' Will acknowledged with what she imagined he thought was a reassuring smile. ''My sister and brother-in-law are the Houston couple who adopted him.''

''I see.'' Lowering her gaze, Tess considered what he'd said. Then, as if it had been only yesterday, she recalled exactly what she'd been told about her son's...parents.

A wonderful young couple...unable to have children of their own...more than able to give your son all that we know you'd want him to have...

She'd thought of them often, the wonderful young couple who'd adopted her baby boy. She'd thought of them each time she'd thought of her son. And she'd hoped that all three of them were happy and healthy.

Healthy...

She raised her head, meeting Will Landon's gaze once again. ''He's all right, isn't he?'' she asked anxiously. ''Please, tell me he's all right.''

''Up until six months ago he was just fine. Then he came down with what seemed like a bad case of the flu. He *had* picked up a virus, a rather deadly virus. The doctors had hoped that it would simply run its course as most viruses do. But about four months ago they found that it had invaded his liver. Since then the infection has destroyed almost seventy percent of the organ.''

All along Tess had known that what Will Landon had to tell her wouldn't be pleasant. However, since she'd dealt with more than her fair share of nasty problems in the past, she'd been fairly sure she could cope with whatever he laid on her plate.

But a dying child…her child…yet, not really *hers*…

As a wave of almost unbearable anguish washed over her, Tess sat back in her chair, her hands clasped in her lap so tightly that her fingers ached. Until a few moments ago, she had believed that giving up her son for adoption had guaranteed he would have a long and happy life. But according to Will Landon that wasn't going to be the case. Unless…

"Why are you telling me this, Mr. Landon?" she asked, though somewhere in the back of her mind, the puzzle pieces had already begun to fit together in a terrifying way.

"Without a liver transplant he won't make it through the summer," he conceded, his voice steady as he held her gaze. "Unfortunately, he's AB negative. Finding a suitable donor has been impossible. In fact, until a few days ago, my sister and brother-in-law had all but given up hope. Then Dr. Wells mentioned the possibility that one of Jonathan's birth parents might have the same blood type he did. My brother-in-law contacted the Amberton Home immediately, and finally, very reluctantly, they gave him your name."

Jonathan…

His name was Jonathan. And *she* had the same blood type he did. Which meant that she could very well be the child's only hope. Maybe somehow, some way, she could save her son's life. Which she would do if she could. She loved her child no less today than she had ten years ago. And just as she had been willing to do anything for him then, she would do anything for him now.

With a mighty effort, she brought her teeming thoughts to heel. Better not to jump to any conclusions…yet.

"And he asked you to find me?"

"Actually, I volunteered so Julie and Philip could stay with—their son."

"Wise move," she murmured. "Especially since I could very well have been a real deadbeat."

For one long moment, he eyed her with obvious dismay. Then, as if realizing that she hadn't taken offense, he smiled slightly. "They've had enough grief already," he admitted. "So, yes, that was a consideration, too."

She'd been right about him. He was a good man, a kind and thoughtful man. And he truly cared about his sister and brother-in-law, as well as the child they'd adopted, in a way that no one had ever cared about her.

In fact, she could only imagine what it would be like to have someone so willing to look out for her best interests, especially someone like Will Landon. Too bad he already owed his loyalty to the...opposition. Not that she thought of his sister and brother-in-law as her adversaries. She simply had to keep in mind that he was here on *their* behalf. And even if he seemed to be concerned about her, as he did at the moment, if push came to shove, he'd be on their side completely.

"Well, then, since you aren't heading for the door, I suppose that means you think I'll suit your...needs," she said as lightly as possible.

"Yes," he admitted, his smile fading. "Because you have the same blood type as Jonathan, there's a good chance you're physically compatible with him in other important ways, which can be verified by a series of tests.

"If the tests are positive, and you then agree to donate a part of your liver to be transplanted into his body, he will more than likely make a full recovery and go on to live a normal, healthy life."

Having the details spelled out in relatively plain English left her at a momentary loss for words. For the past few minutes, she'd had a fairly good idea where their conversation was going. But now she finally began to realize exactly what Will Landon wanted of her.

"A part of my liver..." she murmured, her heart pounding. "Correct me if I'm wrong, but I only have *one* liver, don't I? And I can't survive without it. So...?" Not quite sure how to voice her concern, she shrugged and shook her head.

"The liver regenerates itself. The part you donate to Jonathan will grow along with him, while yours will eventually return to normal. In the meantime, you should be just fine. The liver can function and maintain life even if eighty percent of the organ is missing or unable to function, and the doctors will take less than fifty percent for the transplant."

"I see."

Suddenly unable to meet his earnest gaze any longer, Tess stood and paced the length of the living room, pausing in front of the fireplace. One hand braced on the mantel, she stared at the print of Dunluce Castle hanging on the wall, and wished that Will Landon would just disappear.

He had no right to come into her home and ask her to risk her life for someone else's child. Because the child he called Jonathan wasn't her child. Not in any way that really counted.

Nice try, Tess, very nice try. But you're only fooling yourself.

No matter how she tried to convince herself otherwise, the boy *was* her son in the one way that counted, at least at the moment.

Flesh of my flesh...blood of my blood...

For just an instant, she closed her eyes, remembering his first soft, sweet cries and her single, swift glimpse of him. And she realized that if their roles had been reversed, if she'd needed Will Landon to save her son's life, she'd have been just as audacious as he'd been.

"As I mentioned, you'd have to go through a battery of tests, physical and psychological."

At the close sound of his voice, Tess glanced over her shoulder. Though she hadn't heard him move across the room, she saw that he was standing just a few feet away, shrouded in evening shadows. She thought about turning on the lamp. But she found the growing darkness somehow comforting. It was one thing to silently vow to do whatever was necessary to save her son's life. But the reality of what she would have to undergo to do so terrified her, and she'd rather Will Landon didn't know it.

"And then what?" she asked, turning away again.

"Then, if you're a suitable match, you'd undergo several hours of major surgery. Afterward, recuperation could take anywhere from six to eight weeks, perhaps even longer, depending..."

Yes, indeed, just the thought of what lay ahead made her palms sweat. Not only major surgery, with all the attendant risks, but weeks, perhaps months of trying to regain the good health she'd always enjoyed. And what if she didn't fully recover? How would she support herself if she couldn't teach anymore? As had been the case for most of her life, she had no one to turn to. No one at all.

Yet how could she turn her back on a dying child? *Her* child—her baby. If there was any way at all that she could help to save his life, she knew that she would do it, no matter what the consequences might be.

"What are our odds, Mr. Landon?"

"There are no guarantees for either of you, Professor," he advised quietly. "Major surgery is...major. But you'll both have a better-than-average chance of coming through with flying colors. The staff at the medical center are among the highest-rated professionals in the world. Please believe me when I tell you that you'll have the best possible care."

Touched by the grave concern she heard in his voice, Tess glanced at him again. Obviously he wasn't finding this easy, either. Which made her admire him all the more for pressing ahead.

"Of course I believe you," she assured him, trying to smile.

"I know I'm dumping a lot on you all at once," he admitted. "But our window of opportunity is closing fast. At the rate he's deteriorating, if Jonathan doesn't have the surgery within the next few weeks, he'll be too weak to make it through."

With surprising suddenness the fear that Tess had been feeling for herself turned to fear for her son. She'd hoped to have at least a little time to consider her options. But Jonathan had only a few weeks left. Which meant that her decision had been made.

"So...when do you want me to come to Houston?"

He didn't answer her immediately. For what seemed like a very long time, he simply stood and stared at her, as if he wasn't quite sure he'd heard her right.

"You'll do it, then?" he asked at last, his eyes holding hers. "You'll be tested?"

Not quite trusting her voice, Tess nodded slowly, then turned back to the fireplace.

"The tests will take at least four or five days, and the sooner they can get started, the better,'' he advised. ''So...do you think you could get away sometime Sunday afternoon?''

Again she nodded.

She had to attend the graduation ceremony Saturday evening, but then her time would be her own. She did have some paperwork to complete by next Friday, when final grades were due in the registrar's office. However, if she put her mind to it, she could probably finish it tonight or tomorrow at the latest.

Her gaze lingering wistfully on the print above the fireplace, she thought of her plans to spend the summer in Ireland, plans she might very well have to cancel at the last minute. Richard would be furious. Yet if she proved to be a suitable match for the boy, she certainly wouldn't hesitate to do so. No trip abroad, no matter how long awaited, meant more to her than her son. He needed her help, and nothing would stand in the way of her offering it.

''I planned to drive back then,'' he said, his deep voice interrupting her reverie. ''You're more than welcome to come with me. I'll call Philip and ask him to make arrangements for you to stay at a hotel near the medical center.'' He paused, as if considering his next words carefully, then continued. ''I realize we're asking more of you than we really have a right to, but I want you to know that you'll be compensated for your time and trouble.''

''Compensated?'' Tess asked as she turned to face him. ''What do you mean by *compensated?*''

''In return for what you've agreed to do for Jonathan, Philip will see to it that you receive the best possible care. Your medical bills will be paid, and, of course, you'll also be given a generous financial remuneration.''

''Oh, really?'' she drawled, eyeing him narrowly as a wave of anger coursed through her. ''So, exactly how much is a piece of my liver worth to your brother-in-law, Mr. Landon? You used the word *generous.* Would that be ten thousand dollars? Or maybe more like a hundred thousand? Or are we talking something in the neighborhood of half a million?''

Frowning, he shifted from one foot to the other. ''I'm not really sure—'' he began, his confusion evident in his voice.

"Well, *I'm* sure," she shot back. "Sure that I don't want anything from you *or* your brother-in-law. Not a ride to Houston, not a hotel room and certainly not any *financial remuneration.*"

"What *do* you want, then?" he asked, still visibly puzzled. "Just tell me—"

"For you to have never walked through my front door," she muttered.

Brushing past him, she strode across the living room and switched on the lamp. Then, her back to him, she took several deep, steadying breaths.

Did he really think she was the kind of person who'd expect to be paid for helping to save her own child's life? Did she come across as *that* materialistic? She certainly couldn't deny that she enjoyed having some of the finer things in life, things like a modest home of her own filled with the antique furniture she herself had spent so many hours refinishing. But she'd earned everything she owned honestly, through hard work and perseverance.

"Look, Professor, I didn't mean to offend you. I just thought—"

"I know exactly what you thought," she snapped, barely quelling the urge to throw something at him. Luckily she wasn't one for knickknacks, and her lamp had been too costly to destroy it in such a senseless way. "I'm not for sale, Mr. Landon. I never have been and I never will be."

"I never meant to insinuate that you were," he replied in a conciliatory tone. "I just wanted to be sure you realized we weren't expecting something for nothing."

Slightly mollified, Tess shoved her hands in the side pockets of her jeans, then turned and met his gaze again. "I said I'd do whatever I can to help your nephew, and believe me, I will. But I don't want anything in return, not anything at all. So why don't you just tell me where you want me to be and when, and trust that I'll be there?"

"But you're doing so much for Jonathan," he protested. "At least let me take care of your transportation to and from Houston and see to it that you have a nice place to stay until you have to check into the hospital. It would mean a lot to me. Really, it would."

Her first instinct was to refuse his offer as adamantly as possible. But he sounded so honestly apologetic that she couldn't quite bring herself to say the words.

She'd already concluded that approaching her hadn't been easy for him. Yet he'd taken care to do so in a way that hadn't caused her any real embarrassment. And though she'd been insulted by his offer of payment for services rendered, she didn't really think that was what he'd intended to do. As she'd willingly admitted earlier, he'd had no way of knowing for sure what kind of person she was. So he'd simply done his best to cover all the bases.

Tess knew she was bending over backward to give him the benefit of the doubt. But then one tended to make allowances for a possible ally when faced with a scary situation. Just the thought of what lay ahead for her in Houston made her heart pound and her palms sweat. Saddling herself with the added burden of making her way there on her own, then finding a place to stay—for no other reason than to assuage her wounded pride—was just plain silly.

If Will Landon wanted to run interference for her, why not let him? He seemed like an honorable man, and he'd already proved he could be considerate. She hadn't been kidding when she told him she didn't trust easily. But accepting his offer of a ride to Houston and allowing him to make a hotel reservation for her certainly didn't entail any kind of commitment on her part...or his. In fact, he'd probably deem his duty done once he'd dropped her at the hotel, and more than likely, she wouldn't see him again after that.

Which would definitely be all for the best. She still found him much too attractive, but now, more than ever, she knew better than to imagine that anything would ever come of it. Surely his sister and brother-in-law wouldn't want the birth mother of their adopted child around any longer than necessary. And since he obviously cared about them quite a bit, he'd naturally be inclined to respect their feelings.

Admonishing herself for once again allowing her thoughts

to wander in such a totally inappropriate way, Tess turned her attention back to the matter at hand. Though Will Landon seemed to be in no hurry to go, she couldn't expect him to wait indefinitely for her to make up her mind. And since she could think of a lot worse ways to spend a Sunday afternoon than making the drive to Houston with him…

"If you're sure it won't be too much of a bother for you…" she began, determined to let him know up front that she didn't want him going out of his way for her.

"No bother at all," he assured her, a smile hovering around the corners of his mouth.

"I won't be able to get away until late Sunday afternoon."

"We can leave whenever you want," he said, as if her wish was his command. "Tell me what time you'd like me to be here, and I will."

"But…" He had to have better things to do than hang around San Antonio all weekend. Surely a man like him must have someone waiting for him at home—a wife, a couple of kids, maybe even a big old dog. "What about your family? Won't they mind your being away for several days?"

"Julie, Philip and Jonathan are my only family," he answered easily, his smile widening. "And they aren't expecting me back until Sunday evening."

Realizing that he'd been aware of what she was really asking, Tess blushed furiously as she lowered her gaze. She hadn't any right, not to mention any reason, to question him about his private life, even in a roundabout way. In fact, the less she knew about him, the better. And the sooner she got rid of him…

"How about four o'clock on Sunday, then?"

"Sounds good to me." He hesitated, his smile fading. "I imagine you've got a lot to do between now and then, so I guess I'd better be on my way."

"Quite a lot," she agreed, yet she made no move to show him to the door.

He seemed reluctant to leave, as reluctant as she was to see him go. She had no idea at all why he'd want to linger any longer than necessary. As for her…

Once she was alone in the house she'd be forced to face up to what lay ahead for her in Houston. She'd never been sick a day in her life, probably because she'd never been able to afford to be. When she'd been younger, she'd had to be physically strong simply to avoid emotional devastation at the hands of her mother. Now, because of her physical, as well as emotional well-being, she was able to keep food on her table and a roof over her head. Yet she'd all but *volunteered* to have surgery, the kind of major surgery that would leave her as weak as a newborn kitten for days, or probably weeks.

Just the thought of being so...helpless was enough to make her want to change her mind. But how could she when her child's life hung in the balance?

Suddenly, aware that Will Landon was watching her with growing concern, Tess tipped her chin up and squared her shoulders. She not only could take care of herself, but she *would,* and she wanted him to know it. That way he could save his sympathy for someone who really needed it.

"Are you staying at one of the hotels in town?" she asked, starting toward him.

"At the La Mansion on the Riverwalk." He pulled another of his cards from his jacket pocket and jotted something on the back of it, then offered it to her. "If you have any questions or...anything, don't hesitate to call me."

"I won't." Taking the card from him, she glanced at it and saw that he'd written the hotel phone number, as well as his room number on it. She set in on the coffee table, then turned toward the entryway. "Let me see you to the—"

"Tess...wait."

He rested his hand on her arm as he spoke, and she faced him again, surprised as much by his gentle touch as by the odd way in which he'd said her name. As she gazed at him in confusion, he released her, then pulled what appeared to be another card from his pocket.

He eyed her silently for several seconds, as if he wasn't quite sure about what he planned to do next. Finally he reached out and tucked the small square into her shirt pocket, his fingers barely brushing against the fabric before he lowered his hand to his side.

"What—" Tess began.

"Just something I think you should have," he replied, holding her gaze a moment longer. Then he turned and headed for the door. "See you on Sunday, Professor."

"Yes...of course," she murmured, more bewildered than ever as she watched him take his leave.

For what seemed like a very long time, Tess stood alone in the middle of her living room, not quite sure that he was gone for good. Finally she crossed to the entryway and locked the door. Then, almost as an afterthought, she dug out the card he'd stuck in her shirt pocket. Only it wasn't a *card*...

Suddenly, not quite able to catch her breath, she sat down slowly in the wing-back chair, her gaze riveted on the photograph she held in her hand.

A young boy smiled back at her, a boy with her dark, curly hair and pale gray eyes. Tracing her fingers over his face, she smiled, her heart full of love and pride. Her son...and Bryan's. His square jaw and cocky grin left no doubt of that. Although *she'd* never been the one who'd been unsure...

Ah, well, that was all water under the bridge now, wasn't it? No sense getting worked up all over again. Doing so hadn't done her any good anytime over the past ten years. And it certainly wouldn't do her any good tonight.

Looking back, she knew she'd made her choices the best way she'd known how. She'd only wanted what was best for her baby, and that seemed to be just what she'd gotten for him.

He obviously had two parents who loved him above all else, and he looked so happy, so healthy. Just like a real boy should. But then he *was* a real boy...

And she was no more able to think of letting him down now than she had been ten years ago.

If Will Landon had wanted to guarantee her cooperation, he couldn't have chosen a better way to do it, Tess thought, gazing at the photograph a few seconds longer, then slipping it back in her shirt pocket. Yet she couldn't believe that was why he'd given her the boy's picture. Coercion of any kind simply wasn't his style.

So what had prompted him to do it? She hadn't asked about the boy in any great detail. But not because she hadn't wanted to know. She'd just felt that she had no…right.

And she didn't, she reminded herself as she picked up the lukewarm glass of iced tea Will had left on the coffee table and headed for the kitchen.

Whatever his reasons for doing so, Will Landon had been kind enough to give her a picture of…his nephew. But Tess knew she'd be making a big mistake if she allowed herself to hope for any other concessions where the boy was concerned.

Jonathan had a family, and no matter what she did for him, she had to remember that she'd never be a part of it. In fact, she'd probably be expected to fade quietly into the woodwork once she'd served her purpose, and the less she knew about him, the easier that would be.

"Talk about feeling sorry for yourself," she chided softly as she dumped the iced tea down the drain, then set the glass on the counter.

She thought about fixing herself something to eat, but she wasn't the least bit hungry. Nor did she want to call Richard as she'd thought of doing earlier. He'd want to talk about their trip to Ireland, and she certainly wasn't up to any prevarication.

That left the briefcase full of paperwork she'd brought home with her. She couldn't honestly say she was in the mood to regrade a stack of tests, but she had a lot to do between now and four o'clock Sunday afternoon. The sooner she got started, the better.

"So get your butt in gear," she ordered softly.

Instead of wasting time wishing for the moon…

Will sat in the car outside Tess's house for much longer than he should have. He wasn't quite sure why. He hadn't really expected her to follow him out the door. Nor did he have any good reason to go back and talk to her again. Yet he didn't feel right about leaving her all alone.

Unfortunately he knew she wouldn't welcome *his* company.

But he found himself hoping that maybe someone else would come to the house and spend a little time with her. At least then he'd feel better about going on his way.

He'd laid a hell of a lot on her in the past couple of hours, and no matter how cool and calm she'd tried to appear, he hadn't been fooled. He'd seen the fear and confusion in her pale eyes, and he'd sensed her inner turmoil. Yet he hadn't backed off the slightest bit.

He'd asked her to risk her life for a child who was really no more than a stranger to her, and he'd done so without offering her any guarantees. He'd been so sure that he was doing the right thing when he'd begun his…campaign. Anything to save his sister's son. He hadn't allowed himself to take into account how Tess McGuire would be affected, especially in the long run. But now…

Whether or not she proved to be a suitable donor, thanks to him her life would never be the same. From the look he'd seen on her face when he first mentioned Jonathan, he'd stirred up more than a few painful memories, and that had been just for starters. Whatever plans she'd made for the summer would very likely have to be canceled. And though he'd downplayed the possibility considerably, there was a slight chance that she might not ever fully recuperate from the surgery.

Of course, Philip would see to it that she never wanted for anything. But considering how insulted she'd been by his callous mention of compensation, Will didn't think she'd find that much of a comfort. She'd made it clear she wanted nothing from his brother-in-law or from him.

Talk about one of a kind… She was so proud and so independent…too damned independent for her own good. If she'd had any sense at all, she'd have insisted up front that she be given *x* number of dollars in exchange for what she was doing. That's what Claire would have done.…

"But then your ex-fiancée was always more interested in your brother-in-law's money than she was in you," he reminded himself bitterly.

At least on that score, Tess McGuire wasn't anything like Claire Colson. In fact, Tess had been so angered by his assumption that she'd expect to be paid that she'd been ready to refuse his offer of a ride to Houston, as well as a hotel room.

Of course, she could always change her mind about the money, and she might very well do just that once she realized what she'd gotten herself into. But Will doubted it. The standards she'd set for herself were simply too high. She'd keep her part of the bargain without asking for anything in return, just as she'd said she would.

Making a mental note to advise Philip not to mention the words *financial remuneration* to her under any circumstances, Will turned the key in the ignition and started the car. It was well past eight o'clock, and Tess was still home alone. But he had yet to call his sister and brother-in-law to give them the good news about her, and he knew they were probably growing more anxious by the minute.

As he pulled away from the curb, he glanced at her house one last time. Her living room light was still on, but she'd closed the blinds. Turning his attention to the road ahead, he found himself hoping that she was all right. Maybe he'd call and check on her after he talked to Julie and Philip. Then again, maybe not.

She'd more than likely heard all she wanted to hear from him for the time being. And it wasn't as if he had anything reassuring to add to what he'd already said to her. In all honesty, calling her would be more for *his* peace of mind, and that simply wasn't a good enough reason to bother her any more tonight.

He made his way back to the hotel with relative ease, parked in the garage and headed for his room. As he opened the door, he saw the message light blinking on the telephone, and dialed the operator immediately. He found himself hoping that Tess had called, though he could think of no reason why she'd do so, except to say that she'd changed her mind. Instead, the operator asked him to call his sister at home as soon as possible.

That she was at home rather than at the hospital worried him, until he realized it was Friday. Since Philip didn't go in to the office most Saturdays, he'd probably sent her home to rest while he spent the night with Jonathan.

She answered on the first ring, her voice quavering slightly. Mentally cursing himself for dawdling outside Tess's house as long as he had, Will hastened to assure his sister that all had gone well. Though he and Philip had cautioned her not to pin her hopes on the professor, Julie had believed that Mary Theresa McGuire would be the answer to their prayers, and so far, she seemed to be right.

He related the pertinent details of his conversation with Tess, then answered Julie's questions as best he could, realizing as he did so how little he really knew of Tess personally.

"She sounds like a really nice person," Julie admitted at last. "Did you find out why she put Jonathan up for adoption?"

"She didn't offer the information, and since I didn't really think it was any of our business, I didn't ask."

"Did she...did she ask a lot of questions about him?" Julie continued, obviously not quite as convinced as he that Tess hadn't any ulterior motives for helping the boy.

"No, not really," he answered honestly.

"She didn't want to know anything about him?" Julie prodded, making no effort to hide her disbelief.

"I didn't say she didn't want to know anything about him," Will chided quietly. "I said she didn't *ask.*"

"But, why—"

"Maybe she didn't think it was any of her business."

He'd seen the play of emotions on Tess's face when he'd first mentioned the baby she'd given away, and instinctively he'd known that she'd loved her son. Yet she'd chosen to put him up for adoption. Now, after almost ten years, he was someone else's child.

As far as Will was concerned, Tess had accepted that fact with admirable grace, but convincing his sister of it would be difficult at best. Julie had already made it clear that she felt Tess should have as little contact as possible with her son, and to a certain extent Will agreed with her. But Tess was risking her life for the boy, and she was doing so without asking for anything in return.

For that reason, and that reason alone, he'd given her the picture of Jonathan. Unfortunately he didn't think his sister would understand. But what she didn't know wouldn't hurt her. He'd been completely truthful about Tess's reserve, yet he couldn't see that going on to explain his own lack thereof would serve any purpose at all.

"Maybe not," Julie agreed, her voice soft and tremulous. "But what if she just doesn't...care about him? She could... she could change her mind...."

"Trust me, Julie, that's not going to happen," Will soothed. "Tess will do what she can for Jonathan."

"If you say so."

"I say so," he replied. "Now, tell me, how's the kid doing?"

"According to the doctors, he's holding his own." Julie paused as if trying to collect herself, then continued on a lighter note. "He can't wait to see you on Sunday, but of course, that may have something to do with the *stuff* you promised to buy for him at the Mexican market. Do they really have Bart Simpson piñatas, and if so, do you really have to bring one back for him?"

"Absolutely."

Before he hung up the telephone, Will actually managed to make his sister laugh, and just knowing that he'd raised her spirits made him feel better than he had all day.

As he shrugged out of his suit coat and shoulder holster, he realized that he was hungry. He thought about going out to grab a bite to eat, but it was almost ten o'clock, and he didn't really feel like making the effort. Instead, he called room service and ordered a burger and fries. Then, after removing his tie and unfastening the top buttons of his shirt, he crossed to the balcony doors, opened them wide and stepped out into the dark, sultry night.

Several stories below, the San Antonio River meandered past, rippling lazily against the narrow, tree-lined banks. From where he stood, he could see couples ambling arm in arm along the paved walkways, reveling in the peaceful retreat they'd found amid the bustling city.

As their soft voices drifted up to him on the warm, gentle breeze, he caught himself thinking of Tess and recalling once again how drawn he'd been to her, not only when he'd first seen her, but later at her house, as well. She wasn't a classic beauty, yet in her own way, she was a very lovely woman. She was also bright and funny, as well as kind and considerate. And she was definitely too generous for her own good. If she'd been anybody but the birth mother of his sister's son…

"Don't even *think* about it," he muttered under his breath, turning back into the room.

No matter how captivated he might be by Tess McGuire, he simply could not pursue any kind of personal relationship with her. He had to maintain the same type of professional distance he would with any other…business associate. Otherwise, he'd begin to care about her, really *care* about her more than he already did. And that was one thing he just couldn't afford to do. Once she started to mean something to him, standing by quietly and allowing her to put her life on the line—even for the sake of his own nephew—would be damned difficult to do.

He also had to remember how his sister felt about Tess. He'd tried to reassure Julie that Tess was a decent person, but he knew that Julie hadn't been completely convinced. Somewhere in the back of her mind, she still firmly believed that Tess would manage to steal her son away, either by word or by deed. Until there was no longer any reason for her to be a part of their lives and she'd gone back to San Antonio, never to be seen or heard from again, Julie wouldn't rest easy.

And since that certainly wouldn't happen if he got involved with Tess…

"You just won't do it," he warned as he tossed his overnight bag onto the bed, opened it and pulled out a fresh T-shirt and a pair of shorts.

He'd never intentionally done anything to upset his sister, and he wasn't about to start now. He'd much rather do whatever was necessary to make her life a little easier. And if that meant he had to consider Tess McGuire out-of-bounds, then so be it.

Of course, it wouldn't be easy. Not by any stretch of the

imagination. There was no denying he found her alluring. And he'd be seeing a lot of her over the next few weeks, especially since he'd opted to act as liaison between her and his sister.

Maybe when he got back to Houston he'd make an effort to get together with one of the more attainable women Julie had introduced him to lately. Surely then his interest in Tess would wane. In the eighteen months since he and Claire had parted company, he hadn't wanted to be seriously involved with anyone. But apparently he was more than ready to get back in the saddle again.

Unfortunately his body had decided to relay that message to his brain about the time he'd come face-to-face with Tess McGuire. Considering how long he'd been celibate, any other reasonably attractive woman would have probably caught his attention just as easily at that moment. Which meant that the longing Tess had stirred in him hadn't been as...specific as he'd originally thought it to be.

Or so he'd like to believe, he thought as he headed toward the bathroom.

The room-service waiter had advised him that his meal wouldn't be delivered for at least forty-five minutes, and if the clock on the nightstand was correct, he still had more than enough time to take a shower. With luck, the pounding spray would ease some of the tension thrumming through him. Otherwise, he was going to have one hell of a long, restless night ahead of him. And that definitely wouldn't bode well for the rest of the weekend.

Much to his surprise, Will slept fairly well, and when he awoke early Saturday morning, he was more than ready to make the most of what promised to be a beautiful day.

Since he hadn't been to San Antonio for several years, and the city had changed quite a bit in that time, he decided to spend the morning playing tourist. He made the requisite stop at the Alamo, then took the trolley down to the Mexican market, where he did indeed find a Bart Simpson piñata, as well as a couple of brightly painted, gaily costumed puppets and a huge sombrero, all for his nephew. After lunch at the Mexican bakery, he went back to the hotel to drop off his purchases and pick up the car.

After studying the map for a few minutes, he decided to drive down to the old missions south of the city. But when he pulled out of the parking garage, he didn't immediately head in that direction. Instead, he turned north toward the neighborhood where Tess lived.

He'd been determined to stay away from her, for her good, as well as his own. Yet somewhere in the back of his mind, he'd known that he just couldn't do it. Just as he couldn't stop thinking about her no matter how hard he tried.

Of course, he wouldn't go so far as to approach her again. Not when he hadn't the faintest idea what he could say to her if he did. He'd simply ride by her house a time or two and maybe catch a glimpse of her. Then at least he'd know that she was all right.

Realizing he probably needed his head examined, Will drove slowly down her street, gladly staying several car lengths behind the minivan that had pulled out of a driveway in front of him. The odds that she'd just happen to be outside as he drove by were about a zillion to one. But then, from a couple of houses away, he saw her standing near her front porch and knew that his rather foolish gamble had paid off in the best possible way.

She was wearing white shorts and a hot-pink tank top, and she had her hair pulled back in a ponytail. She appeared to have been working in the yard, but at the moment she was talking to another woman, probably a neighbor. And in her arms she held a toddler.

As Will cruised by, he saw her tickle the child under his chin, then laugh out loud with him. A moment later she handed the boy back to his mother and waved them on their way. Then, without so much as a glance in his direction, she knelt down beside the flower bed and reached for the gardening trowel lying in the grass.

Stopping at the stop sign, Will shifted his attention to the rearview mirror and watched her work for a minute or two.

Finally, aware that another car had pulled up behind him, he drove on.

Yet the image of her laughing stayed in his mind. And he found himself wondering how it would feel to be able to make her that happy. Probably pretty damned good, he mused, cutting back to the road that would eventually take him down to the missions. Maybe he'd be lucky enough to find out one day. But then again, all things considered, maybe he wouldn't....

He spent what was left of the afternoon wandering around first Mission Concepcion, then Mission San Jose. Returning to the hotel *without* any...detours, he changed into shorts, a T-shirt and his running shoes, then hit the streets, jogging until he could think of nothing but drawing in his next breath. He showered, changed and went out to eat at one of the quaint little restaurants along the Riverwalk.

He slept again that night, but only after swimming at least a dozen laps in the hotel pool. And when he awoke Sunday morning, he felt anything but rested.

With more than eight hours to go until he was due to pick up Tess, he wasn't quite sure what to do with himself, especially since the weather had turned rainy during the night. He couldn't jog and he couldn't swim; he couldn't even go for a walk without getting soaked to the skin. So he ate breakfast in the hotel dining room, then stopped in the lobby and bought the San Antonio Sunday papers along with those from several other cities around the state. Back in his room, he read, watched television and paced, alternately cursing the weather and his own ill-concealed impatience.

He wanted to see Tess. Yet he knew that when he did, it would be to take her to Houston and whatever Jonathan's doctors had in store for her there....

By three o'clock Will was ready to start climbing the walls. Instead, he checked out of the hotel, loaded the car and headed to Tess's house. If she wasn't ready to go when he got there, he'd sit in her tastefully decorated living room and wait until she was.

Thanks to a traffic tie-up resulting from a minor accident, he pulled up to the curb in front of her house only fifteen minutes early. Not only had the rain let up by then, but to his surprise, Tess opened the door almost as soon as he rang the bell, as if she'd been anticipating his early arrival.

She was dressed in a simple pale yellow knit dress with short sleeves, a fitted bodice and a long, full skirt. She'd tied her hair back at the nape of her neck with a matching silk scarf, and aside from her watch, the only other jewelry she wore was a pair of simple gold hoop earrings.

As she smiled tentatively, he was struck once again by her quiet courage. Yet, seeing the dark shadows under her eyes, he couldn't help but be reminded of her inherent vulnerability, as well.

For one long moment, he wanted to grab her by the hand, hustle her out to the car and head for the border. He wanted to run with her and hide, to keep her safe....

But then he thought of the consequences.

"Is this everything?" he asked, his voice sounding unusually gruff to him as he gestured toward the hanging bag and small suitcase just inside the doorway.

"Yes..."

"Then I guess we'd better get going."

Determined not to be swayed by the flicker of uncertainty he saw in her pale eyes, Will picked up Tess's things, then turned and walked to the car without so much as a backward glance.

He didn't want her to be hurt. Not for any reason. But he had to think of his nephew first. He just *had* to....

Chapter Three

Watching as Will loaded her things into the trunk of the classy BMW at the curb, Tess slipped into her white cotton cardigan, then slung her purse strap over her shoulder and picked up her briefcase.

She wasn't exactly sure what she'd been expecting of him, but in all honesty, she *had* been hoping for more than a curt suggestion that they'd "better get going." A friendly smile, or at the very least, a polite "Hello, how are you?" would have done very nicely, considering her growing trepidation about what awaited her in Houston.

Unfortunately he seemed too caught up in his own thoughts to spare any real concern for her. But then why should he? She'd already agreed to do what he'd asked of her, and apparently he wasn't worried that she'd go back on her word.

Of course she wouldn't, no matter how frightened she might be. But still, she really could have used a *little* moral support....

"Now, Tess, stop feeling sorry for yourself," she murmured as she took one last look around her house. "The man doesn't owe you anything, and you've already made sure that he knows it."

Having assured herself as best she could that the house was secure, she stepped onto the front porch, pulled the door closed and locked it. She hesitated a moment longer, wondering when she'd be back again. Not that it really mattered. Her next-door neighbor had gladly agreed to look after the place as long as necessary. So, as long as she returned eventually…

Realizing that her thoughts were on the verge of becoming downright morbid, she turned away from the house and moved briskly down the walkway to where Will waited with the car door open.

"Would you like me to put your briefcase in the trunk, too?" he asked, his tone much milder than it had been a few minutes earlier.

"I appreciate the offer, but I'd rather keep it handy. I still have quite a bit of paperwork to finish up." Nothing that couldn't wait until she got to Houston, but she didn't want him to feel obligated to keep up a conversation with her during the long drive.

"If it's inconvenient for you to leave today—"

"Not at all," she assured him quietly.

Meeting his gaze as she slid onto the car seat, Tess saw that his expression had softened somewhat. And suddenly she knew that the past few days hadn't been any easier on him than they had been on her. He wasn't the type to take their current situation lightly. Yet he was doing what he felt he had to do, just as she was.

"You're sure?"

"Very sure."

He nodded once. Then, closing her car door, he crossed to the driver's side.

As he settled into his seat and turned the key in the ignition, Tess fastened her seat belt, then smoothed a hand over the rich leather upholstery.

"Nice car," she murmured appreciatively, unable to help but wonder how an investigator with the Harris County district attorney's office could afford such luxury.

"It belongs to my sister," he admitted, a slight smile on his face as he glanced at her. "She lets me drive it every now and then just to remind me of what I'm missing by not going to work for Drake Oil."

Drake Oil? Frowning, Tess stared out the window as Will guided the car onto the freeway. On Friday he'd referred to his sister and brother-in-law as Julie and Philip, but he hadn't mentioned a last name. Yet, thanks to an article she'd read recently in *Texas Monthly* about the wealthiest men in the state, Tess had no trouble putting two and two together. Will Landon's brother-in-law was Philip Drake, CEO of Drake Oil and Gas, one of the most successful of the independent oil companies that had started operating in the mid-1980s.

Of course, she could be mistaken, but…

"Your sister's married to Philip Drake, *the* Philip Drake of Drake Oil and Gas?" she asked, eyeing Will intently.

"For almost twenty years," he replied, meeting her gaze for a moment.

"I…see…" She turned and stared out the window again, her thoughts spinning.

No wonder Will had talked about compensation as if it wasn't a big deal. To a man like Philip Drake, money certainly was no object. Just as it hadn't been to Bryan's parents.…

Not that she could honestly equate Philip Drake with Ray and Ella Harper. Philip had wanted to pay for her help in saving his adopted son's life, while the Harpers had wanted something else altogether. They'd wanted her to end her child's life before it had barely begun.

Still, Will's brother-in-law and the Harpers *did* have one thing in common. They'd assumed that having money in the bank was more important to her than maintaining her self-respect. Why, she wasn't quite sure. Just because someone wasn't financially well-off didn't automatically mean that she was for sale.

However, there was no sense getting her back up about that again. She'd let Will know exactly how she felt about Philip's offer of *compensation* already.

And, looking on the bright side, at least now she was sure

that she'd done the best she could for her child. He'd never want for anything, not anything at all.

"They're good people, Professor," Will said, as if he'd been reading her mind. "They earned everything they have the hard way, but if it meant saving Jonathan's life, they'd give it all away in a minute."

"They really do love him, don't they?" she asked. Though she had no doubt what his answer would be, she wanted to hear him say it.

"More than anything."

"I'm glad." And she was, because that's what *she* had wanted for him. *More than anything...*

"They're very grateful for what you're doing." He hesitated, as if choosing his next words carefully, then continued. "They realize they've put you in an awkward position, and the next few days or...weeks won't be easy for you."

"I imagine it won't be easy for them, either," Tess replied. "Especially since I'm still something of an unknown quantity."

"Not as far as I'm concerned."

Surprised by his frank admission, Tess gazed at him questioningly. "Is that a vote of confidence, Mr. Landon?"

"Very much so," he admitted, offering her a wry smile.

"Well, then, thank you." For just a moment, she smiled, too.

"Why don't you call me Will?"

"All right..." she agreed, though not without some hesitation.

Maintaining at least a semblance of formality between them seemed a wise thing to do. But insisting on it would have been churlish of her. More than likely, he was only trying to make her as comfortable as possible during their limited time together. He couldn't know that any overture on his part only served to intensify her initial attraction to him.

It was bad enough that he'd chosen to wear faded jeans and a black knit shirt today; he looked even better in them than she'd imagined. Still, she'd have been able to quash her hopeless…desire if he'd remained as aloof as he'd been when he arrived at her house.

Ah, well, they'd only be together a few hours longer. And she did have work to do, she reminded herself, lifting her briefcase onto her lap and unzipping it. Maybe if she kept her mind occupied, she wouldn't be tempted to dwell on foolish fantasies.

As she reached for the folder full of papers she'd tucked into one of the compartments, her fingers brushed against the small silver frame that now held Jonathan's photograph. Recalling that she hadn't told Will how much she appreciated having it, she turned her attention back to him once more.

"By the way, thanks for the picture of Jonathan."

"As I said the other day, I thought you ought to have it."

"He looks so happy and so…healthy."

"That photograph was taken about a year ago, before he came down with the virus. Unfortunately he doesn't look nearly as good right now," he advised, adding quietly, "I thought you'd better know, just so you won't be too surprised when you see him."

"When I see him?" Tess queried uneasily.

"I just thought you'd want to—"

"No, really… I…I don't think that would be a good idea at all," she insisted, unable to mask the sudden surge of panic she felt at the mere thought of coming face-to-face with her son.

He eyed her thoughtfully for several seconds, a frown creasing his forehead. "Why not?" he asked, obviously puzzled by her response.

"I don't know," she replied as honestly as she could. "I just…*don't.*"

While she was quite pleased to have a photograph of the boy, actually spending time with him was more than she could countenance. She didn't want to risk forming any sort of attachment to him. For all intents and purposes, he was Julie and Philip Drake's son. And for her own well-being, she couldn't allow herself to ever think otherwise.

"What about Julie and Philip? They're planning on being at

the hospital tomorrow morning when you meet with Dr. Wells and his team. But if you'd rather not have any contact with them, either..."

In all honesty, Tess hadn't considered the possibility of coming face-to-face with the Drakes any more than she had of coming face-to-face with Jonathan. But they had to be curious about her. *She* was certainly curious about *them*. Yet she didn't want them to think that she expected to be a part of their lives, even temporarily. In fact, she'd actually hoped that she could remain somewhat...anonymous. However, since they seemed willing to make the proverbial first move...

"I'd like to meet your sister and brother-in-law, but only if you're sure that's what *they* want," she admitted.

"But not Jonathan?" he prodded, as if he was having a hard time understanding her reasoning.

"Not Jonathan," she responded in an adamant tone of voice, hoping to avoid any further argument. No matter how much she wanted to see the boy, she just couldn't do it. Because once would never be enough.

He didn't say anything more for what seemed like a long time. Finally, however, he murmured a simple "Whatever you say." Then, as the drizzle they'd been driving through for almost an hour turned into a steady downpour, he cursed softly, upping the speed of the windshield wipers.

Determined to see to it that he let the matter rest, Tess opened her folder and removed one of the dozen or more papers still in need of her personal attention. Though she'd managed to finish most of her end-of-semester work on Saturday, she still had a few final grades to tabulate, as well as recommendations to write for several of her graduate students.

Shifting slightly in her seat, she lowered her gaze and tried her best to concentrate on the essay she held in her hands. But somehow the influx of Christian missionaries into Ireland in the late fourth and early fifth centuries failed to hold her interest. Not that the paper was poorly written. She was just too conscious of Will Landon sitting beside her quietly, his capable hands on the steering wheel, his eyes on the road...mostly.

"You're going to ruin your eyes reading in this gloom," he

muttered after a few minutes, punching a button that switched on the map light.

Since she hadn't *really* been reading, she wasn't in any danger of eye strain, but she didn't dare admit as much to him. Though she was using her work as a way to avoid further conversation, there was no reason why he had to know it. He meant well, but as far as she was concerned, some subjects simply weren't open to discussion. Still…

"If the light's going to bother you, I don't *have* to work right now," she admitted.

"Do whatever you need to do. I don't mind having it on."

"If you're sure…"

"Don't worry about it." He glanced at her and smiled, then reached over and gently squeezed her hand. "All right?"

"All right," she agreed, the tenderness of his touch warming her in an unexpected way.

They drove a while longer, and to her surprise, Tess actually got through several essays, despite her increased awareness of Will. However, when he slowed the car to exit off the freeway, she gladly set aside the paper she was working on.

"Any preferences?" he asked, gesturing toward the fast-food restaurants lining the feeder road.

"They're all the same to me."

"Me, too."

Since neither of them was hungry, they stopped just long enough to stretch their legs. Then, cups of coffee in hand, they returned to the car.

They made the rest of the drive in oddly companionable silence, as if they'd gone beyond being mere acquaintances and had somehow become…friends.

They arrived in Houston shortly after seven o'clock, and as Will turned off one freeway onto another, then finally exited onto a city street, Tess reluctantly gathered up her papers and put them away. After he dropped her at the hotel, she probably wouldn't see much more of him, and that was too bad, because she really did like him. Yet in the long run, she knew it was all for the best.

From her past trips to the city, Tess recognized the area of

Houston they were driving through as the neighborhood near Rice University. What she didn't understand, however, was why they were turning into the curving driveway of what appeared to be an old mansion.

"I thought you were taking me to a hotel," she said uneasily, frowning as she turned to look at him.

"This *is* a hotel."

"But it looks more like somebody's house." Somebody very, very wealthy, she added to herself.

"It used to be, but now it's a hotel." He grinned as he met her gaze. "Trust me."

As if she had a choice, she thought as he climbed out of the car, then walked around to open her door. Ah, well, in for a penny…

He helped her out of the car, took her briefcase from her and guided her up the wide stone stairway. As they crossed the huge covered porch, one of the double front doors inset with panels of beveled glass swung open, and a handsome young man wearing a coat and tie welcomed them inside with a flourish.

"Mr. Landon, so good to see you again. I trust your drive from San Antonio wasn't too tedious despite the bad weather."

"Not at all, Henry. Is Ms. McGuire's room ready?"

"Of course." He nodded at Tess, smiling graciously. "Ms. McGuire, it's a pleasure to have you staying with us. May I show you to your room?"

"I'll take her up, Henry."

"Surely, sir." He offered Will an old-fashioned key. "Number three, on the second floor to the right of the staircase. If you'll give me your car keys, I'll see to her luggage."

"Thanks a lot."

As Will led her across the foyer to the carved wooden staircase, Tess eyed her surroundings with undisguised awe. From the Persian rugs scattered across the inlaid floor and the rich paneling covering the walls, to the massive crystal chandelier hanging from the ceiling and the myriad vases full of fresh-cut flowers scenting the air, the place exuded elegance.

"There's the restaurant." Will nodded toward a large room

off to one side, filled with linen-covered tables already set with fine china and crystal and silver. ''And the bar's tucked under the stairs.''

''Very nice,'' Tess murmured.

Actually it was more than *nice,* so much more that she found herself wondering what in the world *she* was doing there.

''You don't like it, do you?'' Will asked as they started up the grand staircase.

''Of course I like it,'' she hastened to assure him. ''I'm just a little overwhelmed. I've never stayed anywhere so luxurious.''

''Philip wanted you to be as comfortable as possible. He also wanted to be sure all your needs would be met. It's very safe here—also very quiet, and the service is excellent. No matter what you want, day or night, the staff will see that you get it.''

''I appreciate his thoughtfulness. Really, I do.''

''Good.''

Pausing by a paneled door marked with a discreet brass number three, Will inserted the key in the lock and turned it. Then, as the door swung open, he ushered Tess into what was more a suite than a room. As well as a spacious bedroom, decorated in shades of rose and cream and filled with beautiful antiques, there was a small sitting room, surrounded on three sides by floor-to-ceiling windows.

''Oh, Will, it's just lovely,'' she murmured, trailing a hand over the striped satin coverlet on the four-poster bed, then moving on to stand beside one of the overstuffed chairs near the windows.

''So I guess that means you'll stay the night?'' he asked, a hint of teasing laughter in his voice.

''Well, as long as I'm here, I suppose I might as well,'' she replied, smiling as she turned to face him again.

''Henry will be happy to hear that. Won't you, Henry?''

''Happy to hear what, sir?'' Henry inquired as he crossed to the closet, hung her hanging bag on the rod and set her suitcase on a small stand.

''Ms. McGuire has decided to stay.''

''But, of course.'' Turning to Tess, he bowed slightly. ''If you need anything, anything at all, just dial the front desk, and we'll see that you get it as quickly as possible.'' Then, with a courteous nod to Will, he left the room as discreetly as he'd entered.

On her own with Will once again, Tess suddenly wasn't sure what else to say to him. He'd done his duty by her, and then some. Surely he had to be ready to go on his way. But suggesting that he leave seemed rather rude. So she stayed where she was, watching as he crossed to the eighteenth-century bureau and set her briefcase atop it, then switched on a silk-shaded lamp.

''Would you...would you like to have dinner with me?'' he asked as he finally faced her again.

At that moment, Tess couldn't think of anything she wanted to do more. Yet she also knew she had to refuse. Accepting a ride to Houston had been one thing. But agreeing to have dinner with him would be something else altogether. If she allowed herself to share that kind of quality time with him, she'd be more tempted than ever to wish for what she couldn't have. And she'd already done enough of that to last a lifetime. No sense setting herself up, just to be shot down...again.

''I really appreciate the invitation, but I still have quite a bit of work to do. I think I'll just order something from room service later.''

He gazed at her wordlessly for several long moments, as if he couldn't quite decide whether or not to accept her excuse. Finally he turned away from her and started toward the door.

''As Henry said, just call down and order whatever you want whenever you're ready.''

''I will.''

Though she trailed after him, she kept a little distance between them, aware of how easily she could change her mind. In fact, there was a good chance that if she got too close to him, she'd end up flinging herself into his arms and begging him to stay. And that wouldn't do at all.

''Well, then, I guess I'd better be going.'' He glanced over his shoulder at her. ''You're scheduled to meet with Dr. Wells at ten o'clock in the morning, so why don't we plan on my picking you up around nine-thirty, all right?''

''If you'll just tell me exactly where I'm supposed to be, I can take a taxi,'' she offered.

''You know, Professor, I'm beginning to get the feeling that you're not very fond of my company.'' Turning toward her again, he gazed at her searchingly.

''Oh, no, that's—that's not true at all.'' Realizing that she'd hurt his feelings, she moved toward him and rested a hand on his arm apologetically. ''I just don't want you to have to go out of your way for me anymore,'' she added softly, drawing away again.

''I'm not,'' he assured her.

''But you must have to go to work tomorrow.''

''No one will give me any grief if I'm a little late.''

''Then I'll be ready at nine-thirty,'' she agreed, aware that any further protestation on her part would be fatuous.

''Dr. Wells will probably want you to check into the hospital after you've talked, so you'd better plan on bringing your things with you.''

She nodded wordlessly, reminded once again of why they were there together. Not to pursue any kind of personal relationship, but to do what they could to save a dying child...a child who was once hers.

He started to turn away, then hesitated, as if reluctant to leave her. ''You'll be all right here, won't you?'' he asked, his deep voice full of concern.

''I'll be just fine,'' she assured him, forcing herself to smile.

Rather than return her smile as she expected, he frowned as he held her gaze. Then, reaching out, he smoothed a wisp of hair away from her face. ''Try to get some sleep tonight, okay?''

''Okay,'' she murmured as he moved toward the door at last.

Somehow she managed to quell the urge to call him back, watching as he walked out of her room and quietly closed the door. As if rooted to the spot, she stood where she was long after his footsteps faded down the hallway, and wondered if she'd only imagined the gentle brush of his fingertips against her face.

Finally, almost as an afterthought, she crossed to the door and locked it. Then, with a soft sigh, she surveyed her surroundings once again. The room really was warm and inviting, more so than any other hotel room she'd stayed in before. Yet Tess couldn't remember ever feeling quite so lonely in her life as she did here.

Maybe she should have accepted Will's invitation to dinner. At least she would have put off this moment a while longer. But then it would have come eventually, and the more time she'd have spent with him, the harder it would have been to bear.

What she ought to do is call Richard. She'd talked to him yesterday, but only for a few minutes. She'd told him that she had to go to Houston to take care of some personal business, but she hadn't gone into any detail. Perhaps she should tell him what she was really doing there. Why, he might even opt to come and be with her....

"Dream on," she muttered as she retrieved her briefcase from the bureau, then curled up in one of the overstuffed chairs by the windows.

If anything, Richard Bering would view her current situation with shock and disapproval. Bad enough that she'd gotten herself into "trouble" ten years ago. But allowing that same "trouble" to rear its ugly head and disrupt the life she'd made for herself now? Heaven forbid. And what about their trip to Ireland...?

She knew Richard well enough to realize she'd get no sympathy from him. Not that he didn't care about her. He just had certain...expectations where she was concerned, and she'd rather not disillusion him unless she had no other choice. She'd always valued the respect he'd shown her, both personally and professionally, and she wasn't about to risk losing it until she had a very good reason to do so. If the tests proved to be positive and she was deemed a suitable donor, she'd call and talk to him. But not until then.

"So, having dealt with the men in your life, what *will* you do now?" she muttered as she set her briefcase on the floor.

She knew she ought to finish the last of the paperwork she'd brought with her, but she wasn't in the mood yet. Nor did she feel like reading or watching television. Shifting in her chair, she gazed out the rain-streaked windows. Blurry lights from nearby buildings cut through the darkness, but otherwise she couldn't make out much of anything.

Turning her attention to the table beside her chair, she noticed a slim leather folder with the word *menu* stenciled on the front in gold letters. Curious as to what such an elegant place had to offer in the way of food, she began thumbing through it.

A few minutes later, her mouth watering, Tess reached for the telephone. She hadn't thought she was hungry, but her appetite had sharpened considerably at the mention of Caesar salad, snapper Pontchartrain and Key lime pie.

She rarely ate so much so late in the evening. But she couldn't see any harm in splurging a bit, especially since she'd be eating hospital food for the next few days.

She placed her order, then settled back in her chair, content to watch the rain wash against the windows. She could finish the work she had left to do after dinner. And maybe by midnight or so, she'd be able to do as Will had suggested and get a good night's sleep.

Maybe…

Considering she hadn't really expected to do more than doze once she'd finally crawled under the bedcovers around twelve-thirty, Tess awoke early Monday morning feeling surprisingly relaxed and refreshed. As she padded over to the windows, she saw that the sky had cleared during the night, and off in the distance, the sun had begun to edge over the horizon. Accepting the promise of a lovely day as a good omen, she turned and headed for the bathroom.

She took her time dressing in the off-white linen suit and pale peach silk blouse she'd chosen to wear. Then, with more than an hour to spare before Will was due to arrive, she decided to go down to the dining room to eat breakfast and read the morning paper.

Oddly enough, she wasn't as nervous as she'd thought she would be, considering what lay ahead of her. In fact, she was almost relieved that the waiting was just about over. Though she still wasn't thrilled with the prospect of meeting the Drakes, she'd more or less resigned herself to doing so. Under the circumstances, she could understand their need to see for themselves exactly what kind of person she was. And once her interview with them was over, at least she'd finally be able to check into the hospital. Then the testing could begin, which would definitely be a step in the right direction.

Despite her best intentions, she was also looking forward to seeing Will again. She knew it would have been wiser to insist on taking a taxi, even if it had meant hurting his feelings. But in all honesty, she was very glad she hadn't. No matter how independent she liked to believe she was, she found the thought of facing the Drakes and Dr. Wells completely on her own more than a little intimidating. Having Will there to at least figuratively hold her hand would be enormously reassuring.

She returned to her room at nine-fifteen, got the last of her things together and was just touching up her lipstick when she heard a knock at her door. She eyed her reflection in the mirror a moment longer, then nodded at herself encouragingly. With her hair coiled neatly at the nape of her neck, she certainly looked like the chic, savvy, professional woman she'd worked so hard to become, she assured herself as she crossed the room and opened the door.

''I'm not too early, am I?'' Will inquired.

''According to my watch, you're right on time,'' Tess replied, returning his smile with ease.

He was dressed in a dark suit, white shirt and patterned silk tie, much as he had been on Friday. She'd thought he was a handsome man then, but knowing him as she did now, she found him even more attractive today.

''You look really nice,'' he said, his admiration and approval equally evident in his bright blue eyes and his husky voice.

''So do you,'' she admitted, allowing herself a long, lingering, *last* look before she turned to fetch her purse and briefcase from the bureau.

They probably wouldn't see much of each other after this morning, so what harm could a little honest appreciation do? Especially since it was obviously mutual.

"Have you had breakfast yet?" he asked as he picked up her hanging bag and suitcase.

"Did I ever." She grinned and shook her head, recalling how easily she'd downed a mushroom omelet, biscuits smothered with honey and a bowl of strawberries and cream. "The food here is wonderful," she continued, barely resisting the urge to add that the condemned had thoroughly enjoyed her last meal.

Somehow she didn't think Will would find that kind of comment amusing, and she didn't want to say anything that might spoil his affable mood.

"Were you able to sleep all right, too?"

"Oh, yes," she admitted, following him out of the room and down the staircase. "Much better than I thought I would. The room was so quiet and so...comfortable."

"So I take it you'd stay here again, huh?"

"In a minute."

After pausing in the foyer while she thanked Henry for her pleasant stay, Will led her outside. As they crossed the porch, then walked down the steps together, Tess eyed the old Blazer parked in the drive with growing chagrin. Dressed as she was in a short, straight skirt and high-heeled shoes, climbing into the thing was going to be a real challenge.

"So you liked the coach better than the pumpkin, Cinderella?" Will asked, opening the back door and tossing her bags on the seat.

"Actually it's not that." Aware that his question had been only half-teasing, she eyed him admonishingly. "I'm not a snob, Mr. Landon. I'm just concerned about how I'm going to get from here to the passenger seat without hiking my skirt halfway up to my waist."

"Well, gosh, I kind of like *that* idea." Grinning, he opened the door for her, and...waited.

"Why am I not surprised?" she retorted, setting her purse and briefcase on the seat, then standing her ground.

"Going to insist on being modest, huh?"

"I most certainly am."

"In that case..."

Before she knew what was happening, Will slipped his hands around her waist and lifted her effortlessly onto the Blazer's passenger seat.

"Oh...my," she murmured breathlessly, gazing down at him as she rested her hands on his shoulders.

"Liked that, did you?" he growled softly, still holding on to her.

She had, quite a bit, but she wasn't about to let him know it. Not when he was so close that she could smell the spicy scent of his after-shave.

"Has anyone ever told you you're incorrigible?" she queried, slipping neatly out of his grasp as she scooted across the seat.

"Not since I accidentally glued Sally Wilkins's braids together in seventh grade," he admitted with obvious pride.

"Accidentally?"

"Stuff happens, ya know." His eyes glimmered with mischief for a moment. Then, as if considering the words he'd just spoken in another way, his gaze suddenly turned solemn. "Tess—"

"Somehow I can't imagine braids and glue just... happening," she cut in lightly, hoping to keep their conversation from taking a serious turn.

Though he eyed her narrowly for what seemed like a long time, he went along with her in the end. "You and Mrs. Adler," he groused as he closed her door.

"Mrs. Adler?" she asked after he'd climbed into the driver's seat.

"My seventh grade teacher." Glancing at her, he grinned once again, then started the Blazer.

It took them about ten minutes to drive from the hotel to the Texas Medical Center. Traffic wasn't too bad at that hour of the morning, and Will obviously knew his way around the numerous buildings that housed six or seven separate hospitals and several hundred doctors' offices, as well as the world-famous Baylor College of Medicine.

He parked in one of the garages. Then, carrying her bags, he led her through a frightening maze of hallways connected by elevators that sometimes took them up and sometimes took them down. Finally he paused in front of a door marked Jacob Wells, M.D., And Associates.

"Doing all right?" he asked as he reached for the doorknob.

"I'm doing fine. But what about you? How are you ever going to find your way out of here again?"

"I've traveled this route several times already," he admitted, ushering her into a waiting room that looked more like someone's elegantly appointed living room.

Despite the soft lighting and soothing colors, Tess's heart began to pound as she stepped across the threshold. She was more than ready to meet with the Drakes and Dr. Wells, then get on with the necessary tests, yet her earlier bravado seemed to be fading fast. In fact, she was suddenly more than a little afraid of what was to come.

"I can stay if you'd like me to," Will offered quietly, as if reading her mind.

"Oh, no, you don't have to do that," she assured him. "I can take it from here." Tipping her chin up, she smiled as brightly as she could.

Frowning, he eyed her quizzically, then headed toward the sliding glass windows set into the dark wood paneling. "At least let me go in with you and introduce you properly."

"All right," she agreed readily, breathing a sigh of relief.

While she hated delaying him any longer than absolutely necessary, she was truly grateful that he was still there with her.

As she stood beside him, he pushed the button next to the window, and immediately one side of the glass slid open. A handsome woman wearing a pretty pink summer suit smiled at them graciously, then gestured toward the door a few feet away.

"Come right in, Mr. Landon. They're waiting for you and Ms. McGuire in Dr. Wells's office."

"Thank you, Edna."

Pausing just inside the doorway, Will set Tess's bags on the floor next to the reception desk. Then he clasped her hand in his and started down the plushly carpeted hallway.

"Just remember, they won't bite," he murmured, squeezing her fingers reassuringly.

"If you say so," she replied, her whisper-soft voice more than a little shaky.

At the end of the hallway, Will paused again, tapped on the closed door, then opened it. A moment later, Tess followed him into Dr. Wells's spacious office as the three people already there stood to greet them.

"Tess, this is Dr. Jacob Wells," Will said by way of introduction, indicating the gentleman standing behind an old-fashioned partner's desk. "Dr. Wells, Tess McGuire."

"Ms. McGuire, it's a pleasure to meet you."

He was tall and thin with snow white hair, twinkling blue eyes and a smile so warm and engaging that it lit up the entire room. Tess not only liked him immediately, but instinctively knew that she could trust him to take good care of her.

"Thank you, Dr. Wells," she replied, some of her confidence slowly returning as they shook hands.

"And my sister and brother-in-law, Julie and Philip Drake," Will continued.

Turning slightly, Tess faced the middle-aged couple standing a few feet away, near a small sofa opposite the desk. They were just as she'd imagined they'd be: attractive, well dressed and very reserved.

As she met first Julie's gaze, then Philip's, she couldn't help but sense their apprehension. Despite what Will had more than likely told them about her, they seemed determined to judge for themselves exactly what kind of person she was.

Would she really do what she'd said she would without demanding anything in return? Would she prove to be a blessing in disguise or the biggest mistake they'd ever made?

Anxious to put their minds at ease, especially since they

already had enough to worry about, Tess smiled reassuringly as she narrowed the distance between them.

"Of course...Jonathan's parents," she said, extending her hand to Julie.

"Ms. McGuire," Julie murmured tentatively as she shook Tess's hand.

"Why don't you call me Tess?" She turned to Philip, offering him her hand, as well.

"Thank you...Tess. For everything." He clasped her hand for several seconds as he held her gaze. Then he gestured toward one of the wing-back chairs facing the sofa. "Won't you please sit down?" he said, adding as he glanced at his brother-in-law, "You, too, Will."

"I'd like to stay, but I've got to get to work." He kissed his sister on the cheek and shook hands with Philip. "I'll talk to you later."

Then, turning back to Tess, he eyed her searchingly. "Sure you're going to be okay?"

"Oh, yes," she replied, glad that she sounded so much more certain than she actually felt.

"Well, then, goodbye...Professor."

"Goodbye, Will," she murmured.

He hesitated, as if aware of her reluctance to see him go. Not wanting to impose on his kindness any longer, she tipped her chin up and smiled brightly, and finally, with a nod to Dr. Wells, he turned and walked out of the office.

"So, Ms. McGuire, why don't we begin?" Dr. Wells suggested, taking the chair next to hers as the Drakes sat on the sofa. "We have quite a bit to go through before you check into the hospital."

Almost two hours later, Tess realized that Dr. Wells's "quite a bit" definitely qualified as the understatement of the year. Not only did the good doctor explain exactly what was involved in each of the tests necessary to determine whether or not she'd be a suitable donor, but he went on to describe the transplant surgery itself in such a way that left absolutely nothing to her imagination. At one point she wondered if she ought to be taking notes, then realized the *less* she remembered of their conversation the better.

Some people would have been fascinated by his detailed explanations, but Tess wasn't one of them. Though she supposed it was a good idea to know what Dr. Wells had in store for her, actually studying a diagram of her liver—before and after—seemed a little much, at least as far as she was concerned.

Of course, she understood that the interview itself was a kind of test, too. If she didn't run screaming from his office anytime during his presentation, then she imagined they'd finally believe she wasn't going to go back on her word.

As if she could, she thought, watching as Dr. Wells shuffled through his folder full of papers for what she hoped would be the last time. Will had been right when he'd said that his sister and brother-in-law loved their son above all else. She'd seen it in their eyes and heard it in their voices more than once that morning. Just as she'd seen and heard their faith in her grow, until they were finally convinced that she'd do whatever was necessary to save the boy's life, no matter how Dr. Wells tried, albeit unintentionally, to scare her away.

Finally, having apprised Tess of all the attendant risks involved in the various tests, as well as the actual surgery, Dr. Wells concluded their meeting with an offer to escort her to the hospital himself. Knowing she'd never find her way there on her own, she gratefully accepted.

As they all stood up to leave, Philip pulled a card from his jacket pocket and quickly jotted something on the back.

"I've arranged for you to have a private room on the VIP floor," he said, handing her the card. "You'll have the very best of care there, but if you need anything, anything at all, please call us. My office number is printed on the front, and I've written our home number on the back."

Though she knew she probably wouldn't call either of them under any circumstances, Tess thanked him quietly as she tucked the card in her purse. All she could think of needing in the near future was...Will, and he was now strictly off-limits.

Fifteen minutes later, after a couple of elevator rides and

another long walk through several mazelike corridors, Dr. Wells led her up to the twelfth-floor nurses' station and introduced her to the staff. After assuring her he'd be back to see her later in the evening, he left her with a pretty young nurse who escorted her to an elegantly appointed suite that bore so little resemblance to any other hospital room Tess had ever seen that she wondered if that's where she really was. When she said as much to the nurse, the woman laughed. Then she showed Tess how all the necessary medical equipment had been neatly hidden behind what appeared to be wood-paneled walls.

On the nurse's advice, Tess changed into a long gown, matching robe and terry-cloth slippers she'd brought with her, then stashed the rest of her things in the antique armoire standing in one corner.

Hoping to relax a bit, she settled into one of the cushy chairs near the windows with a mystery she'd been wanting to read. However, she'd gotten through no more than a page or two when a lab technician arrived to draw blood. By the time he finally left, having filled almost a dozen vials, Tess had begun to believe they must have a pet vampire hidden somewhere in the place.

She barely had time to finish another page before the nurse returned with her lunch. To her surprise, not only was her meal served on fine china but the food was also as good as what she'd had at the hotel.

Unfortunately, after she'd eaten, Tess couldn't seem to settle down again. When the nurse had come to retrieve her tray, she'd advised her that no tests had been scheduled that day. She couldn't seem to concentrate enough to read, and she wasn't at all in the mood to sit and watch television. In fact, by four o'clock in the afternoon, she was ready to climb the walls.

Aware that she was perfectly healthy and thus had no real reason to have to stay in her room, she ventured out into the hallway. Perhaps there was somebody else on the twelfth floor as desperate for company as she was, she thought as she headed down to the nurses' station.

Someone who wouldn't mind spending a little time with a frightened history professor who'd begun to think that maybe she'd wandered into an episode of "The Twilight Zone" sometime in the past three days, and was only just realizing it now....

Chapter Four

"So, you like the sombrero, huh?" Will asked his nephew early Tuesday evening.

"I *love* it," Jonathan replied, grinning up at his uncle from under the hat's wide, floppy brim. "And the piñata and the puppets, too. Thanks a whole, whole bunch, Uncle Will."

"You're welcome a whole, whole bunch. Now, how about giving me a hug so I can get out of here? Otherwise, you're never going to get to sleep."

"How about okay?" Tossing the hat aside, the boy threw his arms around his uncle's neck.

Will had stopped by the hospital Sunday after he'd dropped Tess off at the hotel, but he hadn't been back to see the boy since then.

When he'd arrived at the D.A.'s office Monday morning, he'd been assigned to track down a new lead in an old case that had put a man on death row several years ago. Over the weekend, someone being held on an unrelated charge had indicated that another man had actually committed the crime. Since Will had been one of the investigators on the original case, he'd been determined to find out whether or not the story was true, because the man he'd helped to convict was scheduled for execution in less than two weeks.

He'd worked until after midnight Monday, going over old interviews, as well as transcripts of the trial. Then he'd started again early this morning, talking once again to as many of the people involved as he could locate. By six o'clock he'd been frustrated as hell by his lack of progress. However, knowing that if he didn't take a break he'd be seeing double soon, he'd decided to drive over to the hospital to visit with Jonathan awhile.

To be honest, he'd also been anxious to see Tess. He hadn't wanted her to think he'd forgotten her. Quite the contrary, actually…

"I'll come and see you again tomorrow evening," Will promised, holding his nephew a moment longer, then releasing him.

"I'll be here," Jonathan replied with a weary sigh.

The boy had been in the hospital almost three weeks now, and it was growing more and more apparent that he'd begun to doubt he'd ever be able to go home again. Still, Julie and Philip had decided not to tell him that a potential donor had been found. Until Tess was proved to be a suitable match, they didn't want to get his hopes up.

They'd also considered what they'd say to him about her if Dr. Wells approved the surgery. They'd finally decided to tell him that Tess was a friend of Will's. Jonathan had grown up knowing he was adopted, and more than likely he'd ask about his birth mother one day when he was older. But for now all concerned believed he'd be better off not knowing Tess McGuire's true identity. Apparently including Tess…

"Hang in there, sport," Will advised, ruffling the boy's dark, curly hair.

"I will."

Turning, Will glanced at his sister, who'd been sitting in one of the chairs by the window, and nodded toward the door. "Walk me out?"

"Of course." Assuring Jonathan she'd be right back, Julie

moved across the room with her brother. "You look tired," she said as they stepped into the hallway.

"I am," he admitted, tucking his hands in his pockets and leaning against the wall.

"Better go home and go to bed, then."

"Actually I thought I'd go up to the twelfth floor and see how Tess is doing."

"Are you sure that's wise?" Julie asked hesitantly, a frown creasing her forehead.

"Why wouldn't it be?"

"She might get the idea that you're...interested in her."

Actually he *was* interested in Tess, very interested, but he didn't think it would be smart to say as much to his sister. Julie had set aside most of her reservations about Tess after they'd met on Monday. Yet he knew Julie wouldn't like it if he seemed to be getting involved with her.

"I just want to make sure she's doing all right," he hedged.

"Believe me, she's doing just fine," Julie hastened to assure him. "When I talked to Dr. Wells earlier, he told me she was a real trouper."

"Yeah, I know."

"Will, please don't—" Julie began, resting a hand on his arm.

"I like her, Julie," Will interrupted. "She's not just a nice lady. She's risking her life for your son, and she isn't asking for a damned thing in return." He paused a moment, willing his sister to understand. "The least we can do is let her know that we're concerned about her well-being."

"Of course, we are, Will. But..." She shook her head as if not sure what to say next.

"But...?" he urged, eyeing her almost angrily. "Have you or Philip gone up there and told her so since you saw her on Monday?"

"Well, no..."

"Why not?"

"We didn't think she'd welcome our company, especially since she was so reluctant to meet with us in the first place," Julie admitted uncomfortably. "She seemed so...so cool and calm and...self-contained. I got the feeling she could get along just fine on her own.''

''I imagine she was reluctant to meet with you because she was afraid you'd judge her harshly,'' Will replied. Taking her hand in his, he continued in a gentle tone. ''And I can guarantee she's no more able to get along on her own than we would be under the same circumstances.''

''Well, in *my* opinion, she's a lot tougher than you'd like to admit,'' Julie retorted, pulling away from him. ''Don't forget she gave away her baby.''

''And don't *you* forget that if she hadn't, Jonathan would never have been a part of our lives.'' He met her gaze defiantly for several long moments. Then, muttering a curse under his breath, he turned away. ''Look, Julie, I don't want to fight with you.''

''I don't want to fight with you, either.'' She touched his arm again, then added, ''All things considered, I...I had no right to make that kind of comment about Tess. But sometimes I just have a hard time understanding....''

''That ten years ago, when you were thirty-two years old, married to a wealthy man and desperate to have a baby, she was a pregnant high school senior who wrote 'no next of kin' on the form she filled out at the Amberton Home?'' he prodded softly.

''Oh, Will...''

''I'd like to believe that she didn't feel she had any other choice but to put her baby up for adoption.'' Facing his sister again, he continued gravely. ''I also intend to remember how much her decision has meant to us over the past ten years, and I hope you'll be able to do the same.''

''I'll try,'' she promised.

''Good enough.'' Smiling, he reached out and squeezed her shoulder gently. ''I'll see you tomorrow, okay?''

''Okay.'' She hesitated, then spoke again as he started to turn away. ''Do something for me, will you?'' she asked.

''If I can.''

''Tell Tess I said hello.''

"Gladly," he agreed, his smile widening for an instant before he headed for the elevator at the end of the hall.

Instead of going straight up to the twelfth floor, Will took the elevator down to the lobby first. There he stopped in the little shop he'd seen earlier and bought Tess a basket full of fresh-cut flowers, as well as a copy of a new novel set in France at the turn of the century and a little foil-wrapped box of chocolates.

Though he couldn't say for sure, he had a feeling she'd told no one she was in the hospital, and that meant she'd not only have no visitors, but no flowers, books and/or chocolates to cheer her up.

Of course, Will knew that since she was on the VIP floor, fresh flowers would be brought to her room daily. There was also a small library full of books available for her use. And if she wanted chocolates, he was certain someone on the staff would see that she got them.

But he wanted her to have something more...personal, something from *him.* For some reason he dared not consider too closely, he wanted her to know that he was thinking of her. Because he *was*...a lot more than he should be.

The door to her room was slightly ajar, but when he tapped on it, he didn't get any response. Not wanting to catch her unawares, he pushed the door open a little more and called her name, but again got no answer. Frowning, he opened the door all the way and immediately saw that her room was empty.

Wondering where she could have gone, he stepped across the threshold. The lamp on the nightstand had been lit, and the bedspread had been turned back on the bed. A paperback mystery novel by an Austin writer whose stories were not for the faint of heart lay open on one of the chairs, and her briefcase and a pile of papers had been left on the table by the window. The wall panel across from her bed had been opened to reveal a large-screen television and VCR, atop which three videocassettes had been stacked—*Out of Africa, A Room with a View,* and...*Blade Runner?*

Shaking his head at her eclectic taste, Will crossed the room and set the flowers, book and candy on the nightstand. As he did so, he noticed the small silver picture frame already atop it. Inside the frame was the photograph of Jonathan he'd given her on Friday.

His frown deepening, Will tucked his hands in his pockets and strolled over to the window. Outside, the sun was sinking into the far horizon, painting the sky vivid shades of orange and red and gold, but the beauty of the sunset was lost on him.

As he had on Sunday, he found himself wondering once again why Tess had so adamantly refused to see…her son. He'd already come to the conclusion that giving him up for adoption hadn't been a casual act on her part. Unless he'd read her all wrong, she'd loved her baby enough to make a difficult decision in what she'd believed would be his favor. And she must still care about the boy. Otherwise, why would she be here? No one was *that* altruistic just on general principles.

Returning to the nightstand, Will eyed the framed photograph thoughtfully. Tess wouldn't have put it there if it hadn't meant an awful lot to her. So didn't it stand to reason that actually meeting the boy would leave her with memories she'd cherish always?

Julie had been more than willing to accept the fact that Tess wanted nothing to do with Jonathan personally. But Will knew better than to take Tess's resistance to meeting the boy at face value. No one kept a silver-framed photograph of a child on her nightstand unless that child was important to her in some very special way.

Tess had the right to spend a little time with the boy whose life she obviously valued as much as her own. Now all Will had to do was find a way to convince her to exercise that right. And not only for her own good—if his sister actually saw for herself how Tess felt about Jonathan, maybe she'd realize Tess would never do anything to hurt him, physically or emotionally. Then maybe Julie would finally be able to rest easier.

Just as *he* would be able to rest easier if he had even a vague idea of where the lovely professor had gone, he thought, walking back to the door again. Maybe someone at the nurses' station would know….

Will was halfway down the hall when he heard Tess's voice

drifting through the partially open doorway of another room. Pausing in midstride, he glanced into the room. Tess was standing with her back to the door, tying what appeared to be the silk scarf she'd worn Sunday around a younger woman's bandaged head. Though he couldn't make out what Tess was saying, her voice held a note of teasing laughter, and the other woman was smiling at her gratefully.

Heading back the way he'd come, Will grinned rather ruefully. He couldn't think of another woman he knew who'd choose to spend her time spreading good cheer if caught in the same situation as Tess. Yet somehow he wasn't surprised that *she* was doing so.

Aware that Tess might not return to her room for a while, Will thought about going on home. But there was nothing, or more important, *nobody* special waiting for him there. And in all honesty, he hadn't come up to the twelfth floor to do no more than catch a glimpse of her.

He'd wanted to see her face-to-face and talk to her a bit so he could assure himself that she really was all right. He'd wanted to make certain that she had everything she wanted or needed. And most of all, he'd wanted her to know that he hadn't abandoned her as she'd apparently been abandoned in the past. He'd wanted her to realize that she could count on him to be with her at a time when she didn't seem to have anyone else to lean on.

Back in her room, Will turned on the television, tuning in an all-news cable network as he shrugged out of his jacket and shoulder holster. He folded his jacket around the holster and set both on the table. Then he loosened his tie, rolled up his shirtsleeves and settled into one of the incredibly comfortable chairs by the window. Until she came back to her room and he had a chance to visit with her, he wasn't going anywhere. No matter how long he had to wait…

Will didn't realize he'd fallen asleep until he slowly started to come awake again. But even before he opened his eyes, he knew he was no longer alone. There had been a subtle shift in the atmosphere surrounding him, the kind of shift caused by another person sharing his space. From somewhere quite close by came the faint scent of lemon and spice that reminded him of the other times he'd been with Tess over the past few days.

She was sitting in the chair across from him, her legs drawn up under her, the book he'd brought her lying open in her lap. She was wearing a plain but very pretty pink-and-white-striped robe with short, puffy sleeves and lace around the collar that enhanced her femininity in a truly enticing way. Her dark hair curled wildly around her shoulders, and her pale eyes glimmered with pleasure as her lips curved into a wide, warm, *welcoming* smile.

As if she was actually happy to see him despite the fact that she'd found him sound asleep in one of her chairs, Will mused as he ran a hand through his hair and sat up a little straighter.

"How long have you been back?" he asked, suddenly feeling strangely self-conscious.

"About fifteen or twenty minutes."

"You should have woken me up."

"You looked so peaceful I didn't have the heart to disturb you," she admitted.

"I wish you had," he muttered, disgusted with himself. "I came to see you, not to sleep."

"How long have you been here?" she asked, gazing at him curiously.

"Since just after seven."

"I'm sorry I wasn't here, but I wasn't really expecting any visitors."

"So you went visiting yourself, huh?"

"Something like that."

"Who's your friend?" he asked, realizing that he was honestly interested in anyone who interested Tess.

He wanted to know as much as he could about her, but she was so damned reticent about herself. However, one could learn quite a bit about people from the friends they chose. And he had a feeling Tess wasn't the type to choose blithely.

"Which one?" Still looking at him, she frowned thoughtfully.

"You've been here less than two full days and you already

have more than one friend?'' he prodded, making no effort to hide his amazement. Only Tess...

''Actually three...so far.'' She grinned, obviously quite pleased with herself.

''So far, huh?'' Unable to help himself, Will returned her smile. ''Well, Professor, tell me all about them.''

''You really want to know?''

''I really do.''

She eyed him quizzically for several seconds, as if trying to decide whether or not to take him seriously. When he said nothing more, however, she finally began.

''There's Lydia Davies. She's down the hall in number ten. She's just twenty-one, and a senior at Texas A&M. Her father's a state senator, and her mother used to be a local news anchor.''

''Why is Lydia here?''

''She had a brain tumor.''

''That sounds pretty serious.'' Will shook his head sadly, aware that Lydia was the young woman Tess had been with earlier.

''Luckily the tumor was benign,'' Tess continued. ''She's doing really well, considering, and unless something shows up on her CAT scan a week from Wednesday, she should be able to go home after that.''

''Are her parents here with her?''

''They were until yesterday, but apparently they have several big political fund-raisers in Austin this week.'' Tess shrugged, a frown furrowing her brow. ''She's a lot more understanding than I would be, but then I imagine she's used to it by now. Still, I feel so sorry for her. She's really a sweet girl.''

Will had met Senator Davies and his wife at one of Julie and Philip's parties a couple of years ago, but hadn't particularly cared for either one of them. They'd been much too fond of themselves for his taste. And as far as he could recall, they hadn't mentioned their daughter once.

''She sounds like a survivor to me,'' he said, wanting nothing more than to ease Tess's mind.

He could certainly understand why she'd been drawn to the

girl. Yet he felt that Tess had enough to worry about at the moment without taking on Lydia Davies's problems, as well.

"She seems to be," Tess agreed. "But still..."

"What about your other friends?" Will prodded, hoping they weren't quite as bad off as Lydia.

"Well, Ina Boggs had eye surgery on Friday. Nothing life threatening, but because of her age her doctor wanted her to stay here for several days so he could make sure that she took it easy. She's a bit crotchety, but she can be a real dear when she wants."

"Ina Boggs? *The* Ina Boggs, grande dame of Houston, Texas?" Will asked, glad to see Tess smiling again.

"You know her?"

"Not personally, but she's a legend in the city. Her family owns half of the real estate in the Galleria area, and she's especially fond of donating huge sums of money to the medical center and Rice University for no reason at all. Neither she nor her older sister ever married. Her sister died several years ago, and Ina's slowed down a bit since then. But she's still seen at all of the city's most important social events."

"And here I thought she was just a nice little old lady with a passion for historical romance novels," Tess replied, her voice rippling with barely suppressed laughter.

"You're kidding."

"I wish." Tess shook her head ruefully. "I've been reading *Love's Driving Fury* to her off and on for the past two days. And since I made the mistake of telling her I'm a history professor, she keeps interrupting to ask if the details, historical and...otherwise, are accurate."

"And are they?"

"As far as I know," she admitted.

Unable to stop himself, Will laughed aloud at the woebegone look on Tess's face. Then, sobering somewhat, he advised her gently, "You know, you don't *have* to read to her. One of the volunteers could do it, or maybe a member of her family. Why, with her money, she could even hire someone."

"But she's so appreciative in her own rather irascible way.

And I couldn't risk hurting her feelings by avoiding her all of a sudden, could I?''

She could, but Will knew better than to think that she would. She'd read whatever the old harridan wanted her to read, and she'd do it with a smile.

''What about your third friend?'' he queried, pressing ahead.

''Oh, he's really nice. And he's smart and funny, too.''

''He?'' Will gazed at her with chagrin. He could only hope the guy was as old as Ina, but something about the sudden sparkle in Tess's eyes warned him that he wasn't going to be so lucky.

''Harry Gamble. He broke his leg rock climbing out in Big Bend. He's been in traction for almost two weeks and he's—''

''Harry Gamble?'' Will cut in, wanting to be sure he'd heard her right, though he really had no doubt about it.

''Do you know him, too?'' Tess inquired, obviously pleased. ''He does something with computers, but I'm not exactly sure what.''

''He doesn't just 'do something with computers.' He owns Technotech, one of the largest computer-software companies in the world.''

He was also a billionaire several times over, one of the most eligible bachelors in the state, and, at least according to Julie, handsome as sin. And Tess thought he was not only nice, but smart and funny to boot. Which left Will feeling more than a little jealous.

''Oh, really?'' Tess replied, appearing to be honestly surprised. ''He never mentioned it. But he does talk on the telephone a lot, and he's always doing stuff on his laptop computer.''

''Probably creating another of his highly touted programs,'' Will grumbled ungraciously.

''Don't you like him?'' Tess asked, frowning once again.

He wouldn't like any man Tess showed an interest in, Will realized with a suddenness that surprised him. But he couldn't very well say as much to her. Not when *their* relationship was so ambiguous. They were much more than mere acquaintances, but he wasn't sure she'd actually claim him as a friend. And as for going beyond friendship…

All things considered, that was probably as much out of the question for her as it continued to be for him. In all reality, he should be pleased not only that she'd met Harry Gamble, but that she seemed to like him, too. He should be pleased, but he damned well wasn't.

"I haven't met him, so I can't say. But from what you've said, he sounds all right," Will conceded. Then, eager to change the subject, he continued on another tack. "So, how have the tests gone so far?"

"So far, so good. The results of the blood work won't be ready until Friday. Today I had an EKG and a chest X ray, and according to Dr. Wells, they were both negative, which I gather is actually positive."

"What about tomorrow?"

"I'm scheduled for an upper and lower G.I. And on Thursday I'm supposed to have a thallium stress test."

Recalling his own round of gastrointestinal tests, Will groaned in sympathy.

"That bad, huh?"

"The stress test is okay. But if I never have another G.I. series in this lifetime…"

"Wonderful."

"At least you're getting them over with in one day."

"I'll keep that in mind," she replied, a flash of humor evident in her voice. After a moment's hesitation, however, she continued in a more serious tone. "Do you mind if I ask how Jonathan's doing?"

"Of course not," Will assured her. "I stopped to see him for a few minutes on my way up here, and so far, he's still holding his own, even though his spirits have been down."

"Dr. Wells said Julie and Philip weren't going to tell him about me until they were certain the surgery could be done."

"At this point, they're afraid of getting his hopes up. He's been disappointed so often lately, and they don't want to risk upsetting him any more than absolutely necessary."

"I can understand how they feel." Again Tess hesitated, as

if she were considering her next words carefully. ‘‘What… what exactly *are* they going to…tell him about me?’’ she asked at last, meeting his gaze.

‘‘They don’t want to lie to him, but they don’t think it would be wise to tell him the whole truth, either,’’ Will admitted.

He’d assumed that his sister and brother-in-law had advised Tess of the decision they’d made. That they hadn’t, angered him quite a bit. They owed Tess more than a few words of thanks. They owed her some consideration, as well, and he had every intention of telling them so later. But for now…

‘‘They’ve decided to tell him you’re a friend of mine who agreed to be tested after hearing about how ill he’s been,’’ Will added. ‘‘As long as it’s all right with you…’’

‘‘That’s fine,’’ Tess replied with obvious relief.

‘‘We *are* friends, aren’t we?’’ he prodded, wanting her verification of it.

‘‘I’d like to think so,’’ she said, lowering her gaze shyly as she smoothed a hand over the book in her lap. An instant later, she looked up at him again, her pale eyes full of chagrin. ‘‘Here I’ve been rattling on about myself without even thanking you for the flowers, the candy and especially the book. I’ve been wanting it since I first read a review of it.’’ She paused, then added softly as she ducked her head again, ‘‘I…I really appreciate your thinking of me.’’

‘‘Hey, that’s what friends are for, aren’t they?’’ he asked lightly, hoping to ease her obvious discomfort.

She didn’t reply for several moments, but finally she met his gaze again, her eyes full of warmth. ‘‘So, tell me something, one friend to another, will you?’’ she asked, a hint of mischief in her voice.

‘‘If I can….’’

‘‘Did you have a bad day at the office today or do you normally doze off during the nightly news?’’

Eyeing Tess curiously, Will tried to decide if she’d asked because she really wanted to know. Or was she just trying to be polite? From the look on her face, she appeared to be sincerely interested in the kind of day he’d had. Yet he wasn’t sure he ought to go into all the gory details.

For Claire, his being a cop had been a turn-on...at first. He'd thought that she'd been interested in him and what he did for a living, but she'd liked the *idea* of it a hell of a lot more than the base reality. And little by little, she'd let it be known that certain changes would have to be made.

He'd transferred from the police department to the D.A.'s office to ease her supposed worries, but that hadn't been enough for her. Eventually she'd let him know that she wanted him to quit his job as an investigator and go to work for his brother-in-law. Then and only then could he make enough money to support her in the style to which she wanted to become accustomed. When he'd refused, their relationship had ended bitterly.

But he'd already determined that Tess wasn't anything at all like Claire. There was something so innately *honest* about her that he couldn't believe she'd feign interest where none actually existed. And frankly he couldn't think of anything he'd rather do at the moment than talk about his job and all it entailed to someone who not only wanted to listen, but might also be able to understand.

"Actually a *couple* of bad days at the office," he said at last, her encouraging smile his ultimate undoing. "That's why I didn't come to see you last night."

"Can you tell me about it, or is it 'classified'?"

"I can tell you about it, but it's kind of a long story." He paused, giving her a chance to change her mind.

"I don't know about you, but *I'm* not going anywhere," she reminded him, her smile widening.

"Well, in that case..."

He returned her smile for one long moment. Then, growing more serious, he told her about Eddie Kaminski, the possibly innocent man he'd helped to put on death row at Huntsville State Prison.

She listened quietly, asking an occasional question, her concern for him, as well as Eddie, more than evident.

"It's not like Eddie is some kind of saint," Will concluded. "He's a career criminal with a record as long as my arm. But that doesn't mean he deserves to die for a crime he didn't commit."

"What about a stay of execution?"

"We have to show good cause, and that's what I've been trying to find. But I hit a wall earlier this evening and decided to give it a rest. Figured I'd be able to think better in the morning. And, anyway, I wanted to see you...and Jonathan."

Actually, he'd *needed* to see Tess, he thought, aware of how much better he felt now than he had a few hours ago. He'd forgotten how heartening it could be to have someone special who wanted to hear what you had to say. And, as far as he was concerned, Tess McGuire was very special indeed.

"Maybe if you get some sleep tonight, you'll be able to go at it from another angle tomorrow," she suggested, interrupting his reverie.

"Trying to get rid of me, Professor?" he asked.

"Oh, no, I wish you could stay all night," she replied, then blushed to the roots of her dark, curly hair. "I...I didn't mean that the way it sounded."

What a shame, he thought to himself. Then, hoping to ease her embarrassment, he continued in a teasing tone of voice. "You're not saying you're bored, are you? Not with three very interesting friends just down the hall."

"I can't say I've had too many dull moments around here. At least, not yet," she acknowledged, avoiding his gaze as she set the book on the table beside her, then stood up. "Well, it's getting late. I really shouldn't keep you any longer."

Taking his cue from her, Will gathered his jacket and holster and stood, too. Though he wanted to tell her she could keep him as long as she wanted, he was afraid that kind of comment would only make her more uncomfortable than she already was.

"We both have busy days ahead of us," he said instead as he started toward the door.

"Thanks again for coming to visit and for bringing me such wonderful gifts. I really appreciate it."

"You're welcome." Pausing near the doorway, he turned to face her again. "Unless you've already got big plans for the evening, I'll be back tomorrow night. Do you want me to bring you anything special?"

"I don't have any plans, but..." She hesitated, frowning as she met his gaze. "You don't have to come and visit me. You're really busy at work, and I know you'll want to spend as much time as you can with Jonathan."

"I want to spend time with you, too, Tess," he stated simply, his eyes holding hers.

She looked as if she was about to argue with him, but something in his expression must have warned her that it would be to no avail. He was going to visit her tomorrow night, come hell or high water.

Smiling slowly, she acceded to his wishes. "I'll look forward to seeing you, then."

"Shall we say around seven or seven-thirty?"

"I'll pencil you into my date book."

"You do that, Professor." Mentally cursing the fact that she was too far away to touch, he gazed at her longingly for the space of a heartbeat or two. Then, aware of how easily he could end up doing something he'd regret, he turned on his heel and headed out the door.

As promised, Will returned Wednesday evening, and again Thursday evening, and both nights Tess was waiting for him in her room. From the warmth he saw in her eyes and the welcome he heard in her voice, he knew she was as happy to see him as he was to see her.

They talked about her new friends, as well as the progress, or *lack* of progress, he was making on his case. He also made a point of telling her about Jonathan without waiting for her to ask. She had a right to know how the boy was doing, and Will had every intention of seeing to it that she did.

He was pleased, too, when Tess mentioned that both Julie and Philip had called to check on her. Though she'd seemed somewhat disconcerted by their sudden interest in her, she hadn't been dismayed by it, thus reinforcing his belief that the little talk he'd had with his sister about common courtesy, and her previous lack thereof, had been worthwhile.

All in all, Tess appeared to be holding up quite well. She'd seemed tired Wednesday evening. But then he remembered that going through an upper *and* lower G.I. in one day had taken a lot out of him, too. Thursday evening she'd been more herself. She'd told him about the stress test, and talked a bit about Ina and Lydia. He noticed that she barely mentioned Harry Gamble, but that was all right with him. The less she saw of him, the better.

After he'd left her Thursday evening, more reluctantly than ever, Will also realized that she'd said nothing about the psychological evaluation he knew she'd undergone that afternoon. According to Julie, Dr. Wells had been especially happy with the results of it. Apparently Tess had proved to be a remarkably stable young woman with a no-nonsense attitude about life in general and the surgery she'd agreed to have in particular. She'd made it clear that she hadn't been coerced in any way, and that she fully understood the risks she was so willingly prepared to take.

That Tess had chosen not to talk about the time she'd spent with the psychologist on Dr. Wells's team only strengthened Will's belief that she was a very private person. She could joke about an upper G.I. or a stress test, she could relate funny stories about the people she'd met at the hospital and she could ask intelligent questions about his work. But she wouldn't reveal anything about herself if she could help it. Considering all the time he'd spent with her, he knew almost nothing about her past, and what little he knew about the kind of life she led in San Antonio, he'd more or less picked up on his own.

Most important of all, he had no idea if she was involved in some sort of relationship with a man. While he doubted it, he didn't know for sure. And even though it shouldn't, the not knowing had begun to make him crazy.

They were just friends, and temporary friends at that. Once she'd gone back to San Antonio, he knew it would probably be better for all concerned if he didn't see her again. Yet he was already having a hard time imagining himself walking away from her without so much as a backward glance....

Late Friday afternoon Julie called him at the office. Her

voice hushed, she told him that Dr. Wells had just advised them Tess had been deemed a suitable donor. He'd already talked to her, and she'd signed the consent forms without hesitation. Surgery had been scheduled for seven o'clock Monday morning, and Jonathan had been given the good news. Despite Dr. Wells's cautiously optimistic approach, the boy was overjoyed. But much to Julie's dismay, he was also asking rather insistently to meet "Uncle Will's friend, Tess."

"You know how I feel about that," Will replied, refusing to side with his sister despite her unspoken plea. "And now that Jonathan wants to see her—"

"And you know how *I* feel about it," Julie cut in. "Anyone seeing them together will know..."

"*We* are the only ones who are going to see them together, and we already know. As for Jonathan, you've told him she's a friend of mine. Unless he's told something different, that's what he'll believe. Since none of us are going to say anything to the contrary, including Tess, I can't see any problem with their spending a little time together."

"How can you be so sure about her? Once she's in the same room with him, she could say or do anything, and it will be too late to stop her," she protested.

"Do you really think Tess is the kind of person who'd say or do something to upset a sick child?" Will asked incredulously, then continued without waiting for his sister to answer. "She no more wants Jonathan to know who she really is than you do, because she doesn't want him hurt, either. She just wants him to be well again, and she's going to risk her life Monday morning to make it possible."

In fact, she could die on the operating table, but Will felt as if he was the only one who realized it and was afraid for her.

"I know that."

"Then give her a little credit, will you?" he retorted, wishing they could discuss Tess just once without ending up arguing.

He'd never seen Julie act that way toward another person in his life. But then she'd never been so scared of losing her child, either. And she was currently faced with what she must see as a double threat. Jonathan, too, could very well die Monday morning. Or he could live and eventually be wooed away by his ‘‘real’’ mother. To Julie, one possibility was as terrifying as the other, and trying to convince her otherwise was a waste of breath.

‘‘Look, I’ve done about all I can around here today,’’ he said in a gentler tone of voice. In fact, he’d about given up hope that Eddie Kaminski’s ‘‘almost identical twin’’ even existed, but that was another story altogether. ‘‘I’m going to come over to the hospital and see Tess. I’ll tell her that Jonathan wants to meet her. Then, if it’s okay with her, I’ll bring her down to his room, all right?’’

Julie didn’t answer immediately, but when she did, Will was heartened somewhat by her reply. ‘‘I’m sorry, Will. I’ve really been behaving...badly. If Ms. McGuire would like to see Jonathan, then it’s all right with me.’’

‘‘Believe me, Julie, she’s not going to say or do anything to upset him. She has his best interests at heart, the same as you do. She always has, and she always will.’’

‘‘I hope so,’’ Julie murmured.

By the time Will managed to clear his desk and head for the hospital, almost an hour had passed. He ended up getting caught in traffic on his way out of downtown, and that delayed him, as well. But when he finally got off the elevator on the twelfth floor, he was still at least an hour earlier than he’d been the past few evenings.

On his way to Tess’s room, he glanced into Lydia’s room, then Ina’s and Harry’s, taking advantage of their partially opened doors. To his relief, she wasn’t with any of them. Considering the news she’d had a short while ago, however, Will wasn’t too surprised.

Agreeing to have major surgery to save a child’s life was a little different than actually knowing you were scheduled to have part of your liver removed at seven o’clock Monday morning. In the space of a few days, possibility had become a potentially frightening reality for Tess. Had he been in her position, Will knew he’d have gone to ground, too.

As he came up to her room, he saw that her door was also half-open. Raising his hand to knock, he heard her voice and hesitated. He didn't intend to eavesdrop, but something about her tone, coupled with the words she was saying, stopped him before he could let her know that he'd arrived.

"I'm sorry, Richard. I can't tell you why I've changed my mind about the trip. I just have."

Richard? Will frowned as he ducked his head and stared at the floor. She'd been planning a trip with someone named Richard?

"All right, then, I *won't* tell you. But, believe me, I'm not canceling on a whim. You know I wouldn't do that to you."

Not on a whim at all, Will thought. Yet why wouldn't she tell him the real reason why she'd changed her mind? Again Will realized what a very private person she was. Richard, whoever he was, probably had no idea she'd had a child ten years ago, and knowing Tess, he never would.

"No, of course, I'm not in any trouble. And I'm not involved with anyone else, either. As I told you a few days ago, I have some personal business I have to attend to, and it's going to take longer than I anticipated."

She paused again, but only for a second or two. When she began speaking again, Will realized that she was very close to tears. Richard obviously wasn't making it easy for her to get out of whatever they'd planned to do together.

"Listen, Richard, I *am* sorry I've disappointed you, but I simply don't have a choice. Have a wonderful time, and I'll talk to you again when you get back."

From where he stood, Will heard Tess cradle the receiver none too gently. Then he heard a muffled sob that tore at his heart, and more than anything, he wanted to bang Richard's head against a wall. Unfortunately Richard was well out of reach. But Tess was just a few steps away, and he had a feeling that although she'd probably never admit it, if she ever needed anyone, it was now.

He tapped on her door, then walked into her room without waiting for an invitation. She stood by the window with her back to him, dabbing hastily at her eyes with a tissue. As she had the other evening, she wore her pretty pink-and-white robe, and her dark hair curled wildly around her shoulders.

The urge to go to her and take her in his arms and vow to beat Richard to a pulp almost overwhelmed him. Instead, he halted a few feet from her, tucked his hands in his pockets and debated whether or not to admit he'd overheard her conversation. Finally, deciding there was already too much left unsaid between them, he asked the question foremost in his mind.

''Who's Richard?''

''Will?'' Obviously startled despite his knock on her door, Tess glanced over her shoulder at him, then quickly looked away again as she blotted up the last of her tears. ''You're... early...''

''And you've been crying. What did that bastard say to you?''

''Investigator for the D.A.'s office or not, you really shouldn't have been lurking outside my room, listening to what was supposed to be a private conversation,'' she scolded gently as she turned to meet his gaze.

From the look on her face, she wasn't pleased with him, but much to his relief, she didn't seem too terribly angry, either.

''I hadn't intended to,'' he admitted. ''But you sounded upset.'' He moved to one of the chairs and sat down. ''Want to tell me about it?''

She shrugged and shook her head, and for an instant Will thought she would put him off again. But she took another tissue from the box on the table, blew her nose, then curled up in the chair across from him.

''Richard is a history professor at the University of Texas in Austin. He was one of my professors when I was an undergraduate there, and I worked as one of his teaching assistants while I was in grad school. He's a friend now, as well as a colleague. We'd planned to go on a research trip together this summer, but because of the surgery on Monday I had to cancel. He...he wasn't too happy about it.'' She glanced at him again, then lowered her gaze before continuing. ''I guess you know that Dr. Wells has decided to do the surgery. It seems that Jonathan and I are a perfect match.''

"Julie called and told me. I came over here as soon as I could."

"They've told Jonathan, haven't they?"

Will nodded.

"So…how's he taking the news?"

"I haven't seen him yet, but Julie said he's pretty happy about it."

"You came to see me first?" Tess asked, obviously puzzled.

"I thought you might like some company. Major surgery is—"

"Major surgery," she filled in for him, as if recalling the first time they'd talked about it.

"Yeah, something like that," he agreed with a slight smile.

"I'm fine, really. Why don't you go down and see Jonathan?" she urged.

"Trying to get rid of me?"

"No." Blushing, she avoided his gaze.

"That's good, because I thought we could go down and see him together," Will said, watching her carefully.

"Oh, no, I can't…." she protested.

"He wants to meet you, Tess."

"How do you know that?" she asked, eyeing him doubtfully.

"Julie mentioned it when she called. Seems he's been rather insistent about it, too."

"But why—"

"He's been told that someone has been found who's willing to donate a part of her liver to save his life, but until he actually meets you, he's going to wonder if it's really true. Spending a little time with him would go a long way to ease his uncertainty," Will prodded shamelessly.

He wanted her to see the boy just once, for her own good, as well as Jonathan's. She, too, had to have some uncertainties about the decision she'd made, but he didn't want her to have regrets, as well. More important, he wanted Jonathan to be more to her than a picture in a little silver frame. Because she wasn't risking her life to save just any child. She was risking her life to save her own son.

Standing, he crossed to her, took her hands in his and slowly drew her to her feet. As she gazed up at him, her pale eyes shadowed with doubt, he smiled reassuringly.

"Come and see him with me, Tess. Please..."

Chapter Five

Her heart pounding, Tess tipped her head back and met Will's gaze, encouraged by the warmth and certainty of his smile. More than anything, she wanted to go with him to see…her son. When Will had first broached the subject on the drive to Houston, she'd been adamantly against it. But over the past few days, knowing the boy was close by, she'd begun to hope that somehow, some way she'd catch a glimpse of him. Now Will was offering her much more than that.

Still she hesitated, unable to banish the feeling that meeting Jonathan face-to-face wouldn't be wise. He wasn't her child, not in a way that mattered much beyond Monday, and she couldn't afford to forget it. Nor could she allow herself to think that she'd ever have a permanent place in his life. More than likely, whatever time she spent with him tonight would be the *only* time she'd be able to spend with him…ever.

She also had to remember that while they were together, she'd have to be careful not to say or do anything to arouse his suspicions. As long as she was with him, she'd have to maintain the same emotional distance any other friend of his uncle's would. And when the time came to leave, she'd have to do so as gracefully as possible.

If she clung to the boy or cried, he'd begin to wonder, and she simply couldn't risk that. He was only ten years old, but she had a feeling he wasn't any dummy. Which meant she'd have to be extremely cautious about giving the game away.

Maybe it would be best not to see him at all, she thought, lowering her gaze wordlessly as she eased her hands from Will's and walked back to the window. But then he'd still be worried about whether she'd really go through with the surgery. She knew enough about kids to realize that Will was right. Seeing *was* believing for them, and until Jonathan saw her, he wouldn't be convinced that she'd come through for him.

If she spent some time with him, he'd gain at least a little peace of mind. And compared to that, Tess had to admit whatever heartache she experienced as a result would be negligible.

"Tess...?"

"I don't want to say or do anything to upset him," she said, turning to look at Will again.

"You won't," he assured her.

"Will you stay in the room with us?" She slipped her hands into the side pockets of her robe and gazed out the window once more.

"If you'd like me to."

"I would."

Somewhere in the back of her mind, Tess realized that she'd begun to depend on Will in a way she shouldn't. Over the past few days, she'd found herself looking forward to his visits more and more. He'd filled the empty hours of her evenings with warmth and good humor, and he'd done so in such a way that she'd known he honestly wanted to be with her as much as she wanted to be with him. She'd tried to remember that their time together was limited, yet it had become harder and harder lately. And now she found herself needing him more than ever.

As long as he stayed with her while she was with Jonathan, she'd be able to hold herself together. And if by some chance she began to fall apart, he'd be there to get her away before any damage was done.

"I'm not very good around kids," she continued by way of explanation.

"Don't worry," he replied, a hint of amusement in his voice. "Jonathan's *really* good around adults."

Tess appreciated his attempt at humor, but she still had serious concerns about meeting the boy. "If I start to say something I shouldn't..."

"Don't worry, Tess. You're going to do just fine."

"How can you be so sure?" she demanded, rounding on him almost angrily.

"You wouldn't be having major surgery on Monday morning if you didn't have his best interests at heart," Will reminded her gently. "I think you always have and always will."

Deeply touched by his faith in her, Tess lowered her gaze. "Thank you for that," she murmured. Then, gathering what little courage she had, she took a deep breath and continued as lightly as she could. "What time is Master Drake expecting us?"

"Anytime you're ready."

"Then I guess we'd better go now." Waiting would only increase her anxiety, and the more nervous she was, the more likely she'd be to make a mistake. "Just give me a minute to freshen up a bit," she added as she crossed to the bathroom.

"Take your time," Will replied. "I'm not in any hurry."

Despite Will's words, Tess hurriedly washed the traces of tears from her face, then ran a brush through her hair as quickly as she could, afraid that if she lingered too long, she'd end up changing her mind about meeting her son. She wanted to believe that spending a little time with him would be good for both of them, but it wasn't easy.

Once she'd actually seen him, he'd be more real to her than ever, but she wouldn't have any more access to him than she'd had for the past ten years. He was and always would be someone else's child, and that was as it should be. Yet with one wrong word she could unintentionally turn his solid, stable world upside down.

"But you're not going to say anything you shouldn't, are you?" she muttered, eyeing herself critically in the mirror. "You're going to remember that you're Will's friend and you're going to act accordingly, because if you don't, you could ruin a little boy's emotional well-being."

Turning away from the mirror, Tess opened the door and stepped out of the bathroom. From where he stood by the window, Will faced her, a questioning look in his eyes. For just a second, Tess wondered if he'd overheard what she'd been saying, then realized it would have been impossible, considering how softly she'd been speaking. Still, something about the way he looked at her made her realize that he knew just how difficult meeting Jonathan was going to be for her.

"I'm ready if you are," she said, forcing herself to smile brightly.

He hesitated a moment, as if he might be having second thoughts about what he was asking her to do. But then he smiled, too, as he moved across the room to join her.

"Anybody ever tell you what a nice person you are, Professor?" he inquired, admiration evident in his deep voice.

Blushing at his compliment, Tess shook her head.

"Well, then, let me be the first," he continued, taking her hand in his as they started down the hallway toward the elevator. "You're one hell of a lady." He squeezed her fingers gently. "And it's a real pleasure to know you."

Aware that he wasn't the kind of person to say something he didn't mean, Tess glanced at him gratefully. He had the most wonderful way of making her feel good about herself when she needed to most.

"Thanks," she murmured. Then, wanting to let him know that the feeling was definitely mutual, she added, "You're not so bad yourself."

"I'd say that was high praise, coming from you," he teased as the elevator doors opened.

"And I'd say you're right."

Actually he was one of the kindest, most caring men she'd ever met, and under any other circumstances, she could have easily fallen in love with him. However, she didn't dare say as much to him. As it was, she shouldn't even be holding his hand, but she couldn't have let go of him if she tried.

Since they had to share the elevator with several other people, they rode down to the fifth floor in mutually agreeable silence.

Standing close to Will, Tess managed to relax a little, but when they stepped off the elevator, her heart began to pound again. As if sensing her unspoken anxiety, Will gently squeezed her fingers once more.

''You're going to do just fine,'' he said. ''Jonathan's a good kid. I think you'll really like him. Just remember, though, he's not going to look quite as healthy as he does in the photograph I gave you.''

As they paused in front of a closed door, Tess saw the boy's name printed on the card fitted into the metal slot on the wall beside it. For just a moment, running as far and as fast as she could seemed like a really good idea. But then common sense came to the fore. He needed to see her, and in her own way, she needed to see him, too.

''Ready?'' Will asked.

''As I'll ever be,'' Tess admitted with a wavering smile.

''Then here goes.''

He knocked on the door, and from within, a young voice invited them to enter. Still holding her hand, Will opened the door and led her into the room.

Tess saw the boy at once and paused, her breath catching in her throat. Nestled against a pile of pillows on the hospital bed, he appeared much thinner than she'd expected him to be. He had dark shadows under his eyes, and there was a jaundiced cast to his skin, as well. But otherwise, he looked much as she'd imagined he would, with his wild mess of dark, curly hair, his eyes full of mischief and a bright smile tugging at the corners of his mouth.

She could see a lot of herself in him, and a lot of Bryan, too. In fact, he seemed to have inherited the best of what each of them had had to offer, she thought, blinking back the sudden prickle of tears in her eyes. *Their* son…

''Hi,'' he greeted her, sitting up a little straighter, his smile turning into a wide, welcoming grin. ''Are you Uncle Will's friend Tess?''

Not quite sure she could trust her voice yet, Tess nodded. Beside her, Will let go of her hand, then slipped his arm around her shoulders. Without hesitation, she leaned against him, more thankful than ever that he was there with her.

''Jonathan Drake, meet Professor Mary Theresa McGuire, better known as Tess,'' he said as he urged her closer to the boy's bed, then moved back a step or two.

From the corner of her eye, Tess saw Julie and Philip standing near the foot of the bed, watching her with obvious concern. Taking a slow, deep breath, she ordered herself to smile as she turned her attention back to the boy.

He was eyeing her intently, as if taking her measure. As she met his curious gaze, Tess silently willed him not to find her wanting.

''You have neat eyes,'' he said at last, grinning again.

''So do you,'' she replied, laughing in spite of herself.

Leave it to him to mention the one way in which they were undeniably alike. And, of course, she had to acknowledge it. He was smart enough that he'd be suspicious if she didn't.

''How long have you known Uncle Will?''

''Not too long,'' she admitted honestly. ''He's a nice guy, isn't he?''

''Yeah,'' Jonathan agreed. ''He brought me a whole bunch of stuff from San Antonio.''

''I know.''

''That's where you live, isn't it?''

''Yes.''

''Are you going to marry Uncle Will and move to Houston?''

''Um, well...'' Tess hesitated, then glanced at Will, hoping for some help, but he merely gazed back at her thoughtfully. Mentally cursing him for putting her in such an untenable position, she turned back to Jonathan. ''No, I'm not. We're just...just friends.''

''Too bad,'' Jonathan replied with obvious regret. ''He was gonna marry Claire Colson, but she didn't want him to work for the D.A. anymore. She wanted him to work for my dad, but he didn't—''

''Jonathan,'' Will interrupted warningly, ''Tess isn't interested in my past history.''

''Oh, but I am,'' she contradicted.

''Do *you* mind that he works for the D.A.?'' Jonathan asked.

''Not at all,'' she said.

The boy arched an eyebrow and shot a wise-beyond-his-years look at his uncle, then turned back to Tess again. ''What do you teach?''

''History.''

''Not *my* favorite subject at all. But Uncle Will likes history a lot. Don't you?'' he asked, waggling his eyebrows at his uncle.

''Oh, yeah, I like it a lot.''

''So maybe you'll end up more than just friends, huh?''

Tess deemed it wise not to say a word, and obviously so did Will. After several moments of silence, Jonathan finally took off on the tack Tess imagined he'd been slowly working up to all along.

''Dr. Wells said you're going to give me a part of your liver so I can get well again,'' he said, gazing up at her expectantly.

''I am, at seven o'clock Monday morning. You *will* take good care of it for me, won't you?''

''Oh, yes, I promise.'' He returned her smile for a moment, then grew serious again. ''Are you scared?''

''A little bit,'' she admitted, reaching out and taking one of his hands in hers. ''How about you? Are you scared, too?''

''Yeah, a little bit,'' he agreed.

''But not enough to change your mind about having the surgery?''

''No...''

''Me, neither.''

''Really?'' He hung on to her hand as he gazed up at her, his eyes searching hers.

''Really.'' With a reassuring smile, she squeezed his hand in the same gentle way Will had done hers, then let him go. Though she longed to gather him into her arms, to hold him close and kiss his cheek, she took a distancing step back. She wouldn't cling and she wouldn't cry, no matter how desperately she wanted to. "So do we have a date Monday morning?"

"You betcha." Once again he flashed his devilish grin.

"You know, we won't get to see each other because we'll be in different operating rooms, but I'll be thinking of you."

"I'll be thinking of you, too," he vowed.

"That's good to know." Still smiling, she took another step back and realized that Will had moved to stand beside her once more. "Now I think we'd both better get some rest, right?"

"Right," Jonathan said, settling back against his pillows with a weary sigh.

She'd only been there a short time, yet Tess had noticed how quickly the boy tired. From what Dr. Wells had told her, she knew that his fatigue was due to his devastating illness. He should be bouncing around the room like a rubber ball, just as any normal, healthy ten-year-old boy would be doing instead of languishing in a hospital bed. And he would be if the surgery was a success. Within a few months he'd be almost as good as new, and by this time next year…

"It was nice meeting you, Jonathan," Tess said, any lingering doubts she'd had about the transplant surgery vanishing in an instant.

"It was nice meeting you, too, Tess."

"Thank you for coming to see him, Ms. McGuire," Philip said, speaking for the first time since she'd entered the room.

"Yes, thank you," Julie echoed softly, her voice thick with unshed tears.

"It was my pleasure," she replied, gazing at Will's sister for one long moment. "You have a wonderful son."

She took one last, longing look at Jonathan, her heart aching. He was as bright and funny as she'd hoped he would be, he had a family who loved him deeply, and very soon he'd be well again. There was little more she could want for him except a long and happy life. But then that went without saying.

"Goodbye, Jonathan," she said, her voice whisper-soft.

"'Bye, Tess."

As she turned toward the door, tears blurring her vision, she felt Will slip his arm around her shoulders again. He said something to his nephew and something more to his sister, but Tess was concentrating too hard on not crying to make any sense of his words.

Finally they were out in the hallway, walking toward the elevator. Just a few minutes more and she'd be back in her room. Then she could weep all she wanted. Once she got rid of Will…

"I thought you said you weren't good with kids," he chided gently as they stepped onto the elevator.

"I'm not. But you were right about Jonathan. He *is* good with adults. He took charge of the conversation from the first. All I had to do was answer a few questions, some of them tougher than others." She glanced at Will as the elevator stopped and they got off. "I could have used a little help on that one about marriage."

"I thought you handled it very well, although I must admit my hopes were somewhat…dashed. Just friends?"

"Don't be silly." She glanced at him again, sure that he must be teasing despite his oddly serious tone of voice. "'Just friends' is pretty good considering we didn't even know each other a week ago."

"Ah, but will it be good enough down the line?" he asked.

"All things considered, I think it's going to have to be," Tess stated firmly, though her heart was pounding again, this time with a new kind of fear.

More than once over the past few days she'd had the feeling that her attraction to Will was mutual. But each time that had happened, she'd always managed to convince herself that she was just indulging in a bit of good, old-fashioned wishful thinking. But what if she'd been right all along? What if he really did find her as appealing as she found him? What would she do? What *could* she do that wouldn't land her in a world of hurt?

"I suppose you're right," Will agreed after a moment or two. Then, as if they'd been talking about nothing more important than the weather, he added lightly, "Shall we see what 'room service' has to offer? I don't know about you, but I'm starving."

As she followed him into her room, Tess had the strangest feeling that Will hadn't really been kidding around at all, but rather testing the waters. But why? He had to know as well as she that they had no hope of ever having any kind of future together. And she didn't think he was any more interested in casual sex than she was.

Maybe he'd just been trying to take her mind off her visit with Jonathan so she wouldn't break down while he was there. Not that he seemed to be in any hurry to go. Still he *had* succeeded in giving her something else to think about, albeit something she was afraid to consider too closely.

Or maybe he was simply on the rebound from his apparently failed romance with Claire Colson, whoever *she* was. With Jonathan being so ill, Will probably hadn't had a chance to meet anyone else yet. And having obviously taken on the job of looking after her, he wasn't exactly free to get out and about right now. Of course, he'd said that he wanted to be with her, but she knew him well enough to know that he was too nice to say otherwise even if that was how he really felt.

"Earth to Tess, earth to Tess...come in, please," Will quipped.

"I'm sorry." Drawn from her reverie, Tess turned away from the window and met his teasing gaze. "Did you say something?"

"I was just wondering if you'd eaten yet?"

"I was supposed to have dinner at six-thirty, but we were with Jonathan then. If I call the nurse, she'll bring me something whenever I want, though."

"How about if I try to mooch a meal, too? Then we can have dinner together and maybe watch a movie, depending on what's available in the video library."

Tess liked Will's idea more than she wanted to admit, yet she didn't feel right about taking up any more of his time than she already had. He'd spent almost every evening that week with her, which wasn't the least bit necessary. She was perfectly capable of looking after herself. She'd done so for years.

As she'd realized earlier, she was growing much too dependent on him for her own good, and that had to stop.

"Surely you must have something else you should be doing...." she began.

"Not a thing," he replied, taking off his jacket and holster, setting them aside, then loosening his tie in what had become his evening ritual. "What about you? Got any big plans for tonight?"

"Well, no—"

"All right, then, let me wander down to the nurses' station and see what I can scrounge up in the way of eats. On my way back, I'll pick up a couple of movies at the video library, too."

Before Tess could stop him, he walked out the door, rolling up his sleeves as he went. She thought about going after him, making some sort of excuse and then asking him to leave. If she insisted that she wanted to be alone, she knew he'd honor her wishes. Only she didn't really want to be alone at all....

She'd been on an emotional roller coaster since Dr. Wells had come to tell her the surgery had been scheduled. She'd been oddly relieved yet frightened. As the doctor had made sure she understood before she signed the consent forms, anything could happen while she was on the operating table. Still she hadn't been even vaguely tempted to change her mind. And she wouldn't as long as Jonathan's life hung in the balance.

Then, after Dr. Wells had gone, she'd had to call Richard and tell him she couldn't go to Ireland with him after all. He'd been just as furious as she'd expected he'd be, yet she couldn't blame him for it. She was the one behaving totally out of character. Good old dependable Tess had let him down for the first time in all the years he'd known her, and he'd had a hard time dealing with it. Especially since she'd refused to give him what he thought to be a valid excuse.

What she'd done ten years ago, not to mention what she was doing now, wasn't any of his business. Though they'd been friends and colleagues for a long time, she had no desire to share the intimate details of her past with him. And after their conversation today, she had a feeling she probably never would.

He'd made it clear that she wasn't on his list of favorite people anymore, and while that didn't bother her as much as she'd thought it would, she knew she'd miss the camaraderie they'd shared. She'd always valued the friends she had, because she didn't have a lot of them. Losing one was never easy. But sometimes it became unavoidable.

And, of course, she'd just finished with Richard when Will arrived and began insisting she go to see Jonathan with him. Though the experience had been as heartrending as she'd imagined it would, she was so glad that she'd gone through with it. No matter what happened, she'd always know that she'd done what was best for her child, both ten years ago, as well as today. He was happy and very soon he'd be healthy again, too. She wished her life had been different when he was born, that she had been able to care for him herself, but there was no changing the past. And as for the future, at least she'd always know that he was deeply loved.

"Dinner is served, Professor," Will announced as he strode into her room, somehow managing to juggle two trays full of plates, cups and cutlery along with a couple of videotapes all at once.

"Here, let me," she murmured, catching the tapes as they inevitably slid from his grasp.

"Thanks." He set the trays on the table by the window and pulled the two chairs closer. "They had your pasta and chicken ready and luckily didn't mind fixing another plate for me. How about the movies? Are they all right?"

"*Terminator* and *Enchanted April?*" She eyed the videotapes she held, then glanced at Will quizzically. "You have rather *interesting* taste in movies."

"Talk about the pot calling the kettle black. Or did you pick up *Blade Runner* by accident the other day?" he asked, lifting the covers off their plates.

"Not exactly..."

"In that case..." He grinned as he took the movies from her and gestured to one of the chairs. "Tell me which one you want to watch first, then make yourself comfortable."

"Might as well start with *Terminator,*" she said.

It *was* one of her favorites, as was *Enchanted April.* But surely Will couldn't know that. Which meant that he must like both movies, as well.

"*Terminator* it is." He slotted the tape into the VCR and switched on the television, then joined her at the table and dug into his pasta.

Her own fork poised in midair, Tess gazed at Will with more gratitude and affection than she'd felt toward anyone in a very long time. He'd known what she'd needed earlier when he'd taken her to see Jonathan. And he knew what she needed now. She wished she could find the words to tell him how much his kindness meant to her. But words alone simply weren't adequate to express the gratitude and affection welling up inside her. And words were all she had to offer him.

"You'd better eat, or your food will get cold," Will said, glancing at her, then focusing on the television screen again.

"Nag, nag, nag," she muttered in reply as she speared a piece of chicken.

"Hey, it's a nasty job, but somebody has to do it."

"Yeah, sure, tell me about it."

By the time they'd finished eating and watched both movies, it was well past ten o'clock, and the nurse on duty had begun to hint that visiting hours were definitely over.

Enchanted as she always was by *Enchanted April,* Tess smiled at Will as he stood and stretched. "Thanks for dinner and the double feature," she said.

"You're quite welcome." He gathered his suit coat and holster, but didn't immediately head for the door. Instead, he eyed her thoughtfully, as if he had something important on his mind.

"What's wrong?" she asked, her smile fading.

"Nothing. I was just thinking...."

"About what?"

"Tomorrow. What time would you like me to pick you up?"

"Pick me up?" she echoed in confusion.

"While I was down at the nurses' station, I got you a pass for tomorrow." He pulled a card from his shirt pocket and handed it to her. "You're not scheduled for any more tests, and you're certainly not sick, so there's no reason why you have to stay here all day. I thought maybe we could take a ride to Galveston. That is, if you feel like it.''

At a total loss for words, Tess stared at the card giving her permission to leave the hospital for a maximum of twenty-four hours the following day.

Even with her visits to Lydia, Ina and Harry, she'd been going slowly stir-crazy over the past couple of days. She'd been so looking forward to summer, to being free to go outside and work in her garden whenever she wanted instead of spending hours inside teaching classes or attending meetings. Being cooped up in a hospital room, no matter how luxurious, had become harder and harder to bear. She couldn't have asked for a better gift than a whole day away, and Will was offering her just that.

''If you'd rather stay here, I'll understand,'' he added.

''Oh, no. I...I'd love to get out of here for the day, and I'd especially love to go to Galveston. I haven't been there in a really long time.''

''What time can you be ready to go, then?''

''Whenever you want.''

''How about nine o'clock?''

''Nine will be fine.''

She smiled as she stood and walked to the door with him, putting all the ''shouldn'ts'' out of her mind along the way. He'd offered to spend the day with her, and she'd taken him up on it without hesitation.

''Is the weather supposed to be nice?'' she asked.

''Sunny, hot and humid—a typical Gulf Coast summer day. So wear something cool and comfortable.'' He paused just inside the doorway and turned to face her. ''Maybe the dress you had on Sunday,'' he suggested with a smile.

''I was thinking the same thing myself.''

''Well, I'll see you at nine o'clock.''

''Okay. See you then.''

He stood there, just looking at her for several long moments, and Tess had the strangest feeling that he wanted to kiss her. But he didn't. He reached out and touched her cheek, then drew his hand back and turned away.

"Good night, Tess."

"Good night, Will."

She watched him walk down the hallway, wishing she had a valid reason to call him back. Unfortunately wanting to be held and kissed and caressed didn't exactly fall into that category. In fact, it would be best not to even think of *that* kind of wanting, much less mention it to him. She'd finally gotten to the point where she could accept his kindness, but she didn't dare make too much of it. Just as she didn't dare expect more of him than he was prepared to give.

Keeping her company for a few hours in the evening wasn't much in the total scheme of things. Nor was a Saturday drive to Galveston. And she'd do well to remember it. They'd been thrown together by unusual circumstances, and he was trying to make the best of it in his own way. Taking advantage of his generosity would be a terrible thing to do, not only to him, but to herself as well.

Tess was ready and waiting for Will long before nine o'clock the next morning. She'd slept much better than she'd expected, probably due to the fact that she allowed herself to think no further ahead than Saturday. And though she had awakened earlier than she intended, she'd felt better than she had in days.

She slipped into her pale yellow dress and a pair of sandals. Then, keeping in mind that it was going to be hot and humid outside, she twisted her hair into a neat coil at the nape of her neck. With the addition of her gold hoop earrings, she felt ready for anything, from a walk on the beach to lunch in one of the funky restaurants along the Strand.

After breakfast she looked in on her three new friends to let them know she'd be gone for the day. Back in her room again, she tried to read the morning paper, but she couldn't seem to settle down at all. She ended up standing by the window, barely able to contain her excitement as her gaze drifted from the bright, sunny sky above to the bustling traffic on the street below. Not only was she going to be outside all day, but she was going to be out with Will, and she couldn't imagine a more wonderful way to spend such a beautiful day.

"I guess I don't need to ask if you're ready to go," Will said as he walked through the open doorway of her room.

"Only since about seven o'clock." Tess turned to face him, smiling as she grabbed her purse off the table and started toward him.

He was dressed in tailored navy blue shorts, a white knit shirt and leather deck shoes. With his broad shoulders, flat belly and muscular arms and legs, he looked more attractive to Tess than ever. For just an instant, she wondered what it would be like to make love with him. Then, feeling her cheeks warm with the beginning of a blush, she forced the all-too-vivid image from her mind. They were nothing more than friends sharing a day together.

"One would think you weren't too fond of hospitals, Professor," Will teased, clasping her hand in his as they walked down the hallway.

"They're nice places to visit, but staying in one for any amount of time..." She shrugged and shook her head. "The past few days have really made me appreciate that old saying, 'there's no place like home.'"

"Would you like me to make sure everything's all right there?" he asked as they boarded the elevator. "You've been away almost a week, and now, with the surgery..."

"I appreciate the offer, but everything's under control. My neighbor's been picking up my mail and watering the yard and generally looking after the place for me. I talked to her yesterday and told her I'd be gone another two weeks or so." Tess hesitated, then added quietly, "I also gave her your telephone number in case of an...emergency. I hope that was all right."

"Of course."

"I guess I ought to give you her telephone number, too, so if anything happens to me..."

"I think that would be a good idea," he admitted. Then, as if trying to reassure himself, as well as her, he continued rather hastily. "But you're going to be all right, Tess. Dr. Wells and his people are one of the best transplant teams in the country."

"I've always believed that when it's your time to go, you...go, regardless."

"I've kind of always felt that way myself," he agreed quietly, then tightened his hold on her hand for a moment. "However, *you're* not going anywhere but back to your pretty little house in San Antonio, and I want you to remember that."

"I promise I will, but only if you promise not to talk about it any more today." She glanced at him and added almost pleadingly, "Today I want to get as far away from here as I can, mentally, as well as physically."

"Whatever you want, Professor. Your wish is my command."

"Well, then, why don't we hop on a Learjet and fly to Paris for lunch?" she queried in a teasing tone of voice.

"As soon as we get downstairs, I'll call Philip and see what he can arrange," Will replied so seriously that Tess had a feeling they'd be heading out over the Atlantic in a few hours if that's what she really wanted. But it wasn't.

"Actually I'd much prefer to go to Galveston as we planned."

"Are you sure? Paris isn't completely out of the question, you know."

"I'm positive," she assured him. "Absolutely positive."

Tess had no idea how Will found his way to the parking garage where he'd left his Blazer. She only knew that had she been forced to find her way back to her hospital room, she couldn't have done it, even at gunpoint.

Though she could have easily climbed onto the passenger seat in the longer, full-skirted dress she wore, Will helped her up with the same casual ease he had on Monday. And though his hands lingered at her waist a bit longer than necessary, as they had then, too, Tess didn't mind at all.

Neither of them said much as Will navigated the busy city streets around the medical center, but once he had the Blazer on the freeway heading south to the island, he picked up where he'd seemingly left off.

"Were you going to Paris with your friend Richard?" he asked, putting "friend" and "Richard" together in a way that made both words sound like a slur.

"No, I wasn't."

Tess hesitated, not really wanting to discuss Richard or her canceled trip to Ireland. Yet she didn't feel right about letting Will think the worst of a man who really had been a good friend in the past.

"He's really not a callous brute," she said. "He's actually a rather nice person most of the time. He was angry with me yesterday, and he had good reason to be. Of course, that upset me. But I imagine we'll patch up our differences eventually."

"You didn't tell him about Jonathan, did you?"

"I wasn't prepared to discuss what happened ten years ago with him. So...no, I didn't."

"What *did* happen ten years ago?" Will asked, his gentle voice a lure she found hard to resist.

"I made a mistake," she stated flatly. Then, desperate to change the subject before she was tempted to say more than she should and curious about something Jonathan had mentioned last night, she turned the tables on him. "What about you and Claire Colson? Are you still friendly with her?"

Will glanced at her, an amused look in his eyes. "Our relationship didn't exactly end amicably, so I haven't seen her since then."

"How did you meet in the first place?" Tess prodded, not minding that he knew what she was doing, especially since he seemed willing to go along with it.

"Her father owns a drilling company. He does a lot of work for Philip. Claire came to one of Julie and Philip's parties with her parents, and I happened to be there, too. We got together, and for a while, I thought we'd stay together, but what Jonathan said was true. She wanted me to go to work for Philip, and I refused."

"She didn't like your being an investigator for the district attorney's office?"

"I was on the police force when we met. She seemed to like the idea at first. Then she started making noises about the odd hours and the danger involved. So when I heard about an opening at the D.A.'s office, I applied for it. I'd just finished working on the Kaminski case and had a pretty good rep as a homicide detective already, so I got the job.

"I thought she'd be satisfied, but she wasn't. What she really wanted was for me to make a lot of money at what she considered a prestigious job, so she could keep up with her friends in the Junior League. When she realized that wasn't going to happen, we parted company. Last I heard, she was seeing an attorney who's a partner in one of the city's biggest law firms."

Staring out the window at the strip shopping centers, car dealerships and restaurants lining the freeway, Tess thought about what Will had said and understood why he'd mentioned financial remuneration the way he had. Coming off a relationship with a woman who'd been more interested in how much money he made than in the kind of person he was, he'd expected the worst of her.

That also must be why he'd been so hesitant to talk about his work when she'd first asked him about it. But she thought he had an interesting job. And from what he'd told her, she knew that he was not only good at it, but enjoyed it enormously, as well.

Though he might not agree, she thought him well rid of Claire Colson. As far as Tess was concerned, he was much too good for her. But, of course, she couldn't say that to him. Not when he'd once been engaged to the woman.

"Speaking of your job," she said, once again deeming it wise to change the subject. "Have you had any breaks in your case?"

"I wish. I drove up to Huntsville yesterday morning and talked to Eddie again. He's still insisting he's innocent, but that's nothing new. I also went over to the county jail and talked to the guy who tipped us that someone else committed the murder Eddie was convicted of. He wasn't any more help than he was the first time around.

"I'd really like to chuck the whole mess, but I keep getting the feeling there's something to all this. We never found the murder weapon, and our eyewitness was shaky at best. Still, by his own admission, Eddie *was* in the vicinity that night. And the modus operandi of the breaking and entering was his, if not the senseless violence.

"I've got some feelers out, but otherwise I'm about at the

end of the line.'' He glanced at her again and smiled. ''I needed today as much as you, Professor. To be honest, if I'd gone in to work today, I'd be climbing the walls by now.''

''Well, then, why don't we try to forget about the hospital *and* the D.A.'s office for the next few hours and just enjoy ourselves?'' she suggested, returning his smile.

''Sounds like a winner to me,'' he agreed readily as he drove over the bridge connecting the mainland to the island. ''What do you want to do first? We can tour the old Victorian homes, walk through the rain forest at Moody Gardens, go shopping on the Strand or just wander along the beach.''

''Did you say rain forest?''

''A man-made rain forest growing in a ten-story glass pyramid. It's really something to see.''

''Sounds fascinating. Let's go there first, then the Victorian homes, then the Strand and finally, the beach.''

Tess wanted to do as much as possible in the hours ahead so she'd have lots of wonderful memories to keep her company when Will could no longer be a part of her life.

''As I said, your wish is my command. Just don't get too tired out, or Dr. Wells will be furious. I promised him I'd take good care of you.''

''You've done that for over a week already,'' she murmured. In fact, he'd taken better care of her than anyone ever had in her life, and she'd never forget it.

''I hope so, Professor.'' Reaching out, he touched her cheek as he had the night before. ''I certainly hope so.''

The rain forest was as intriguing as Will had said it would be. Hand in hand, they spent almost two hours wandering along brick paths that meandered through an incomparable array of exotic plants, pausing occasionally to watch the ducklings paddling in one of the small pools or to gaze at a brightly colored butterfly flitting among the foliage.

When they'd seen all there was to see at Moody Gardens, they drove to the historic district and toured first the Bishop's Palace, then Ashton Villa, admiring the elegant antique furnishings that had been used to recreate an era long past. They went on to the Strand for a late lunch, and spent the rest of the afternoon and early evening browsing in the shops and stores lining the sidewalks there.

Just after six o'clock, they returned to Will's Blazer and headed for the beach. Bypassing the still-crowded east end of the island, they drove west for several miles until they reached a residential area called Pirate's Beach. Turning left, they followed a narrow road that led past several dozen homes and, to Tess's surprise, pulled into the driveway of a house set off by itself at the end.

Though built up on pilings, the white clapboard house with dark green trim looked like the kind of summer house Tess would have expected to find on Cape Cod. But the storm shutters covering the windows indicated that the place was vacant.

"Do you know the people who own this place?" she asked as Will switched off the ignition.

"It belongs to Julie and Philip. I told them I'd check on it while we were here. They haven't been able to come down to the island since Jonathan's been sick." He glanced at her questioningly for a moment. "I hope you don't mind."

"Of course not."

She walked up the steps with him, then admired the beautiful view of the gulf from the old-fashioned, wraparound porch while Will checked the locks on the doors and the seals on the shutters.

"Would you like to take a look inside?" he asked, joining her at the porch railing several minutes later.

Though Tess was tempted, she shook her head after only a moment's hesitation. The day was almost over, and more than anything she wanted to be outside, where she could breathe in the salty sea breeze while the last rays of sunshine warmed her skin.

"Let's go for a walk," she suggested, smiling as she held out her hand to him.

They ran down the steps and quickly crossed the wooden bridge over the dunes. As if by mutual agreement, they paused just long enough to take off their shoes. Then Will took her hand in his again and led her down to the water's edge. As the sun dipped toward the horizon, they splashed through the ankle-deep waves lapping lackadaisically against the packed sand.

They walked for what seemed like a long time in the same companionable silence they'd shared off and on all week at different times in different places. Though she tried, Tess couldn't remember when she'd ever felt so…peaceful. Being there with Will warmed her heart and settled her soul in a way she'd never expected could be possible. If only she could have made time stand still, she would have. If only…

"We'd better go back," Will said, drawing her to a halt all too soon. "Otherwise, we won't have time to stop for dinner, and there's somewhere special I want to take you tonight."

Tess wanted to protest that she didn't really care about eating another meal, but her growling stomach begged to differ with her.

"Do you come down here often?" she asked as they turned and started back along the nearly deserted beach.

"I haven't been on the island for a while, either. Claire didn't care for the beach much. It was too quiet for her. And then, with Jonathan being sick and my being busy at work, I haven't really had the time. But I'm really glad we came today."

"Me, too," she said as she glanced at him. "But then I've always loved the beach because it *is* quiet. In fact, I think it would be wonderful to be able to come down here and stay for several days or weeks and just do nothing."

"Yeah, I think it would be, too," he agreed, meeting her gaze as he threaded his fingers through hers in a way that had become devastatingly familiar. "With the right person."

Feeling as if he'd read her mind, Tess ducked her head wordlessly. When she'd thought of spending days or weeks on Galveston Island, she hadn't honestly imagined being there by herself. But what she *had* been considering was totally impossible.

"Did you stop to see Jonathan this morning?" she asked after a while, deftly changing the subject.

Though she'd been thinking about the boy all day, she'd avoided talking about him just as she'd avoided talking about anything to do with her stay at the hospital. Now, however, she felt both she and Will needed a reminder of why they were together and why they'd soon be apart once again.

"He's doing great. His spirits are way up, and he finally seems to believe he's going to get well. You were a big hit, Professor."

"I'm glad."

"Me, too."

"What about Julie and Philip? How did they feel about my visit?" she asked curiously.

Will hesitated so long that Tess turned and looked at him. "They're really...grateful that you came and talked to him, especially since you put his mind at ease," he answered at last.

"But...?" Tess prodded, aware that he was leaving something important unsaid.

"But..." Avoiding her gaze, he paused again. "My sister has always been afraid that Jonathan's birth mother would appear out of nowhere one day and find a way to take him away from her."

"Oh, Will, I could never do that," Tess cried. "I may have given birth to him, but Julie and Philip are his parents. They've loved him and cared for him for almost ten years. I'd never do anything to come between them...*never.*"

"I know that," Will assured her. "And I've tried to convince Julie of it, too. But she seems to be having a hard time believing me."

As she listened to what Will said, Tess realized that the past week must have been much more difficult for him than she'd originally thought. Feeling the way she did, his sister wouldn't have wanted him to be any more involved with her than absolutely necessary. Yet he'd taken it upon himself to look after her, even though he'd more than likely done so without Julie's approval.

Though she was touched by Will's vote of confidence, Tess hoped that she hadn't come between him and his sister in an irreparable way. So far, she doubted that she had. But the sooner she got out of their lives, the better for all concerned.

"Well, I'll be gone in a couple of weeks. Maybe then she'll

finally be able to accept the fact that she has nothing to worry about where I'm concerned.''

''One can only hope,'' Will replied in a surprisingly solemn tone of voice.

From the island they drove north to the small town of Kemah on Galveston Bay. There they stopped for dinner at a little seafood restaurant overlooking the channel into Clear Lake. As they sat outside, eating boiled shrimp and fried soft-shell crabs, boats of all sizes and styles cruised by, heading either out to the bay or back to one of the many marinas lining the lake.

They drove back to the hospital in relative silence, one as sorry as the other that their day together was almost over. By the time Will parked in the garage and they made their way back to the twelfth floor, it was after ten o'clock. They stopped at the nurses' station just long enough for Tess to check in again and have her wristband ID replaced. Then, after a reminder from the nurse on duty that Will couldn't stay more than fifteen or twenty minutes, they walked down the hallway to Tess's room.

Someone had been there to turn on the lamp on the nightstand and turn down her bed, but otherwise the room was just as she'd left it that morning. Standing inside the doorway, Tess wondered if she'd only imagined that she'd been out with Will all day.

As if reading her mind, he slipped an arm around her shoulders and held her close for a moment. ''I feel like a real crud bringing you back here,'' he muttered against her hair, then released her reluctantly.

''I must admit I'm not all that thrilled to *be* back here. But if I wasn't, Jonathan wouldn't have nearly as good a chance of getting well again.'' Somehow she managed to keep her tone light as she moved away from Will. ''Thanks for today. I had a really nice time,'' she added, turning to face him.

''So did I.'' He didn't say anything more for several seconds, then finally continued. ''You said something earlier about giving me your neighbor's telephone number....''

''Oh, yes.''

Glad to have an excuse to put even more distance between

them, Tess crossed to the nightstand, pulled out a sheet of paper and a pen and wrote down her friend's name, address and telephone number. When she faced Will again, however, she saw that he'd followed her and now stood no more than an arm's length away, leaving her nowhere to go but up against the bed.

"Her name's Susan Wylie. She lives in the redbrick house with blue trim to the right of my place. She's been working at home since she had her second baby, so you shouldn't have any trouble reaching her there. Her husband's name is Mark. They're really nice people...."

Tess knew she was rattling on, but Will was so close and he was watching her much too intently. Lowering her gaze, she offered him the paper. As he took it from her, his fingers brushed hers, and she met his gaze again. He tucked the paper in his pocket. Then, his eyes still holding hers, he rested his hands on her shoulders and drew her closer. Before she could say a word, he bent his head and kissed her ever so gently on the lips.

"Tess..." He murmured her name as he put his arms around her. Then he kissed her again, not nearly so gently, his mouth covering hers.

More like a lover than a friend, Tess thought as she parted her lips for him, welcoming the possessive glide of his tongue over hers with an eagerness she refused to deny. He tasted of sun and sea breezes, and she couldn't seem to get enough of him. Sliding her arms around his neck, she threaded her fingers through the silky hair at the nape of his neck and pressed against him longingly, wanting to be held, *needing* to be held by him.

When he finally raised his head, she murmured a word of protest. Soothing her, he brushed his lips over her cheek and along her jaw as he pulled the pins from her hair. Then, tangling his fingers in her curls, he took her mouth again with a hunger that made her heart ache.

He shouldn't be kissing her, and *she* certainly shouldn't be kissing *him,* but rather than move away from him, Tess clung all the more tightly to him, whimpering softly as his hands stroked over her breasts once and then again. Somewhere deep in her soul, she'd wanted him to hold her, to kiss her and caress her from the moment she'd found him standing outside her office doorway. And now...*now*...

Now she ought to have more sense, she warned herself, easing away from him as he raised his head again.

"You'd better go," she muttered, not quite meeting his gaze as she rested her hands against his chest.

"Yeah, I guess I'd better," he agreed, yet made no move to leave her. "I...I guess I shouldn't have kissed you, huh?"

"And I shouldn't have kissed you back."

"But I'm not sorry I did. Not after spending all of last night being sorry I *didn't.*" He feathered his lips along her cheek again as he smoothed his hands over her hair. "What about you? Are you sorry?"

"Oh, Will, we *can't*..." She knotted her fingers in the fabric of his shirt, then made a liar out of herself as she turned her head so that his mouth covered hers again.

He kissed her nearly senseless, then muttered softly, *"Are you sorry?"*

"No, but—"

"No buts," he growled, hugging her close for several long moments.

Then, stepping back, he finally released her. Somehow she managed to let go of him, but only because it was the best thing she could do...for both of them. Yet, as she shoved her tangled curls away from her face, he gazed at her with such blatant desire that she almost put her arms around him again.

"Thanks again for...for today," she said, offering him her hand as she ducked her head.

"You're welcome, Professor," he replied, taking her hand in one of his as he tipped her chin up with the other. "Very welcome indeed." He brushed his lips over hers as lightly as he had the first time. "See you tomorrow."

He squeezed her hand as if sealing a very special pact, then turned and walked to the door.

Part of her wanted to beg him not to go while another part

of her wanted to insist that he stay away. But she did neither. When he glanced over his shoulder at her questioningly, she nodded her head reluctantly.

"Yes...see you tomorrow."

Chapter Six

Muttering a string of curses, Will shoved the jack under the front bumper of his Blazer and began to hoist the right end into the air. Though it was already well past six o'clock Sunday evening, the heat and humidity of the day had yet to dissipate, and he was bone weary to boot. Had he been able to do so, he couldn't have chosen a worse time *or* place to have a flat tire.

He'd planned to spend the day at the hospital with Jonathan and Tess. Instead, he was stuck on a back road between Beaumont and Houston, miles from anywhere, fighting with the lug nuts securing the wheel while precious minutes slipped away steadily, one after another.

For the umpteenth time, he wished he'd tried to call Tess again before he started back to Houston. But he'd been so anxious to see her that he hadn't wanted to waste any more time trying to get in touch with her, especially since he'd been unsuccessful more than once already.

Of course, he could have left a message for her with one of the nurses, but he hadn't wanted to go into the details of his trip to Beaumont with a stranger. And since he wasn't sure when he'd get back to Houston, he was afraid Tess would worry if she was told nothing more than that he'd called.

He hadn't felt good about asking Julie to relay a message, either. She was still annoyed that he'd been with Tess all day Saturday, and he hadn't wanted to antagonize her any more if he could help it.

By now Tess was probably beginning to wonder why he'd said he would see her today but had yet to show up. And here he was, nowhere near a telephone, with a thirty-minute tire change and at least an hour's drive still ahead of him. If only he hadn't been so cheap about buying a cellular phone, he could have called her from where he was. If only…

The last thing Will had expected to end up doing today was driving ninety miles to Beaumont. But when he'd gotten a call from one of his more reliable snitches at six o'clock that morning regarding the guy who was supposed to have committed Eddie Kaminski's crime, he hadn't had any choice but to follow the lead he'd been given.

Armed with a name and a Beaumont address, he'd spent half the morning trying to find a judge to issue a search warrant. Then, when he'd reached Beaumont, he'd hooked up with the local police and gone to check out Walter Hodges. Walter hadn't been home, but that hadn't kept them from going through his garage apartment with a fine-tooth comb.

They'd found a .38 that Will believed would prove to be the missing murder weapon, and eventually they'd found Walter, too, hiding out at a friend's place. His distinct resemblance to Eddie had been enough to convince Will that he'd found the perpetrator he'd been looking for.

So Eddie Kaminski wasn't going to die after all, or at least not as scheduled by the state of Texas. Once he was free, he'd more than likely resume his life of petty crime. But, then again, maybe not. Several years on death row could very well have been just the kind of rehabilitation he'd really needed all along.

In between completing the paperwork necessary to ensure Hodges's transfer to Houston the following day, and making the calls he'd had to make on Eddie's behalf, Will had managed to get in touch with Julie to let her know where he was. But each time he'd phoned Tess he hadn't gotten any answer.

Knowing her, he suspected she'd been visiting Lydia or Ina or...Harry Gamble. Of all days, today wouldn't be one he imagined she'd want to spend alone. Which was one of the main reasons why he'd intended to be there with her.

She put on a brave face, but Will knew the prospect of major surgery scared her. She could talk all she wanted about accepting death as a natural part of life. But he simply couldn't believe that she wasn't concerned about what might happen to her tomorrow.

For his part, he was concerned as hell. In fact, if anything went wrong with her surgery, he wasn't sure he'd ever be able to forgive himself. He'd been instrumental in getting her to agree to risk her life, and while he still felt he'd been right in doing so for Jonathan's sake, he couldn't forget that he hadn't really considered Tess's best interests, at least not at the outset. But now...

Now he wanted her to be well and...happy. And as he'd realized last night as he held her in his arms and kissed her, he wanted her to be a part of his life.

"Which happens to be just about as likely as your flying to the moon," he muttered, pulling the flat tire off the axle and replacing it with the spare.

For one thing, they lived and worked in different cities. But that was actually a minor inconvenience compared to some of the other problems they'd have to contend with if they became any more involved with each other than they already were.

All his life he'd shared a loving, trusting relationship with his sister, but he knew that getting involved with Tess in any kind of permanent way would very likely put an end to that. Especially if Julie insisted on continuing to think the worst of her. His sister had found it hard enough to accept that he'd become friendly with Tess. He could only imagine how she'd react if she discovered how he really felt about her. And considering how much he owed her, upsetting Julie was something he simply could not easily do.

He had to think of Tess, too. While she might be as attracted to him as he was to her, if she got seriously involved with him, she could end up in a potentially painful position where Jonathan was concerned. After seeing her with the boy Friday night, he'd realized that she cared about him more than she'd ever admit. Yet he'd also gotten the feeling that being with him had been very hard on her emotionally.

If Tess and he had any kind of permanent relationship, and if Julie brought herself to accept it, then Jonathan would also be a part of Tess's life, albeit in a peripheral way. If, on the other hand, Julie couldn't accept Tess, then Tess wouldn't be able to have anything at all to do with the boy. Either way, she could be deeply hurt. And either way, eventually she could very well have to deal with an older, wiser Jonathan who might not only be curious about the identity of his birth mother, but also be quite capable of putting two and two together where she was concerned. Especially if she was a part of his extended family, whether welcome or not.

Will realized that probably the best thing he could do for all concerned was back off. But how could he? He was already half in love with Tess, and he couldn't, *wouldn't,* leave her alone, either literally or figuratively. Yet, at the same time, he knew he'd be better off not thinking beyond the next couple of weeks.

He'd be there for her when she needed someone the most, come hell or high water. But then he'd have to try to let her go back to San Antonio and the life she'd made for herself there. Given time and distance, they'd more than likely be glad to go their own ways. Or at least maybe Tess would. As for himself…

He'd never met anyone like Tess before in his life. Nor had he ever been so drawn to anyone as swiftly and surely as he'd been drawn to her. He'd never believed in love at first sight, but over the past few days he'd been converted. And already he couldn't quite bring himself to contemplate the time when he'd no longer be able to look forward to seeing her again.

He shouldn't have kissed her last night, but heaven help him, he couldn't have stopped himself if he'd tried. He'd wanted to hold her, touch her, taste her since the first moment they'd met, just as he now wanted her in an even more primal way. Not for just a day or a week or a month, but for always.

And since he'd never been one to start something he was almost positive he couldn't finish…

Once again, Will knew he'd be better off putting some distance between them. But knowing and doing were two altogether different things. Right now all he really wanted was to be with her, to let her know he hadn't forgotten about her. As if he ever could.

He finished with the tire at last and, back in the Blazer again, drove well beyond the speed limit the rest of the way to Houston. Feeling hot and gritty, he stopped at his apartment just long enough to shower and shave, then climbed into the Blazer again and headed to the hospital.

He planned to stop by Jonathan's room first. Although the boy would be asleep, he knew Julie and Philip would be there and he wanted to see them. Then he'd go to Tess and stay with her as long as she'd let him. He didn't like the idea of her being alone tonight any more than he liked the idea of being alone himself. And he could see no reason why they should be.

Tess rested her forehead against the cool glass of the window in her room and stared out into the night. All around, the lights of the various buildings comprising the medical center glimmered in the darkness, while on the street below an occasional car flashed past, trailing a streak of red. Closing her eyes, she crossed her arms over her chest, took a deep, steadying breath and willed away the hurt that had settled in her soul.

She'd believed Will when he'd said he would come to see her, but it was almost nine o'clock and he hadn't called or…anything. Not that he was obligated to spend time with her. But she'd really thought he *wanted* to be with her as much as she wanted to be with him. Especially after last night.

Of course, after what had happened between them, maybe he'd decided it would be wiser to stay away from her. Tess couldn't say she blamed him. She'd thought the same thing herself off and on all day. They'd been playing with fire, and she had a feeling he couldn't afford to get burned any more than she could. Still, somewhere deep in her heart, she'd hoped that somehow they'd find a way to work things out, despite all they had going against them. Which only went to prove that she never seemed to learn.

With her track record, she should have had more sense than to depend on a man to stand by her when she needed him most. Her father hadn't done it, and neither had Bryan. Considering Will's situation with his sister, Tess could understand why he wouldn't, either.

He owed his first loyalty to Julie. And though Will hadn't said it in so many words, Tess gathered that his sister didn't want her around any longer than absolutely necessary. She was too afraid of losing her son to trust that Tess would never try to steal him away, physically or emotionally.

Maybe Julie had asked him to choose between them, and that's why he was keeping his distance. After what he'd told her about his sister yesterday, Tess knew she should have expected it. But she hadn't. She'd actually thought that he'd be here today to help chase her fears away. And her blind trust had made the waiting a little more painful with each hour that had passed.

She'd filled the day as best she could. After poring over both morning papers, she'd read to Ina until the old woman had fallen asleep. She'd played gin rummy with Harry for the rest of the afternoon, winning, losing, then winning again. And earlier in the evening, at Lydia's insistence, she'd washed her hair, then allowed Lydia to fashion it into French braids for her.

Her new friends had gone out of their way to keep her spirits up. But eventually she'd had to return to the solitude of her room, where she had much too much time to think.

In less than ten hours, they'd put her to sleep. Then Dr. Wells would cut her open and…and…

With a shiver, Tess opened her eyes again, preferring the view from her window to the mental images she'd had of the surgery the good doctor had described in such exacting detail.

"Think of Jonathan," she reminded herself softly.

The boy would be well again because of her, and that was

all that really mattered right now. In the past, she'd faced worse things than surgery on her own without falling apart. She could and *would* do it again. The time she'd spent with Will Landon had been nothing more than a pleasant interlude. And while she'd never forget it, dwelling on impossible hopes and dreams was foolish at best.

Two weeks from today she'd be back in San Antonio again, picking up the pieces of her quiet, albeit satisfying life. She had books to read and a paper she ought to at least *think* about writing. And she had two new classes she'd be teaching in the fall that she had to prepare for, as well. After several weeks away, her garden would need a little TLC, and she couldn't forget the old kitchen cupboard out in the garage, just waiting to be refinished.

She'd probably have to take it easy at first, but she had a lot to keep her busy. If she put her mind to it, she'd be as good as new by the end of the summer, in mind as well as body. And the hours she'd spent with Will would be no more than a fading memory—

"I sure as hell hope you're a believer in better late than never, Professor," Will muttered from somewhere close behind her.

Startled, Tess glanced over her shoulder and saw him standing less than a foot away, hands tucked in the pockets of his worn jeans, his shaggy auburn hair curling damply around the collar of his black knit shirt. Though his tone had been teasing, and he wore a sheepish smile, the wary look in his eyes assured her that he wasn't really taking the situation as lightly as it seemed.

She had no idea how he'd managed to cross the room without her hearing him. But then she'd been a millon miles away, trying desperately to convince herself that she didn't need him after all.

Heart racing, she turned back to the window, unsure what to say or do. He'd come to see her, and she *did* believe that late was better than never. Still part of her wanted to tell him to go away. Unfortunately another, more vulnerable part of her wanted to throw herself into his arms and beg him to stay. To her dismay, she found one prospect as frightening as the other. Having told herself more than once that she could get along fine without him, she really ought to just do it. But she didn't want to. Not when she didn't have to.

"I...I thought you'd changed your mind about...about..." She shrugged and shook her head.

"I got a tip from one of my sources on the Kaminski case early this morning. I had to drive to Beaumont to check it out. I tried to call you several times this afternoon, but you were gone. Leaving a message would have been kind of complicated, and I thought I'd be here a lot sooner. But then I had a flat tire." He moved a few steps closer to her so that she could feel his breath against the back of her neck. "I...I hope you didn't think I'd forgotten about you."

"I thought you'd changed your mind and decided to spend the day with Jonathan," she admitted quietly.

"I wouldn't have done that without telling you. If it hadn't been six in the morning, I wouldn't have gone off to Beaumont without telling you, either." He put an arm around her waist and drew her close. "And I *did* try to call you in the afternoon once things settled down a bit...."

She tensed for a moment, then relaxed, savoring the feel of his warm, hard body against hers. Just knowing he'd wanted to be with her went a long way toward easing the hurt she'd been feeling.

"When I realized you probably weren't going to make it after all, I went visiting," she said, resting her hands on his forearms.

"How is everybody?"

"Ina's as feisty as ever, Harry cheats at cards in the worst way, and Lydia's a real sweetheart." Tess smiled as she recalled Lydia's increasing interest in Harry; she obviously had a crush on him, and if Tess did nothing else before she left the hospital, she vowed to get the two of them together.

"You did something with your hair, too," he murmured, teasing the curve of her neck with his lips.

"Actually Lydia did the braids for me," Tess replied, leaning closer to him and tilting her head slightly as longing stirred deep inside her. "She thought it would be a good idea since I won't be able to do much with my hair for several days. Do you like it?"

"Let me see." He turned her to face him and studied her quite seriously. "Yeah, I like it a lot. But I like it best all wild around your shoulders like it was...last night."

Drawing her closer, he bent his head and kissed her with a hunger that had her clinging to him just as she had the night before, despite her best intentions.

"Ah, Tess, you have no idea how much I wanted to be here with you today," he said, hugging her close.

She held on to him for as long as she dared, then took a step back. "Can you tell me what happened in Beaumont?" she asked, struggling to regain her balance.

"Why don't we sit down? Then I'll tell you all about it."

With a wicked grin, he scooped her into his arms, carried her over to one of the chairs, sat down and settled her in his lap so swiftly that she didn't have a chance to object.

"I don't know if this is such a good idea," she said, gazing up at him with concern after a moment's hesitation.

"Under the circumstances, it's the best I can do. I want to hold you," he growled, his voice husky. "So we either sit together in this chair or on the bed. And since I'm having a hard enough time behaving myself as it is..."

"Oh, Will..." Smiling, she shook her head in mock dismay as her heart warmed with tenderness.

"Stop looking at me like that, or I'm going to throw caution to the wind and ravish you right here," he warned, his bright eyes glimmering with something quite...elemental.

"Whatever you say," she murmured agreeably, lowering her gaze as she rested her head on his shoulder.

"How I wish," he groaned.

Then, one hand resting on her hip, the other slowly stroking her arm, Will told her about his trip to Beaumont and the quarry he'd caught there.

As she listened to him talk, Tess became so engrossed in his story that she all but forgot about the following day. She was amazed at how one piece of information in the hands of the right individual could end up saving one man's life and perhaps ending another's.

"So what happens now?" she asked when Will finally paused for a moment.

"A stay of execution will be granted for Eddie while the case is reopened and the new evidence assessed. If Hodges's .38 proves to be the murder weapon and our witness can identify him in a lineup, then he'll go to trial and Eddie will be freed."

"Poor Eddie..."

"I told you he wasn't any choirboy. Granted, he got a raw deal, but he won't go away empty-handed. More than likely he'll slap the state with a lawsuit and win. And maybe he won't be so eager to go back to a life of petty crime."

"Not if he wins his lawsuit, he won't," Tess replied.

"Yeah, he'll probably end up rolling in dough."

"Did you have a chance to see Jonathan before you came up here?" she asked.

"He was asleep already, but I'll have a chance to see him in the morning before they take him into the operating room. I talked to Julie and Philip for a few minutes, though. They said he was in pretty good spirits all day, and they seemed to be upbeat themselves." He paused and brushed a kiss against her cheek. "Julie said to tell you they'll be thinking of you tomorrow along with Jonathan."

"I'll be thinking of them, too," Tess admitted, trying not to read too much into his sister's obvious overture. "They must be scared to death right now, especially if Dr. Wells gave them as many details about Jonathan's surgery as he gave me about mine. Sometimes ignorance really can be bliss."

"You know, Tess, if I could take your place tomorrow, I would," Will said, tightening his hold on her.

"I know." She tipped her face up and met his gaze. "But since I'm the one who can help him..." She shrugged as she offered him a wry smile.

"Ms. McGuire, Dr. Wells wants you to get some sleep tonight, so he's ordered some medication to help you relax. Since it's almost ten o'clock, I thought you'd better take it."

Eyeing the two of them unabashedly, the nurse crossed the room, stopped beside the chair where Tess sat in Will's lap and handed her a couple of tablets and a cup of water.

Blushing at being caught in what could be termed a compromising position, Tess took the pills, then handed the cup back to the nurse with a murmur of thanks.

"I think you'd probably be more...comfortable in the bed," the nurse added, then turned her attention to Will. "Dr. Wells told us you'd be staying the night. That chair opens into a bed." After staring at them for a moment or two longer, she finally turned and left.

"You're staying here all night?" Tess asked, unable to hide her surprise.

"Unless you want me to go." Still holding her in his arms, he stood easily and walked over to the bed. The covers had been turned back and the pillows plumped up already.

"But what about work tomorrow?"

"Everything's under control, and I'd planned to be here anyway." He set her on the bed, then stood back and braced his hands on his hips. "So, Professor, what'll it be? Do you want me to stay or go?"

As Tess kicked off her slippers and unbuttoned her robe, she considered her alternatives. With the pills the nurse had given her, she'd sleep no matter what. But just knowing Will was there with her would mean that she'd rest much easier. For some reason, his very presence made her feel stronger and more sure of herself than she'd ever felt before. And tonight of all nights she needed as much strength and certainty as she could muster.

She tossed her robe to the foot of the bed. Then, taking care that her pink flowered cotton gown didn't hike up embarrassingly, she scooted across the bed and slipped her legs beneath the blankets.

"Stay," she said, smiling up at him, then patted the empty place beside her. "Here..."

"I'm not sure that's such a good idea," he said, tossing her own words back at her with a devilish grin.

"Don't worry. You're safe as houses." She yawned daintily

and settled back against one of the pillows. "Those pills are already starting to knock me out."

"Well, in that case..." His grin softening into a heartachingly sweet smile, Will kicked off his deck shoes, switched off the lamp and stretched out beside her atop the blankets. "Come here."

He reached for her, and she went to him willingly, snuggling against his masculine warmth with a sigh of utter contentment.

"Thanks, Will. I...really appreciate...this." Yawning again, she closed her eyes and suddenly felt as if she were floating.

"My pleasure, Professor," he muttered, his lips brushing hers tenderly. "My pleasure..."

Shortly before midnight, one of the nurses stopped by Tess's room to check on her. Though the woman frowned and shook her head when she saw Will lying on the bed, holding Tess in his arms, she didn't say anything about it. Which was just as well, since Will had absolutely no intention of moving. Not when Tess was sleeping so peacefully. Morning would come soon enough, and he was determined not to allow her to be disturbed until then.

When the nurse whispered a reminder not to let Tess eat or drink anything after midnight, Will nodded in agreement, then turned his full attention back to her as the nurse left the room. He couldn't remember ever experiencing the same mix of emotions that he was at this moment, with Tess lying close beside him.

She was so warm and soft and so damned...fragile. She smelled of lemon and spice and everything womanly nice. And she curled against him with such implicit trust that he couldn't help but feel deeply honored. She'd let him know early on that she tended to be wary, yet over the past few days she'd welcomed him into her life in a way he'd never expected she would.

He had never felt so happy or so scared. He could have searched his whole life for someone like Tess and never found her. Fate had brought them together. But fate could also keep them apart.

If anything happened to her during the surgery, he wasn't sure how he'd ever manage to deal with it. And that wasn't the only risk he had of losing her. In two weeks she should be well enough to go back to San Antonio, and he'd have no choice but to let her. What he did or didn't do after that would depend a lot on Tess....

Stuck in a big city hospital completely on her own, with no close family or friends to depend on, she'd obviously needed someone to keep her company the past week. And while he had to admit she'd seemed pleased by his presence, her choices *had* been limited. Once she was home again, she wouldn't need him in quite the same way, if she needed him at all.

For his part, he'd meant only to fill a few empty hours for her. At least at the outset. But his being there had gone far beyond that days ago. Granted, part of her attraction was physical, a *good* part of it. But more than that, Will enjoyed just being with her in a way he'd never enjoyed being with a woman before. She made him feel good about himself, about who he was and what he could do. Given the opportunity, he'd never get tired of coming home to her. Never in a million years.

But they weren't going to have a million years, he reminded himself as he gently brushed a wisp of her dark hair away from her face. They had tonight and a few tomorrows, and then...

As he had earlier, Will warned himself not to think too far into the future. Better to let Tess get through the surgery and start to recuperate, then give her—as well as himself—a little time and space to consider the future. They'd known each other only a week, and not under the best of circumstances. Both of them had been dealing with a fair amount of fear, and he'd had an added burden of guilt to contend with.

Once they were back in the "real world," following their normal routines, they'd have a better idea of how they really felt about each other. Then, considering the myriad problems they'd have to face, they could decide whether or not to deepen their relationship.

They were both thoughtful, caring, intelligent adults. Either they would or wouldn't choose to be together. It was as simple as that. Which wasn't really that simple at all...

Though he'd thought he would stay awake all night, the trying day he'd had finally caught up with Will and he slept after a while. However, when one of the nurses came down to prep Tess for surgery, he was awake again.

He woke Tess gently, as best he could, considering she was still groggy from the medication she'd taken the night before. Reluctantly he left her with the nurse, then spent the next thirty minutes or so pacing up and down the hallway. Finished at last, the nurse finally let him back in her room with a quiet admonition to mind the shunt in her left hand.

Sitting up against her pillows, Tess smile bravely when she saw him. She'd exchanged her pretty pink flowered nightgown for a standard-issue hospital gown. Her neatly braided hair had been tucked under what looked like a pale blue shower cap.

As he moved toward her, the full realization of what she was about to do hit Will like a brutal punch in the gut. Only the thought of Jonathan, lying in another hospital bed, waiting to be well again, kept him from scooping her into his arms and spiriting her away as far and as fast as he could.

''Hey, how are you doing?'' he asked, trying unsuccessfully to return her smile.

''Okay, I guess. I'm feeling kinda woozy. The nurse gave me an injection. She said it was something to keep me from tensing up when they start the anesthesia.'' She tipped her head back against her pillows, holding his gaze as he stopped beside her bed. ''Thanks for staying last night and for being here with me this morning.''

''I *wanted* to be here,'' he said, taking her right hand in his as he sat on the edge of her bed. ''And I'll be here when you wake up, too.''

''Excuse me, Mr. Landon. It's time for us to take Ms. McGuire down to the O.R.''

Glancing over his shoulder, Will saw that the nurse who'd prepped Tess had returned with an orderly and a gurney. He nodded to her, then turned back to Tess as she tightened her hold on his hand.

''I'm scared, Will,'' she murmured, her defenses suddenly seeming to crumble.

"Me, too," he admitted, holding on to her as determinedly as she held on to him. "But you're going to be all right, sweetheart. Dr. Wells is the best. He'll take good care of you. I know he will."

"And Jonathan, too?"

"And Jonathan, too," he assured her, aware that her fear wasn't only for herself. "You're both going to be just fine."

"Mr. Landon…" the nurse interrupted, her tone insistent.

"Can I go down with her?"

"Yes, of course. But we have to get her on the gurney now."

"All right." He met Tess's gaze again. "I'll be waiting for you out in the hallway, okay?"

"Okay," she said, her voice whisper-soft as she slipped her hand from his.

Less than five minutes later, Will walked alongside the gurney where Tess lay, her hand once again in his. Ahead of them were the double doors that opened into the O.R., doors through which Tess would be whisked all too soon.

Whatever the nurse had given her had really begun to work. Her breathing had slowed, and she was fading in and out as they halted for a moment. Bending over her, Will brushed his lips against hers.

"Take care, Professor," he muttered, blinking back the sudden sting of tears in his eyes.

"You, too." She opened her eyes and gazed at him steadily. "Do something…for me if…if I don't…don't…"

"Anything you want. Just tell me, and I promise I'll do it."

"Someday when…when Jonathan's older…tell him…tell him I…loved him."

"I think you'll be able to do that yourself when the time comes." He kissed her again, ever so gently. "But if you can't, I will. I promise."

"Thanks." Smiling, she closed her eyes again.

"The waiting room for the O.R. is just down the hall, Mr. Landon. Would you like me to show you where it is?" the nurse asked.

"I'll find it," he replied. Letting go of Tess's hand, he took a step back as the doors opened and they began to wheel her away.

"One of the team will keep you posted on how she's doing at regular intervals."

"Thanks."

As the doors closed, he turned on his heel and headed back to the elevator, digging in his pocket for a handkerchief. Tess was going to be all right. She *was*...

By the time he reached the fifth-floor pediatric wing, Will had managed to get his emotions under control again. The last thing he wanted to do was upset his nephew or his sister and brother-in-law, none of whom, to his knowledge, had seen him cry anytime in his adult life.

Jonathan wasn't scheduled to go down to the O.R. until ten o'clock. The first part of the transplant surgery, Tess's part, included clamping off blood vessels to her liver, which would take some time. Her gall bladder would then be removed, and after that, the portion of her liver she was donating to the boy.

At Jonathan's room, Will tapped on the door, then entered at Julie's invitation. She and Philip were sitting near the window, while Jonathan lay on the bed, watching cartoons.

With a nod to his sister and brother-in-law, Will crossed to the bed. He needed to see his nephew, not only to reassure himself that allowing Tess to go through with the surgery had been the right thing to do, but because the boy was now his only link to her.

"Hey, buddy, how are you feeling?"

"Kinda sleepy."

"Tess was, too."

"Did you see her this morning?"

"Right before they took her into the operating room."

"Was she thinking about me like she said she would?" the boy asked, meeting his uncle's gaze.

"Yes, she was...." More than he could say, Will thought. "How about you? Are you thinking about her, too?"

"A whole, whole lot," Jonathan assured him fervently. "Do you think she knows?"

"Yeah, I think she does, and I think she's really glad. So don't stop, okay?"

"Okay, Uncle Will."

Moving away from the bed, Will joined Julie and Philip. Tucking his hands in his pockets, he stared out the window wordlessly.

"How was she?" Julie asked after a while.

"Scared," Will answered quietly.

"That makes three of us," Philip said.

"*Four* of us," Will corrected, rubbing a hand along his whiskered jaw.

"You look like hell," Julie murmured.

"Thanks a lot, sis. You don't look so good yourself."

"Did you stay with her last night?"

"Yes, I stayed with her," Will admitted.

"I'm...glad," Julie said after only a moment's hesitation.

"So am I," Will agreed.

Eyeing his sister curiously, he wondered if her change of heart was only temporary. He supposed time would tell. But any warming toward Tess on her part gave him reason to hope.

"Is Jonathan still scheduled to go up to the O.R. at ten o'clock?" he asked.

"As long as everything goes as planned with Tess."

"Well, then, I'll see you in the waiting room after they take Jonathan in."

"You're not going to stay here with us?"

"The nurse told me someone would come out regularly and let me know how Tess is doing. I want to be there when they do."

"You ought to at least get something to eat," Julie urged.

"Do you feel like eating right now?"

"No..."

"Neither do I." Pausing by Jonathan's bed, he ruffled his fingers through the boy's dark, curly hair. "See you later."

"See you, Uncle Will."

Will spent the hours waiting for news of Tess alternately pacing and staring out the bank of windows lining one wall of the room set aside for the families of patients undergoing surgery. Each time one of the members of Dr. Wells's team came out to talk to him, the prognosis was good, and just after ten o'clock Julie and Philip joined him there. They, too, paced and stared as one hour after another slowly passed.

Much to Will's relief, word came that Tess had been taken to the recovery room. Her part of the procedure had been completed. But now the most technical part, transplanting a portion of her liver into Jonathan's body, would take place. Knowing that he wouldn't be able to see Tess for several hours, he stayed with Julie and Philip, lending them what moral support he could as they waited for word of the doctors' progress.

Near seven o'clock, almost twelve hours after Will had watched Tess being wheeled away, Dr. Wells himself joined them in the waiting room, beaming with obviously well-deserved pride.

"Your son's doing just fine. Blood is circulating through his new liver, and though we're not completely out of the woods yet, from my experience, it looks as though the surgery was a definite success."

Sobbing softly, Julie clung to her husband as Philip thanked the doctor.

"How's Tess?" Will asked. "Have you seen her since she was taken to the recovery room?"

"I stopped to check on her on my way here. So far, she's doing just fine, too. She's being moved to intensive care, probably as we speak. According to the nurses, she came around for a minute or two in recovery, but we've got her pretty knocked out right now. More than likely, she won't really wake up until sometime tomorrow. But I've left orders that you can see her for ten or fifteen minutes every hour or so."

"Thanks a lot, Doc." Will turned to his sister and brother-in-law. "If you don't mind, I'd like to go and see her now."

"Go ahead," Philip urged. "We'll be up, too, just as soon as we finish talking to Dr. Wells."

The nurse on duty allowed Will to see Tess immediately. Aware of the physical trauma she'd endured, he tried to prepare himself for the worst. Still he was surprised at how small and frail she appeared as she lay on the bed, unmoving except for the gentle rise and fall of her chest. Her skin was much too pale, and the shadows under her eyes much too dark for his peace of mind, while the array of tubes and wires connecting her to a variety of blinking, beeping machines intimidated the hell out of him.

She looked as if she was just sleeping, but the dregs of the anesthesia she'd been given, coupled with the pain medication Dr. Wells had ordered for her, guaranteed she wouldn't awaken for quite some time. And that was just as well. More than anything, she needed to rest so her body could begin to heal.

Tracing his fingers along the back of her hand, he murmured her name, but she gave no response at all. Yet Will wanted to believe that somehow she knew he was there with her just as he'd promised.

"Time's up, Mr. Landon." The nurse touched his arm sympathetically, turning him toward the doorway. "You can come back in about an hour."

He glanced over his shoulder, taking one last look at Tess before he stepped out into the open area separating the nurses' station from the ICU rooms.

"I'll be in the waiting room," he said. "Will you let me know just as soon as I can come back?"

"Certainly, Mr. Landon."

He spent the night in the ICU waiting room along with Julie and Philip, visiting both Tess and Jonathan as permitted and napping in between.

Sometime just after dawn, as he sat beside Tess, holding her hand, she stirred slightly, then opened bleary eyes. After a moment or two, she focused on him and smiled.

"Hi..."

"Hi, yourself," he replied. "How are you feeling?"

"I...hurt..." she murmured, her smile fading as she closed her eyes again.

"I'll call the nurse."

He pressed the button beside her bed, and when the nurse answered, he told her that Tess had awakened in pain. A few seconds later, the nurse hurried in, carrying a syringe. She gave

Tess an injection and checked her vital signs. Then, allowing him to stay a little longer, she left again.

"Better?" Will asked after a few minutes.

"Getting there," Tess admitted, meeting his gaze again. "How's Jonathan? Is he...is he all right?"

"He's doing just great. He's in the room next to yours. He hasn't woken up yet, but Dr. Wells said he should anytime now, too."

"And the surgery?"

"A success as far as the doctor's concerned. Jonathan's new liver seems to be functioning perfectly so far."

"I'm...glad." She closed her eyes again as the drug obviously began to take effect. "Is it still Monday?"

"Actually it's early Tuesday morning."

"You haven't been...home...."

"How'd you know?"

"You...need a...shave." She smiled again, then slowly began to drift away.

"You want me to shave, I'll shave," he said, bending over to kiss her cheek. "As long as *you* promise to get well."

"For you...anything..."

"I'm going to hold you to that, Professor. Believe me, I am.

Chapter Seven

For the first day or so after her surgery, Tess was pretty well out of it, thanks to the pain medication Dr. Wells had prescribed in order to make her as comfortable as possible. Still, each time she awoke while she was in the ICU, as well as later when she was moved back to her room on the twelfth floor, she was conscious of the fact that Will was there with her.

He'd come to see her on his own early Tuesday morning, but that afternoon Julie and Philip came with him, too. Their reassurances that Jonathan was doing just fine, coupled with their overwhelming gratitude for what she'd done, went a long way toward making her physical discomfort more bearable.

Tuesday evening Will came on his own again. After making sure that she knew Jonathan was all right, however, he seemed more than content to sit on the chair beside her bed, quietly holding her hand in his.

Tess wasn't the least bit surprised. Sometime between his early-morning and afternoon visits, he'd obviously gone home to shower, shave and change clothes. But other than that, she had a feeling he'd not only been at the hospital since Sunday night, but hadn't gotten any rest at all while he was there.

Aware that Will had to go back to work the next morning, and knowing *she* probably wouldn't be doing much besides sleeping over the next twelve hours anyway, she insisted that he spend the rest of the night at home. Finally, reluctantly he agreed, but not before vowing to return the next morning on his way to the office.

On Wednesday Lydia, Ina and Harry, along with the Drakes and Will, saw to it that Tess's room was filled with baskets of flowers and her nightstand covered with a variety of get well cards, both sweet and silly. And over the next few days, her new friends, as well as Will, made every effort to spend as much time with her as possible.

Mornings Lydia came down to visit on her own, then returned with Ina for a while each afternoon. The younger woman's latest CAT scan had been negative, and she could have gone home anytime, but her parents' busy schedules precluded their driving her back to Austin until the following Monday. However, since she'd also been visiting Harry, ostensibly in Tess's place, Lydia didn't seem to mind the delay at all.

Now able to get around in a motorized wheelchair, Ina not only came to see Tess in the afternoons along with Lydia, but also began showing up in the evenings, about the time Tess and Will had finished eating dinner. Insisting that she and Tess just had to find out what happened next in the novel Tess had been reading to her, she somehow managed to get Will to read to both of them for an hour or so. Good sport that he was, Will went along with her, even though he ended up blushing more than once when he came to some of the…steamier passages.

Poor Harry was still in traction, but he called several times a day to check on her. And to Tess's delight, more and more often Lydia seemed to be his favorite topic of conversation.

Tess appreciated her friends' thoughtfulness and concern more than she could say. Yet, despite the fact that she knew it wasn't wise, she looked forward to Will's visits more than anything.

As promised, he stopped by her room early each morning on his way to work, then again in the evenings on his way home. By late afternoon, she caught herself watching the clock, counting the hours until he strode through the doorway, a wide smile on his devilishly handsome face. At his charming request, the nurses brought an extra tray for him along with Tess's, and as they ate dinner together, they traded bits and pieces of what had happened while they'd been apart.

Will also kept her informed of Jonathan's progress each day. And, of course, he read to her and Ina until their eyelids began to droop. Then he'd take Ina back to her room, and return to say a more leisurely good-night to Tess.

To Tess's dismay, he seemed perfectly satisfied with a chaste peck on her cheek, and she had no alternative but to hide her disappointment. Obviously she'd read more than she should have into his earlier ardor. He'd probably meant only to soothe her fears, and now that the worst was over, he apparently thought she no longer needed that kind of…reassurance. Which she didn't, she reminded herself on a regular basis.

Still, with each day that passed, she felt closer and closer to him, especially after he'd spent the entire weekend after her surgery with her. They watched old movies together, took turns reading to Ina and allowed themselves to be conned into a card game with Lydia and Harry, who'd finally graduated to a wheelchair. Much to the nurses' chagrin, but Tess's friends' delight, Will also made several forays out to the real world for tacos, fried chicken, burgers and pizza, each time vowing not to do it again with his fingers neatly crossed behind his back.

By Sunday night, Tess felt as if she and Will had been together a lot longer than a couple of weeks. She'd never been so at ease with anyone in her life. Nor had she ever had so much fun with another person, man or woman. Yet, as she sat alone in her room after he'd finally gone home, she realized that the time they had left together was growing shorter and shorter.

Slowly but surely her body had begun to heal. By Thursday the worst of the pain from her incision had diminished to the point where she no longer needed anything stronger than Tylenol to ease the occasional dull ache she felt. And although she was still weak enough not to relish any extended physical activity, she'd been getting out of bed and walking around a little more each day, thus regaining her strength in ever-increasing increments. All of which meant that she'd probably be ready to return to San Antonio to complete her recovery as scheduled.

According to Will's daily reports, Jonathan was recuperating well, too. They'd had a bad scare Thursday night when he'd been rushed back to the operating room to stop some minor internal bleeding, a not-uncommon occurrence with transplant recipients. But after that, he'd been just fine. That weekend he'd finally been moved out of ICU, and more than likely he would be able to go home within a couple of weeks, as well.

So Tess had done what she'd come to Houston to do. She'd donated a part of her liver so that a young boy—her son—could be well again. And since that seemed to be exactly what was happening, obviously she was no longer needed there.

That meant only one thing. Her relationship with the Drakes—and with Will—would soon be coming to an end. Rationally she'd known all along that it would, but actually facing it was more difficult than she'd ever anticipated. Despite all the odds against it, somewhere in the back of her mind Tess had hoped for a miracle, the kind of miracle that would have allowed her to remain a part of their lives forever. But she'd learned long ago that miracles rarely happened, and the sooner she remembered it, the better.

After saying a tearful goodbye to Lydia on Monday, Tess decided the time had finally come to start distancing herself from Will. But knowing what she had to do and doing it weren't quite the same thing. Not when Will absolutely refused to cooperate.

Now that she was ambulatory again, she tried hiding out in Ina's or Harry's room about the time Will usually arrived. But he wasn't the least bit put off. He just came looking for her, then whisked her away possessively before she had a chance to protest. She couldn't even complain about his being rude to her other friends, since they both seemed to assume she'd rather be with Will anyway.

That she did and…didn't, left her feeling more confused and frustrated each day. Yet she couldn't think of anything to say to him that wouldn't end up either hurting his feelings or sounding like a pitiful plea for sympathy.

Wednesday afternoon she said goodbye to Harry. He was now able to get around on crutches and was more than anxious to get back to work on a full-time basis. He was also planning a trip to Austin to see Lydia in a couple of weeks, which pleased Tess more than she could say.

Friday morning Ina was finally ready to go home, too. The older woman could now see well enough not to be a hazard to herself. And with a live-in housekeeper and a chauffeur to look after her, she'd be just fine.

As Tess helped her gather the last of her books together, she thought of how much Ina, as well as the others, had come to mean to her over the past few weeks.

"I'm going to miss you, you know?" she said, securing the flap on Ina's overnight bag.

"I'll miss you, too, my dear. But you *will* write to me, won't you?" she asked as she settled into the wheelchair for her final ride down the hallway.

"I've already said I will," Tess reminded her gently.

"And you'll come to see me when you return for your checkup in a few weeks, too," she added. "My house is huge. You can have your choice of rooms…a different one every night if you want."

"If I can," Tess replied.

"Don't be silly. Of course you can," the older woman retorted querulously. "And you can invite me to your wedding, as well."

"What wedding?" Tess asked, eyeing the woman askance.

"*What wedding?*" Ina looked at her as if she needed her head examined, which Tess couldn't wholly discount. "Why, *yours.*"

"But, Ina, I'm not getting married," Tess protested.

"You most certainly are. To your young man…Will Landon,'' she insisted. ''Anyone with two good eyes, and some of us with only one and a half, can see you two are in love with each other.''

''Actually we hardly know each other. We're just... friends,'' Tess said, feeling herself blush to the roots of her hair.

''Oh, piddle. You're *just friends* with Harry Gamble. You're in love with Will Landon,'' Ina replied in a voice that brooked no argument. ''I know there are problems, what with your... relationship to the boy and all, but if you love each other, you'll work 'em out. And mark my words, you love each other. I've been around long enough to know the real thing when I see it. He's a good man, Tess. Don't turn him away.''

''Oh, Ina...'' Wishing it was that simple, she hugged the other woman. ''You don't know what you're saying....''

How she knew about Jonathan, Tess had no idea. She'd never said anything specific, but Ina had seen his picture on her nightstand and she wasn't any dummy. Still...

''At my age, I know better than most, missy.'' Ina touched Tess's face for a moment in a kind of gentle benediction. ''And I know you deserve some happiness,'' she added, holding Tess's gaze before continuing more caustically. ''Now, where in blazes is Barnes?''

''Waiting right outside the door with Mrs. Terry,'' Tess soothed, waving Ina's chauffeur and housekeeper into the room again.

''Well, then, get me out of here.''

''As you wish, madam,'' Barnes replied, winking at Tess as she walked to the elevator with them.

Smiling, Tess winked back. ''Take care, Ina,'' she said as Barnes wheeled her onto the elevator.

''You, too. And don't forget what I said.''

Although doing just that would be for the best, she wouldn't, Tess thought, heading back to her room as the elevator doors slid shut.

Feeling more lost and alone than she had in weeks, Tess sat by the window and wished that she, too, could leave the hospital. But although Dr. Wells had removed her stitches a couple of days ago, he hadn't said anything about discharging her yet. And even when he did, she wouldn't be up to getting herself back to San Antonio on her own. Not that she'd have to. Will had already made sure that she knew he'd take her home just as soon as she was allowed to go.

As if Dr. Wells had read her mind, that afternoon when he stopped in on his daily rounds, he finally pronounced her far enough along in her recovery to be on her own at home. He advised her of what she could and couldn't do, cautioning her to keep her physical activity within reason and to call him if she became ill in any way, then insisted on seeing her back in his office in exactly four weeks.

Tess gladly agreed to everything he said, more ready than she could say to get on with the rest of her life. For almost three weeks, she'd been living in an odd kind of limbo, especially where Will was concerned, and she was finding it more and more difficult to deal with the emotional toll of her increasing uncertainty. With luck, Will would be able to drive her to San Antonio in the morning, they'd say their goodbyes, and that would be…that.

With a heartening hug, Dr. Wells wished her all the best and went on his way. Alone again, Tess called her neighbor, Susan, to let her know she'd be back the following day, then gratefully accepted her offer to pick up a few things for her at the grocery. While Tess had stocked up on frozen food and nonperishables before she'd left, she needed some staples like milk and bread, as well as eggs and cheese, to tide her over until she was up to going shopping on her own.

Next she called Will at his office. If he couldn't take her to San Antonio tomorrow, she wanted to make other arrangements. Unfortunately, according to his secretary, he was at the courthouse testifying in a case and wasn't expected back until late that afternoon.

Tess left a message for him. Then, as she'd been doing off and on all week, she ran through the litany of things she had to do at home as she began gathering up her books and papers. One way or another, she was going home in the morning and she was glad. Because she had to be…

She'd thought that Will would return her call eventually. Instead, he showed up at the hospital an hour or so earlier than usual, walking in on her as she was busily folding her extra nightgowns and tucking them into her overnight bag.

"So Dr. Wells *finally* decided to let you go home, did he?"

"Just this afternoon," Tess admitted, glancing over her shoulder at him.

As he met her gaze, the solemn, almost sad look in his eyes belied his lighthearted tone of voice. Praying that he wouldn't make their parting more difficult than it had to be, she took a deep, steadying breath as she turned back to the task at hand.

"I wasn't sure you'd be able to get away tomorrow morning to drive me back to San Antonio. If not, I can always—"

"No problem," he cut in smoothly, pacing to the window. He peered out for several seconds, then turned to face her. "If you're sure that's what you want to do."

"Well…yes," she said, puzzled by his words.

What other choice did she have? She certainly didn't want to stay in the hospital any longer, and she had nowhere else to go but home.

"You're going to be there alone, aren't you?" he asked, his concern more than evident. "Do you think that's wise?"

"I've lived alone for years," she replied with a negligent shrug.

"But you've just had major surgery."

"Dr. Wells said that as long as I take it easy, I should be all right. And I'll be able to drive in another week or two."

Though she couldn't say for sure, Tess had a good idea of where Will was heading. But she had no intention of allowing either one of them to get into something they'd only end up regretting. Better to make a clean break of it tomorrow than go on as she had been, hoping against hope that there was a chance of their having a future together.

She couldn't deny that she cared for Will more than she'd ever cared for any man. Nor did she doubt that he cared for her in his own way. But enough was enough. There were too many obstacles in their path. And she'd rather walk away from him now than be the one left behind when he finally realized she wasn't worth the trouble she'd caused him.

Aware that he was watching her from his place by the window, Tess glanced at him again as she slipped the last gown into her bag and fastened the zipper. From the set expression on his face, she knew he was getting ready to argue with her and she just wasn't up to it.

"Don't worry about me, Will. I'm a big girl and I'm more than capable of taking care of myself. Although I will need a little help getting this thing off the bed," she added, pasting a bright smile on her face as she gestured toward her overnight bag.

For what seemed like an eternity, he stared at her searchingly, as if he couldn't quite bring himself to accept what she was saying. Finally he crossed to the bed and shifted her bag to the floor.

"Do you need help with anything else?" he asked.

"Thanks for the offer, but I think I've got everything just about ready to go."

One of the nurses had helped her put the plants she was taking home in a cardboard box, and she'd already packed away her books and papers, as well as most of the clothes she'd brought with her.

"I guess you're pretty anxious to get home," Will said with a noticeable lack of enthusiasm.

"I've been away almost three weeks," she reminded him as she perched on the edge of her bed. "And I've got a lot to do there." She ticked off the list she'd been going over in her head earlier, then added, "The sooner I get started, the better."

"I thought you said Dr. Wells told you to take it easy," Will chided, sitting down across from her on the other side of the bed.

"Oh, I will," she assured him. "I won't mow the yard for at least a week, and I'll wait at least two weeks before I start rearranging the furniture."

"Not funny, Professor," he growled.

"I'm just kidding."

"You'd better be."

"Or else what?"

"I don't know. But believe me, I'll think of *something*." He caught her hand in his and squeezed it gently. "You know, Tess, you could come and stay with—"

"I know," she interrupted hastily, refusing to let him finish. "But I not only have to go home now. I really *want* to go home."

"All right, then. If you insist." He paused for a moment, holding her gaze. Then, smiling just a bit, he changed the subject.

"According to Julie, Jonathan's been asking about you all afternoon. Dr. Wells mentioned you were going home, and the kid's afraid you'll leave without saying goodbye to him. So why don't we take a walk down there and pay him a little visit?"

"I'd like that very much," Tess admitted softly without the slightest hesitation.

Thoughts of Jonathan had never been far from her mind over the past couple of weeks, and more than anything, she'd wanted to see him again one last time. Yet, even considering all that she'd done for him, she hadn't felt right about insinuating herself into his life any more than she had already. But now that she had an invitation…

Though Will did offer to take her down to the fifth floor in a wheelchair, Tess insisted on walking. She really was much stronger and she wanted him to know it. She intended to go home tomorrow, and she didn't want to have to argue with him about it again.

By the time they reached Jonathan's room, the nurses were serving dinner. At Julie and Philip's urging, and the boy's insistence, Tess and Will ended up eating with them. At first Tess was a little uneasy, especially since she'd thought they would be there only a few minutes at most. But after a while, she finally began to relax.

However, she refrained from joining in the conversation flowing so freely around her. She was more than content to sit and listen while Julie, Philip and Will discussed the events of their respective days. And as she did, she couldn't help but realize that they shared a very special kind of closeness, a closeness she vowed she would never do anything to destroy.

As for Jonathan, Tess hadn't been sure what to expect. Will's daily reports had been increasingly positive, but even a young boy took time to recuperate from major surgery. And the doctors had had to operate on Jonathan a second time just a week ago.

But to Tess he looked just wonderful. Gone was the weariness that had seemed to weigh him down two weeks earlier. Gone, too, was the jaundice that had discolored his skin. And the dark shadows under his eyes had almost completely faded away. He was still a little pale, but he fairly radiated energy and excitement. She could just imagine him bouncing off the walls in another week or so, and as she did, her heart swelled with pride and joy.

She'd given him life not once but twice, and that was very special indeed. Deep in her heart she knew that, partly because of her, he had a wonderful future ahead of him. And no one could ever take that away from her.

Hanging on to that thought as he began to yawn, she stood slowly, as ready as she'd ever be to say her final farewell.

"I wish I could go home tomorrow, too," Jonathan groused, squirming on his bed.

"I know how you feel," Tess agreed, trading smiles with him. "But you want to be sure you're all healed up first."

"That's what Dr. Wells keeps saying." He paused, his smile fading as he gazed up at her. "Am I ever going to see you again?"

From the corner of her eye, Tess saw Julie watching her and waiting, as if everything she held dear was riding on her answer.

"Maybe one day. But you know I live and work in San Antonio, and I don't get to Houston very often at all," she responded carefully.

"But you're going to see Uncle Will again, aren't you?"

"That might be…hard. He lives and works here. And we're both really, really busy," she said, praying that Will wouldn't choose to contradict her.

"Oh..." Jonathan stared at her doubtfully. "I thought you were friends."

"We are, but we're...we're the kind of friends who don't get to see each other too often." With an effort, she smiled at the boy. "So it looks like this is going to be goodbye."

"Okay." He nodded rather solemnly as he extended his hand. "Goodbye, Tess."

"Goodbye, Jonathan." She held on to him for one long moment. Then, reminding herself that crying and clinging weren't allowed any more tonight than they had been two weeks ago, she drew her hand away and took a step back. "Have a wonderful life." Shifting her gaze to Julie and Philip, she added quietly, "You, too."

"And you, Tess," Philip said, his voice husky.

"Thank you for...for everything," Julie added, smiling despite the tears in her eyes.

"I think maybe I'm the one who should thank *you,*" Tess replied.

Then, straightening her shoulders, she turned and walked out of the room, barely aware of Will's comforting arm around her shoulders.

They made the trip back to her room in silence, and once there, Tess moved away from Will, crossed to the bed and sat down wearily. While saying goodbye to Jonathan had drained her emotionally, the walk had taken a physical toll. Suddenly, more than anything, she wanted to curl up and have a good cry. And that was exactly what she planned to do after she sent Will on his way.

"You look beat," he said, smoothing a hand over her hair as he came to stand beside her.

"I think I overdid it."

"Maybe I'd better call the nurse," he said with obvious concern.

"I'm just really tired." Plucking at the fabric of her robe, she avoided his gaze, afraid that he'd see how upset she was. She didn't want him hanging around any longer than absolutely necessary. Tonight she had to deal with her heartache as she'd always done, and would always do in the future—on her own.

"I think maybe I'd better call it a night, especially with the long drive tomorrow."

"We can wait until Sunday..." he began.

"Oh, no. I want to go home *tomorrow.* And I'll be just fine as long as I get some sleep."

"In that case, I guess I'd better get out of here." He paused, and as the silence stretched between them, Tess had a feeling he was hoping she'd ask him to stay. When she didn't, he continued almost formally. "What time would you like me to pick you up in the morning?"

"Would nine o'clock be too early for you?"

"Not at all. I'll be here then."

Bending, he brushed his lips against her cheek so gently that Tess almost flung her arms around him and begged him not to go. Only the realization that she'd be prolonging the agony of their inevitable parting held her still. Spending tonight alone would be good practice for all the nights to come.

"Sleep well, sweetheart," he murmured, sliding a finger under her chin and tipping her face up.

"You, too." Drawing on the last of her dwindling courage, she offered him a small, shaky smile.

He wasn't the least bit fooled. She could see it in his eyes. Yet somehow he must have known how very close to the edge she was, because after another moment or two, he finally left her, quietly pulling the door closed behind him.

She sat where she was a little longer, then slipped out of her robe and switched off the lamp. Lying on the bed, staring into the darkness, she thought of all that had happened in the past three weeks and how rich her life had been as a result. She thought of Lydia, Ina and Harry, of a little boy named Jonathan, his parents and most of all, his kind and generous Uncle Will. And for the first time in ten long, lonely years, she allowed herself to cry for all that had never been and all that could never be.

She slept eventually, too exhausted to do anything else, but when she awoke she felt anything but rested. Ignoring the heaviness in her heart, she bathed, slipped into the pale yellow dress

Will liked so much, then did her best to hide the last traces of the tears she'd shed.

Will arrived on time and within a matter of minutes had her officially checked out of the hospital. Carrying her things, he led her down to the front entrance where he'd parked his sister's car, and settled her solicitously into the passenger seat.

To Tess's relief, after gaining her assurance that she was feeling all right and making a few comments about the weather, Will seemed as eager as she to make the rest of the three-hour drive in silence. She'd hoped that her spirits would rise once she was out of the hospital and on her way home. But just the opposite seemed to be happening. The farther they got from Houston, the more forlorn she felt. In fact, more than once she was tempted to ask him to turn around and take her back, but somehow she managed not to.

At her house, Will took her key and unlocked the door for her, then brought in her things while she stood in the entryway, watching. Thanks to Susan, who'd thoughtfully turned on the air conditioner, the house was wonderfully cool and inviting. Just the sanctuary she needed, she thought as Will returned from the kitchen, where he'd taken her plants.

"You still have my card with my phone numbers on it, don't you?" he asked as he paused beside her.

"Tucked in my wallet."

"If you need anything, anything at all, day or night, even just to talk, I want you to call me."

"I will," she assured him, though she knew in her heart that she wouldn't. She had to make this break a clean one or she'd end up paying in the worst way.

"When are you supposed to come back to Houston to see Dr. Wells again?"

"In four weeks."

"If you give me a date, I'll come and get—"

"No, really, that won't be necessary. I'll be driving by then, and I'm sure I'll be able to make the trip on my own."

"I'd feel better—"

"And *I'd* feel better not putting you out any more than I

already have.'' She took a step back, anxious to end their conversation before he talked her into something she'd regret.

''But you'll call me while you're in town so we can get together.'' He didn't make it a question, but rather a statement of fact.

''Yes, of course,'' she agreed again, but only because she wasn't up to arguing with him.

''Well, then, I'll see you in four weeks, Professor.''

Not trusting her voice, she nodded her head. Then, afraid that he'd touch her and she'd fall apart completely, she took another step away from him.

''Take care,'' he muttered softly.

''You, too,'' she replied, the hurt look in his eyes making her heart ache.

He hesitated a moment longer, then turned away without another word. As he headed down the walk, Tess moved forward and slowly swung the door closed. Standing all alone in her quiet little house, she tried not to dwell on the fact that she was never going to see him again, but she just couldn't do it. With a soft whimper, she rested her head against the smooth, cool wood of her front door, and though she'd been sure she hadn't any more tears left, she suddenly began to sob.

In a few short weeks, her world had been turned upside down, and somehow she knew that she'd never be the same again. She'd learned long ago how devastating shattered hopes and dreams could be. Yet she'd always been able to pick up the pieces and go on. But now…

Now she wasn't even sure she wanted to try.…

Swearing softly, Will cradled the receiver for the umpteenth time that night. Four weeks had passed since he'd taken Tess back to San Antonio, four long, lonely weeks during which he'd waited in vain for some word from her. He'd been determined to give her the time and space she'd seemed to need, but now he was afraid he'd made a big mistake.

Not that he'd cut himself off from her completely. He'd called her several times over the past few weeks, but each time he'd gotten her answering machine. And although he'd left messages for her, she'd never returned his calls.

He'd tried to give her the benefit of the doubt. She'd been through a great deal of physical and emotional trauma, and he knew she was the kind of person who'd want to deal with it in her own way. If that meant keeping to herself for a while, he could understand.

But she'd promised to call him when she came to see Dr. Wells, and she hadn't done it. In fact, she hadn't come to Houston at all, as far as he knew. And he wasn't about to back off any longer. She meant too damned much to him....

When he hadn't heard from her by late afternoon, he'd called the doctor's office. According to the receptionist, Tess had not only missed her two o'clock appointment, but she hadn't called to reschedule, either. And when the receptionist had tried to contact her, she'd gotten no answer at all, not even from Tess's machine.

For the rest of the afternoon and evening Will had been trying unsuccessfully to contact Tess. Out of desperation, he'd finally gotten in touch with Ina and Harry. But neither of them had heard from her, either, despite the calls they'd made to her and the letters they'd sent.

As he paced from one end of his living room to the other, Will wasn't sure if he was more angry or afraid. He shouldn't have stayed away from her so long. When she hadn't responded to his calls, he should have driven to San Antonio and confronted her face-to-face.

But he hadn't wanted to take advantage of her in any way. And he certainly hadn't wanted to push her into a relationship she wasn't ready for. So he'd ended up all but abandoning her, at a time when she could very well have needed him more than she'd been able to admit.

She was so proud and so damned...independent. She'd leaned on him for a little while, but only because she hadn't had much choice. Yet he'd hoped that once she felt as if she was in control again, she'd actually *want* him to be a part of her life. Now it seemed that she'd cut herself off from everyone, or at least everyone she'd been involved with at the hospital.

But why? Did she honestly want nothing more to do with any of them? Was she so busy with her own life that she hadn't a few minutes to spare to call or send a note to those she'd seemed to care about only a month ago? That certainly didn't seem like the Tess he'd come to know.

And if she was progressing in her recovery, why hadn't she kept her appointment with Dr. Wells? She had to know how important it was that she be monitored by him over the next year or so. A part of her liver had been cut out of her body, and while other donors had so far suffered no ill effects, the surgery was still too new for anyone to be sure that no problems would crop up as a result.

Tess was a smart lady, too smart not to take care of herself. But what if she couldn't?

Therein lay the source of his growing fear. Maybe her recuperation *hadn't* gone as well as it should have. Maybe she hadn't been able to drive herself to Houston after all, and hadn't wanted to ask anyone, including him, for help. But Tess wouldn't be that foolish. If she needed help, she'd ask for it. If she could....

As he paced back to his desk, an awful image of Tess lying alone in her house, either sick or hurt, flitted through his mind. She lived by herself, and if she'd chosen to be as reclusive as it seemed she had over the past several weeks, who would know if something had happened to her?

Eyeing the telephone again, he thought of her neighbor. Tess had given him the telephone number of the woman who lived next door to her, hadn't she? Surely the woman wouldn't mind checking on her for him.

Mentally cursing himself for not thinking of contacting her sooner, Will strode into the bedroom and retrieved his wallet from the top of the dresser. Tucked inside it was the slip of paper Tess had handed him at the hospital what seemed like a lifetime ago.

He crossed to the telephone on his nightstand and dialed Susan Wylie's number without hesitation. She answered after several rings and listened quietly as he told her who he was, then explained why he was calling so late on a Friday night. When he finished, she didn't say anything for a moment or two, and Will found himself imagining the worst all over again.

"She is all right, isn't she, Mrs. Wylie?" he asked, more than a hint of fear in his voice.

"She seems to be," Susan replied. "In fact, I saw her for a few minutes this morning." She paused, as if weighing her next words carefully, then added, "I have to admit, I've been kind of worried about her, though. To be honest, I'd even been thinking of calling *you,* Mr. Landon. But when I mentioned it to Tess, she made me promise not to. She got so…upset that I…I told her I wouldn't."

"Has she been sick?" Will prodded.

He doubted Tess had told her neighbor any details about what she'd done while she was in Houston. But considering how healthy she'd been before the surgery, surely the woman would have noticed if she'd been physically ill any time during the past few weeks.

"No…" Susan replied. "But…"

"But?" Will questioned when she seemed to hesitate.

"She looks like she's lost weight. And she hasn't really seemed like herself. Since she's been back, she's hardly been out in her yard at all. She has someone mowing the lawn, which I can understand, but she hasn't bothered with her flower beds, and she used to love to work on them.

"Come to think of it, she's hardly been out of her house at all lately. She hasn't wanted to come over to visit with me and the kids. I've been going to the store for her, too. And worst of all, several times when I stopped by her house, I got the feeling she'd been crying. She seemed so…so sad."

He should have known not to leave her all alone in that house, Will thought. He should have taken her home with him and looked after her himself, no matter how much she protested. He'd been responsible for disrupting her peaceful existence. He'd asked her to risk her life for the child she'd given up for adoption ten years ago, a child he'd insisted she meet for what he'd thought would be her own good. And then he'd left her alone to cope with the emotional aftershock of it all.

He couldn't blame her for being sad. But he *did* blame himself. She'd asked for nothing in return for what she'd done. In fact, she'd gone out of her way to make sure that Julie, Philip and Jonathan understood that they'd probably never see her again.

And he hadn't said anything to the contrary. He'd been so damned determined to follow her lead that he hadn't let her know he intended just the opposite to be true. He'd let her go back to San Antonio thinking he, as well as his sister and brother-in-law, was glad to be rid of her, and that had to have hurt her deeply.

"Are you still there, Mr. Landon?" Susan asked, interrupting his reverie.

"I'm sorry. I was just thinking about what you said." He glanced at his watch and saw that it was almost ten o'clock. Even if he left immediately and drove like a maniac, he wouldn't arrive in San Antonio until after one. Better to wait until morning. "I'm going to drive over first thing tomorrow and look in on her myself. But I think it would be best if you didn't say anything to her." He didn't want Tess running off on him, and he had an idea she might do just that if she knew he was coming. "I'll plan on being there about nine or nine-thirty."

"I'll plan to be home then, too. Just in case you need to...use my key."

"I'd appreciate that," he admitted.

If Susan Wylie had been standing there beside him, Will would have hugged her. She obviously understood the situation and seemed to be on his side. And where Tess was concerned, he had a feeling he was going to need all the allies he could muster. One way or another, he was going to bring her back to Houston with him and make sure that she saw Dr. Wells. After that, he wasn't sure what he'd do. He had some vacation time coming. Maybe he'd spend some of it with her.

"Thanks again for all your help, Mrs. Wylie," he said, aware that he'd taken up enough of her time already.

"No problem, Mr. Landon. I'm really glad you called. Tess is a very special lady. I just hope you'll take good care of her."

"Believe me, I will," he vowed, meaning it with all his heart.

Chapter Eight

Though Will would have preferred to take Julie's car, it was too late to call her Friday night when he finished talking to Susan Wylie. Nor could he call her in the morning, since he wanted to be on the road no later than six. So he drove his battered old Blazer and hoped that the ride back to Houston wouldn't be too rough for Tess. Because she *was* coming back with him.

Just past nine o'clock, he pulled into her driveway. Her car was out of the garage, but from the dust on the windshield, it looked to Will as if it hadn't been driven in a couple of weeks or more. At least it seemed that she was home. But if by some chance she wasn't, she couldn't have gone farther than a neighbor's. Not without her car.

As he walked to the front door, he noticed that the lawn had been freshly mowed, but as Susan had said, the flower beds had been left to run wild, the weeds steadily encroaching on the impatiens, pansies and petunias. Reaching out to ring the doorbell, Will also saw that the blinds were closed. Of course, it was still fairly early on a Saturday morning. Still he didn't consider it especially encouraging to find her house looking as if no one lived there.

He counted to ten after ringing the doorbell, and when he got no answer, he rang it again, more insistently. He was on the verge of pounding his fist against the door when he heard the click of the lock being released. A moment later, Tess peered out at him warily.

"Will?" She frowned as she met his gaze. "What are you doing here?"

"It's nice to see you again, too, Tess," he said as nonchalantly as he could.

She looked…awful. Granted, she'd apparently just stepped out of the shower, which explained why her hair hung in damp strands around her shoulders. But otherwise…

She wore an old terry-cloth bathrobe that appeared to be several sizes too big for her. Her face was much too pale, and there were dark shadows under her red-rimmed eyes. And she'd definitely lost weight. Not a lot, but enough that he could see it in the sharper angles of her cheekbones and the gaunter line of her jaw.

"I'm sorry." She had the good grace to blush, but she still didn't step back and ask him to come in. "I didn't mean to be rude. I was just…surprised to see you here." She hesitated, shifting uncomfortably as she lowered her gaze. "Why…why are you here?"

When he didn't answer her immediately, she glanced at him again, a frightened look in her eyes. "Is Jonathan all right?" she asked, her voice quavering.

"Jonathan's just fine. He's home now and already begging to ride his bike."

Actually the boy looked a hell of a lot better than she did, but he couldn't very well say as much to her. She seemed distraught enough as it was. And he hadn't come there to hurt her feelings.

On the contrary, he'd come there to put his arms around her and hold her close, to kiss her and caress her and tell her just how much she meant to him. But he didn't dare do that, either.

She was hanging on, but just barely. And any false moves on his part could cause her to fall apart completely.

A faint smile flickered across her face, then her frown deepened once again. "Then, why—"

"Why don't you let me come in so we can talk about it?" he cut in softly, taking a step toward her.

She backed away from him, but still seemed intent on blocking the doorway. For one long moment, she eyed him with such obvious uncertainty that Will wondered if maybe he ought to just haul her into his arms and kiss her senseless after all. But then, as if reading his mind, she shivered slightly, shrugged and turned away.

"Suit yourself," she muttered listlessly as she padded into the living room.

He closed the door, then followed her into the semidarkness and watched as she curled up in a corner of the sofa. When she just sat there, staring at him, he crossed to the windows and opened the blinds, letting in as much sunlight as he could.

Turning back to her, he realized why she hadn't wanted any light in there. Dust marred the surfaces of her lovely antique furniture, and the coffee table was also littered with books and papers, as well as dirty plates and empty cups.

"You missed your appointment with Dr. Wells yesterday," he began as he sat across from her in the wing-back chair. "I was worried about you, especially since you didn't return my calls, so I contacted your friend Susan last night. She seemed to think you weren't feeling well." Barely resisting the urge to grab her and shake her, Will paused as she turned her face away. She wasn't going to make this easy, but then he hadn't really expected that she would. "I thought I'd better drive over and see for myself how you were doing."

"I'm doing just fine," she said, tipping her chin up defiantly.

"And I'm going to be the next king of England," he shot back with unrestrained sarcasm.

"Look, I just forgot about my appointment with Dr. Wells, all right? I'll...I'll call and schedule another one for sometime next week."

"Actually I took the liberty of rescheduling for you. Dr.

Wells agreed to meet us at his office this afternoon. We can leave as soon as you're dressed.''

''Oh, no—'' She faced him again, her pale eyes full of anger and uncertainty.

''Oh, *yes,*'' he retorted, steadily meeting her gaze.

He didn't enjoy acting like a bully, but if that's what it took to get her to Houston, that's what he'd do.

''You can't make me,'' she muttered, suddenly sounding a lot like Jonathan on a bad day.

''I wouldn't bet on that if I were you.''

She gazed at him with obvious surprise, then wordlessly turned her face away.

As he sat back in his chair, Will didn't say anything, either, hoping that the silence stretching between them would work in his favor. He knew she wasn't up to fighting him for long. In fact, he had an idea that her resistance was perfunctory at best. Yet, for some reason, she seemed determined to convince him that she didn't want or need his help.

''I...I really appreciate your concern,'' she said at last, her voice quavering once again. ''But I'm perfectly capable of taking care of myself. I'll drive to Houston next week to see Dr. Wells. I promise.''

''Do you want to get dressed, Tess? Or would you rather make the trip to Houston in your bathrobe?'' he asked as if she hadn't spoken. ''It's your choice, but one way or another, we're leaving here in thirty minutes.''

She stared at him as if she'd never seen him before. Will Landon, the original Mr. Nice Guy, telling her what he was going to do in no uncertain terms. Even he was amazed at his audacity. But at this point, if he had to hog-tie her and toss her in the back of his Blazer to get her to Houston, that was exactly what he would do.

Something of his determination must have shown in his face, because instead of arguing with him any more, Tess stood slowly, then started toward her bedroom with a kind of weary resignation that made his heart ache. Feeling like a real crud, despite knowing that his coercion had been for her own good, he rose also.

"You'd better pack an overnight bag, too. We won't be coming back tonight. In fact, we might not be coming back for several days." In for a penny, in for a pound, he reminded himself resolutely.

"Whatever you say," she murmured without so much as a backward glance.

Will watched her disappear into one of the rooms off the hallway leading out of the living room. Then, gathering up the plates and cups from the coffee table, he headed for the kitchen and the telephone he remembered seeing there four weeks earlier. He wanted to call Susan and tell her that Tess would be away for a while, and he'd also promised to let Dr. Wells know approximately what time to expect them at his office.

Much to his relief, the kitchen wasn't in too bad a shape. There were a few more dirty dishes in the sink, the plants she'd brought home from the hospital needed watering, and the table was piled with newspapers, magazines and a combination of opened and unopened mail. But he could set everything to rights within the half hour he'd allotted.

He made his telephone calls, loaded the dishwasher and watered the plants. Then, intending to sort through the stuff on the table and pull out anything that looked as if it needed immediate attention, he turned away from the sink and started back across the kitchen. As he did so, he noticed what appeared to be a bank check lying in a crumpled wad on the floor near one of the chairs. From the looks of it, it hadn't ended up there by accident. But why—

With sudden dismay, Will bent and picked up the check.

"Damn you, Philip, you *didn't,*" he growled as he stared at the wrinkled paper in his hand.

However, one look at the signature on the check left no doubt that despite Will's warning, his brother-in-law had apparently decided to offer Tess "compensation" after all. And, of course, Philip being Philip, he'd done so in a six-figure amount that would have guaranteed Tess more than a modicum of financial security for years to come.

Knowing how Tess had reacted to just the mention of financial remuneration, Will could easily imagine how upset she had been when she'd received what must have seemed to her like payment for services rendered. Rather than considering it her just due, she'd have thought of it as a slap in the face, even though Philip wouldn't have meant it that way at all.

Still the man should have had more sense, Will thought, as he folded the check and tucked it in the back pocket of his jeans. And he had every intention of telling him so the first chance he had.

As quickly as he could, he went through Tess's mail, setting aside the envelopes that appeared to contain bills, as well as the unopened letters she'd received from Lydia, Ina, and Harry. Since her purse was on the table, he took a look inside it, too, just to make sure her wallet and checkbook were there. Then he slid the bills and letters into an inner pocket, zipped the purse shut and carried it into the living room.

If she was going to be away as long as he planned she'd be, she'd probably want to have some of her books and papers handy. He packed the things she'd left on the coffee table into the briefcase he found lying on the floor beside the sofa. When he finished, he glanced at his watch and saw that the thirty minutes he'd given her were just about up.

"Are you ready?" he called over his shoulder as he set the briefcase next to her purse.

"Do I have a choice?" she inquired as she walked down the hallway.

She was wearing a short, straight denim skirt that hung just a little too loosely around her hips, a plain white cotton T-shirt tucked in at the waist and a pair of white leather moccasins. She'd tied her hair back with a blue-and-white bandanna, but she hadn't put on any makeup or jewelry. She looked a bit better than she had in her old bathrobe, but not much. Yet he couldn't help but feel that several nights of sound sleep and a few decent meals, coupled with some good, old-fashioned TLC, would work wonders on her. Especially once he convinced her to cooperate.

"No," he advised her succinctly, then smiled at her encouragingly as he took the overnight bag she offered him. "I sorted through your mail and put a few things that looked important in your purse. I also packed the books and papers you left on the table in your briefcase. Is there anything else you want to take with you?''

''Not really,'' she replied with an indifferent shrug. ''But I *would* appreciate it if you'd answer one question for me.''

''If I can....''

''Are you aware that kidnapping is a federal crime, and if convicted, as you surely will be, you'll end up spending the rest of your life in prison?'' she queried in a saccharine-sweet tone of voice.

If she hadn't been eyeing him quite so angrily, Will would have laughed aloud. Instead, he reached out and gently touched her cheek. ''I'm not kidnapping you, Tess. I'm placing you in...protective custody.''

''But I'm not in any danger from anyone,'' she insisted, taking a step away from him.

''Except yourself,'' he said quietly, lowering his hand to his side.

''Oh, come on,'' she protested. ''I'm *not* suicidal, you know. I've just been a bit...down.''

''Then a little vacation will be the best thing for you.'' He slung the strap on her overnight bag over his shoulder. ''You did pack some extra clothes in here, didn't you?''

''A nightgown and robe, some shorts and T-shirts and a pair of sandals.'' She gazed at him with honest curiosity as she reached for her purse. ''What exactly have you got in mind anyway?''

''I'm not really sure yet. But as soon as I am, I'll let you know.''

''Gee, thanks.''

''You're welcome.''

His smile widening into a grin, he hefted her briefcase off the table and headed for the front door. For the first time since he'd walked into her house, he felt as if she really was going to be all right. And once again he'd begun to believe that *they* would be all right, as well. Not only because he wanted it, but because Tess wanted it, too. If she hadn't, she would have done a lot more than mutter and grumble. No matter what kind of coercion he used, she would have fought him tooth and nail.

Now, if only he could find a way to make her realize that needing him wasn't a sign of weakness, he'd really be happy. Because *he* needed *her,* too, in a way he'd never needed anyone in his life. And he had no intention of ever abandoning her again, no matter what she said or did.

As he'd expected, Tess slept most of the way to Houston. She hadn't just looked exhausted; she was. For whatever reason, she apparently hadn't gotten much rest over the past few weeks, but that was about to change, along with a lot of other things.

Dr. Wells was waiting for them at his office, as promised. Will couldn't help but notice the worried expression on his face as he greeted Tess. However, when she apologized for forgetting her appointment, he brushed her concerns aside with a sympathetic smile, then led her back to one of the examining rooms.

Alone in the waiting room, Will paced restlessly, battling his sudden fear that Tess might actually be seriously ill. There was no guarantee that her fatigue and weight loss had been caused by her seemingly depressed state of mind rather than something more deadly. Aware of how easily he could lose her, simply because he'd waited so long to go to her, he tried desperately to think positive and failed.

After what seemed like an eternity, Dr. Wells finally returned to the waiting room alone, looking no happier than he had when he'd left with Tess.

"What's wrong?" Will demanded as he met the doctor's solemn gaze.

"Physically, nothing serious," he replied reassuringly. "She's lost a little more weight than I'd like, but she admitted she hasn't been eating as well as she ought to be. She also said she hasn't been sleeping much, either."

"What about emotionally?"

"From the little she told me, I think she's been rather...despondent. That would account for the weight loss and fatigue, and it's not all that unusual considering what she's been through.'' Pausing, he eyed Will thoughtfully, then continued. ''Though I didn't say anything to her, I considered putting her back in the hospital for a few days. But I'd hate to do that to her, especially since I don't really think she's a danger to herself. Still she does live alone, and I'm not sure she'll take care of herself the way she should if she's on her own again right away.''

''What if she wasn't going to be on her own?'' Will asked. ''What if she was going to be with me for the next couple of weeks?''

''That depends on what you've got in mind,'' the doctor replied with a wry smile.

''I have some vacation time coming. I thought maybe we could head down to Galveston and stay at my sister's beach house,'' he said. ''She told me once that was something she'd like to do.''

''I can't see any problem with that idea. At least not as long as you remember that she's a bit fragile emotionally. You obviously care for her quite a bit, Will, so I know you'll understand when I say it wouldn't be wise to rush her into anything she doesn't seem *completely* ready for.''

''Are you telling me not to make love with her?'' he asked bluntly, refusing to beat around the bush where Tess's best interests were concerned. He'd follow the doctor's orders no matter what they happened to be, but he preferred hearing them in plain English.

''I'm *asking* you to consider how both of you might be affected if you…deepened your relationship. I wouldn't want to see either of you hurt. But Tess especially would have a difficult time handling a casual affair right now.''

''I'd never do anything to upset her. Not after all she's been through already. Believe me, *if* I make love to her, it will only be because we *both* want it. And there certainly won't be anything *casual* about it at all,'' Will vowed.

''In that case, have a nice time in Galveston,'' Dr. Wells advised, offering his hand to Will.

''We will, sir. And thanks again for…today,'' he added as Tess finally joined them.

She, too, thanked the doctor for seeing her on a Saturday. Then, promising not to miss her next appointment the following month, she said goodbye to him.

By the time they'd walked back to the garage where Will had parked the Blazer, she was fading fast. Without a word, he boosted her onto the passenger seat, fastened her seat belt around her and crossed to the driver's side.

"Do you want to stop and get something to eat?" he asked as he backed out of the parking space.

"Not especially," she admitted.

"We can grab a bite later, then."

"So...where are we going now?" she asked, gazing at him warily.

"To my apartment."

"Oh..."

He expected some sort of protest, but when he glanced at her, he saw that she'd tipped her head back against the car seat, closed her eyes and fallen asleep again. Even though she'd slept on the drive to Houston, the hour or so she'd spent with Dr. Wells had obviously wiped her out.

And that suited Will just fine. The more amenable she was, the easier the next day or so would be on both of them. After that, they'd be in Galveston, and with luck, he could just sit back and let the sun, the wind and the sea work their healing magic on her.

She followed him into his apartment without a word, and when he asked if she wanted to lie down in the bedroom, she readily agreed. He'd put fresh linen on the bed that morning, so all he had to do was turn back the bedspread for her. After telling her to rest as long as she wanted, he closed the bedroom door so they'd both have a little privacy. Then he returned to the living room, where he crossed to the desk, reached for the telephone and dialed his boss's number.

Though he was working on several cases that would be coming to trial within the next few months, he had nothing on his desk that couldn't be put on hold for a couple of weeks. And since he wasn't scheduled to testify in court during that time, either, he had no problem getting the approval he needed to use some of his vacation days.

Next he called his sister. She answered after a couple of rings, sounding slightly harried but happy. From the noise he heard in the background, Will gathered that Jonathan must have several friends over to play.

After exchanging greetings with her, Will quickly got to the point of his call.

"I've decided to take a couple of weeks off starting tomorrow, and I was wondering if you'd mind my using the beach house."

"Not at all," Julie readily agreed. "In fact, if Jonathan's feeling all right and Philip can take a few days off, maybe we'll come down and join you."

At any other time, Will would have welcomed their presence. But unfortunately he didn't think either Tess or Julie was ready for that kind of family togetherness yet. And to be honest, even if they had been, Will still would have wanted Tess all to himself the next couple of weeks. They needed time to get to know each other better, and to at least begin to work on some of the problems they were going to have to face in the future.

"Tess is going to be with me, and frankly I'd like to spend as much time alone with her as possible."

"Oh..." As Julie hesitated, Will braced himself for the worst. But to his surprise, she seemed more confused than angry when she continued. "I didn't realize you'd kept in touch with her. How...how is she?"

"She's doing all right, considering..." He thought of the bank check in his back pocket, but decided it would be wiser to broach *that* subject when he'd be less likely to say something he'd regret.

"Does she...does she want to see Jonathan?" she asked fearfully.

"She hasn't said that she does," he hedged. Knowing Tess, she probably would have accepted an invitation to see the boy, but she'd never ask to do so.

"What if she does?"

"She won't."

"How can you be so sure?"

"Look, Julie, regardless of what you'd like to think, Tess hasn't come here to disrupt your life. She's here to spend some time with me at my invitation." *More or less,* he added to himself, then continued. "If I'm not mistaken, she told you at the hospital she didn't intend to see you or your son again, and she's definitely a woman of her word. So don't get your knickers in a twist, all right?"

"But I thought she didn't intend to see *you,* either," Julie retorted.

"She probably didn't. But then she probably didn't realize that *I* intended to see *her* again."

"Oh, Will..."

"You know how I feel about her."

"And you've obviously forgotten how *I* feel about her."

"I don't want to hurt your feelings, Julie. Honestly I don't. But I consider Tess a very special lady, and I want her in my life. I wish you could understand...."

"Well, I can't."

"Or won't?" he prodded softly.

"I guess I could try," she muttered without much conviction.

"Yeah, you could." Though he'd hoped for a little more than that from her, he'd take what he could get. "So, what about the beach house? Can I still use it even though I'll probably be sleeping with the enemy?" he teased.

"You really are incorrigible, you know?"

"So I've been told," he admitted rather proudly. "Now, about the house...?"

"Of course you can use it. I'm not an ogre."

"Neither is Tess. She's just a nice lady who probably saved your son's life."

"You really do care about her, don't you?"

"Yes."

"Then I hope you're right about her."

"I *know* I am."

"Well, take care, then. And call me when—"

"When she's gone?" he asked, wishing Julie could set aside her fear once and for all. He didn't like feeling as if he had to choose between them. Yet he had no intention of walking away from Tess just to make his sister happy. "Yeah, I'll do that."

He sat at his desk for a few minutes after he cradled the receiver. Then he realized that afternoon had turned into evening, and he hadn't heard a sound out of Tess since he'd left her in his bedroom. He walked down the hallway and eased the door open. With the blinds drawn, the room was almost completely dark, but as he crossed to the bed, he could see Tess huddled under the blankets, sleeping deeply. Freed from the bandanna, her hair curled wildly across the pillow and over her bare shoulders. She'd taken off not only her skirt, but her bra and T-shirt, as well, he realized as he eyed the pile of clothing on the chair in the corner.

For the space of a heartbeat or two, he thought of stripping out of his jeans and shirt and crawling under the covers with her. He wanted only to hold her as he'd done that night in the hospital, to feel her body close to his. Yet he didn't want to risk waking her. Not when sleep was what she needed most right now. Nor did he want to tempt fate. That he'd do only when she was stronger and more sure of herself, as well as of him.

He backed away from the bed, then quietly turned and left the room, closing the door behind him. He took an extra pillow and blanket out of the hall closet and tossed them on the sofa. Then, feeling hungry, he wandered into the kitchen, made himself a ham-and-cheese sandwich, grabbed a can of beer out of the refrigerator and headed back to the living room.

He'd watch the news while he ate, and when he finished, he'd make out a list of things they'd have to take to the island with them. He had beach towels, bug spray and suntan lotion on hand, but they'd have to stop at the grocery store and buy some food. Other than that, however, everything they needed would be at the house. And best of all, they'd have each other.

Somewhere close by, someone was brewing coffee. Sighing with contentment, Tess shifted beneath the blankets as the rich aroma slowly but surely drew her out of sleep. For the first time in a long time, she felt truly rested, and when she caught the scent of bacon cooking, she realized that she was hungry, too. *Really* hungry, she amended as her stomach growled in a most unladylike way.

Smiling slightly, she rolled onto her back and opened her eyes. In an instant, her smile faded into a puzzled frown as she surveyed her surroundings. She'd thought she'd been sleeping in her own bed, but she wasn't. The sunlight slipping through the slats of the blinds on the windows left no doubt of that. The bed in which she lay was quite a bit bigger than hers, the linens on it a classy combination of burgundy and white stripes and plaids unlike anything she owned. The dark wood dresser, chest and nightstand were unfamiliar, too.

All in all, the room was quite nice. Yet it didn't have the impersonal feel of a hotel room. Not with framed photographs on the dresser, a stack of papers atop the chest of drawers and a science-fiction novel spread open on the nightstand. But if she wasn't at home, and she wasn't in a hotel room, then where on earth—?

Suddenly, startlingly Tess finally came fully awake. As she did, she remembered most of what had happened the previous day. And with those memories came the realization that she'd spent the night in Will Landon's bed.

Flinging an arm over her eyes, she groaned with utter dismay. Of all the things she could have done, allowing him to coerce her into coming to Houston with him had to be the worst. She'd spent four of the most awful weeks of her life trying to get over him. Yet here she was, lying in his bed, back to square one…at best.

Desperate to deny the reality of it, she shook her head again, then moved her arm away from her face, opened her eyes and groaned once more.

If only she'd had some warning that he was coming, she could have gotten in her car and gone away. Although, considering the zombielike state she'd been in lately, she probably wouldn't have made it very far before she ran off the road.

What she really should have done was make some effort to

keep track of time. Then she wouldn't have forgotten her appointment with Dr. Wells. Or at the very least, she should have returned one of Will's calls. Then he wouldn't have worried about her. But she hadn't felt up to talking to him. Not when there was a good chance that she'd break down completely in midreassurance. That would have definitely defeated her purpose.

To be honest, she hadn't felt up to much of anything but sitting alone in her house and crying, even though she'd known that hadn't been wise. She'd been doing better the past week, though. Really, she *had.* She'd made more of an effort to eat and she'd been sleeping a few hours each night. She'd even tried to do some of the reading for the new classes she was scheduled to teach in the fall.

Surely she would have pulled herself out of her blue funk in another week or so. She'd have gotten herself together and gone on with her life just as she'd always done. Time had healed her wounds in the past. And with every day, every week and month that went by, she'd have found it easier to accept the things she couldn't have and eventually begin to enjoy those that she could again. In fact, she'd been very close to that point.

But then she'd opened her front door yesterday morning, and there was Will, standing on her porch. It had been all she could do to keep from flinging herself into his arms. And as she'd met his cool, steady gaze, she'd realized that she was no closer to getting over him than she'd been four weeks ago. Otherwise, she'd have slammed the door in his face.

Instead, she'd let him into her house. Then she'd gotten dressed as docilely as a little lamb, packed a bag and allowed him to drive her to Houston. Oh, she'd put up a token bit of resistance, but nothing like what she could have done if she'd honestly tried, even in her somewhat weary state of mind. No matter how she wished she could convince herself to the contrary, she'd wanted nothing more than to be with him for however long she could, and damn the consequences.

Now that she'd awakened in his bed, however, she was having some serious second thoughts, probably thanks to the best night's sleep she'd had in a month. Yet in all honesty, she couldn't say she wanted to go back to her solitary existence any more than she wanted to end up under a bus.

She'd meant it when she'd told Will she wasn't suicidal. She'd just been sad and lonely until…yesterday. Then she'd been angry and uncertain and even a little afraid. But she'd also been filled with the kind of joy she only experienced when she was with Will. However, as for today…

Tess shoved the blankets back and sat up, then eyed herself with amusement. She'd been so out of it when they'd arrived at the apartment that she hadn't bothered to put on the nightgown she'd packed before crawling into bed. Thank goodness Will had been gentleman enough to sleep on the sofa, or she might have found herself in a compromising position.

Although, she couldn't say she'd have honestly minded. She'd loved sleeping in his arms that night at the hospital. If he'd climbed into bed with her last night, she would have gladly curled as close as she could to him, even in her sleep. And if he'd wanted to make love with her? She'd have done that gladly, too. Because no matter how she tried to tell herself differently, she knew that she loved him. And regardless of what happened in the future, she always would.

But she wasn't going to think too far ahead right now. Now she just wanted to be with him for however long she could. And when the time came for them to go their separate ways, as it surely would, she'd find the courage to accept it and get on with her life again.

No more weeping and sighing for her. She'd done enough of that to last a lifetime. There wasn't going to be any happily-ever-after for them. She'd known that all along. But that didn't mean she couldn't have today and perhaps a few tomorrows with him. Nor did it mean that she had to remain…aloof while they were together. She'd tried that already because she hadn't wanted to be hurt, and she'd been hurt anyway. But not anymore. She planned to take each day as it came, savoring every moment she spent with him and allowing what would be…to be.

As her stomach growled again, she glanced at the clock on

the nightstand. It was almost nine o'clock, which meant that she'd slept at least fifteen hours. And it had been almost twenty-four hours since she'd last eaten.

"Time to get your lazy butt out of bed, Tess," she advised herself softly.

Somewhere beyond the closed bedroom door, Will was waiting for her, and that thought alone was enough to send her spirits soaring.

She took a quick shower in the adjoining bathroom, then dressed in a pair of white shorts and a kelly green T-shirt. She didn't bother with makeup because she hadn't brought anything but a lipstick with her, and she left her hair to curl damply around her shoulders because she didn't feel like tying it back.

Ready at last, she took a deep, steadying breath, opened the door and ventured down the hallway toward the mouth-watering aromas that had originally awakened her. As she walked into the living room, she saw Will sprawled on the sofa, surrounded by the Sunday papers.

He saw her at almost the same instant and sat up quickly, offering her a tentative smile. "Hey, sleepyhead. I see you finally decided to rise and shine."

"Hey, yourself." Warmed by the welcome she saw in his eyes and heard in his voice, Tess smiled, too, any lingering doubts she'd had that he wanted her there disappearing completely. He was wearing the same jeans and shirt he'd had on the day before, and he hadn't bothered to shave yet. But to her he'd never looked better than he did right then. "I guess I was kind of tired. I…I hope I'm not keeping you from anything."

"Not a thing." He set aside the page he'd been reading and stood up. "How are you feeling?"

"Much better," she admitted. Then, remembering that she hadn't given him an easy time of it yesterday and knowing she owed him an apology, she continued quietly. "About yesterday… I'm really sorry I gave you so much grief. I was just surprised to see you, and I didn't want to cause you any more trouble."

"So does that mean you're not going to press kidnapping

charges against me after all?'' he asked, his eyes glinting with mischief.

Recalling the sarcastic words she'd spoken to him, Tess blushed as she lowered her gaze. ''That really was an unforgivable thing for me to say.''

''Not necessarily. I *was* throwing my weight around a bit. So, what do you say we call it even?''

''I say okay.'' She smiled as she met his gaze once more, then rolled her eyes in embarrassment when her stomach growled yet again.

''I hope that means you're hungry.''

''*Hungry* is putting it mildly,'' she admitted with a laugh.

''Then come and sit at the counter while I make you some waffles. I've got orange juice, milk and coffee, and there's some bacon warming in the oven, too.''

''Waffles? Homemade from scratch?'' she asked, eyeing the electric waffle iron and mixing bowl full of batter by the sink as she climbed onto a stool.

''But of course. They happen to be one of my specialties.'' He poured juice and coffee for her, then filled the waffle iron with batter and closed the lid.

''Sounds as if you like to cook.''

''I live alone, so it's either cook for myself or eat out. On my salary, I can't afford to go to a restaurant more than a few times a month, and Julie's only good for a free meal once a week, max, so...''

''I know what you mean,'' Tess admitted. She sipped at her coffee, enjoying the rich taste of it, then asked curiously, ''What are your other 'specialties'?''

''How about if I surprise you with a few of them over the next couple of weeks?''

''The next couple of weeks?'' Staring at him, she set her cup down slowly.

''Yeah, while we're down at the beach house,'' he answered as he slid a waffle onto a plate, added several strips of bacon, then set the plate in front of her along with a napkin, silverware and a small pitcher of syrup.

Tess knew she ought to voice some sort of protest. When

she'd decided to go with the flow, she'd thought they'd have no more than a day or two together, but two *weeks* at the beach.... Yet, no matter how much she wanted to insist that spending all that time together wouldn't be wise, she couldn't seem to get the words out her mouth.

"It'll be just the two of us," Will added nonchalantly, starting a second waffle.

"I...see."

"Of course, we can go somewhere else if you'd prefer. I'm open to suggestions."

"Oh, no. The beach house is...fine." Actually spending two weeks at the beach house with Will would be downright wonderful. But still...

"Does your sister know I'm going to be there with you?" Tess asked with very real concern.

She'd all but promised that she wouldn't see them again, and at the time, she'd meant Will, as well. And while it didn't sound as if she'd be spending any time with the Drakes, to some extent she *was* going back on her word, and that bothered her.

"I mentioned it last night when I talked to her about using the beach house," he admitted as he fixed a plate for himself.

"What did she say?"

"That I'm incorrigible, among other things."

"So she agrees with me and Mrs. Adler, huh?" Tess asked, smiling though she knew he wasn't exactly being straight with her.

They ate in companionable silence for a few minutes, then Tess gave in to her curiosity once again.

"You and Julie are pretty close, aren't you?"

"We have been," Will said. "But then she practically raised me after our mother died. I was about eight and Julie was sixteen. We were both devastated, but our father..." Will shrugged and shook his head. "He had a really hard time handling it. He went to work every day just like he'd always done. But when he came home, he ate whatever Julie had fixed for dinner, then he locked himself in the bedroom and listened to old records the rest of the night. He didn't play them loud enough to be a nuisance, but we could always hear the music in the background, even at one or two o'clock in the morning.

"Weekends he'd work on the yard or do odd jobs around the house, but he hardly said a word to us. And evenings, after dinner, he'd go back to his room and his records. If I hadn't had Julie to look after me..." Will shrugged again. "Guess I was just really lucky to have a sister like her."

More than he'd probably ever know, Tess thought as she recalled her own nightmarish childhood. If only she'd had a brother or sister to lean on, maybe she wouldn't have been so desperate for Bryan Harper to love her. But then she wouldn't have had Jonathan. Nor would she have ever met Will. Talk about fate...

But as fate would also have it, Will's sister saw her as a threat to what she held most dear. Jonathan was Julie's child in every way but one. Yet, no matter how anyone, including Will, tried to convince her that Tess would never "steal" the boy away, Tess couldn't help but get the feeling that Julie still feared she would. Which had to mean that she couldn't possibly want Tess anywhere near *anyone* in her family.

Of course, Will seemed to be having no problem ignoring his sister's wishes at the moment. But Tess had sense enough to know that wouldn't always be the case. Julie had meant too much to him for too long. He'd never allow Tess to come between them permanently. Nor would Tess herself.

But what could two weeks hurt? Will and she were both adults. They could enjoy each other's company, then go their separate ways. Other people did it all the time, didn't they?

"You really were lucky," she said at last. "Julie is a wonderful person, and so is Philip. I couldn't have chosen better parents for Jonathan."

"I'm glad you feel that way, especially after what Philip did."

"What do you mean?" she asked, frowning as she met Will's gaze.

"I tried to tell him how you felt about any kind of payment, but I guess he didn't believe me. I know he didn't intend to insult you by sending that check, though."

"You knew about the check, but let him send it anyway?" Tess asked, unable to hide her puzzlement.

"Actually I didn't know about it until I found it on your kitchen floor yesterday."

"I guess that was a silly thing to do with it, but I didn't want it. I *don't* want it," she said with utter conviction. What she'd done for Jonathan she'd done out of love, and she refused to have that love tainted in any way.

"Then I'll see that he gets it back."

"Please do."

She ate half of another waffle and two more pieces of bacon, then had a last cup of coffee while Will cleaned up the kitchen. After he finished, he went into the bedroom to take a shower. Left on her own, Tess curled up on the sofa and glanced through the papers as she waited for him.

He returned to the living room dressed in khaki shorts and a pale yellow T-shirt, carrying her overnight bag, as well as his. Telling her to stay put, he loaded the Blazer with the things he'd gotten together the night before, and by noon they were on their way.

The weather was typical of the Texas Gulf Coast in the summer—hot and humid with lots of sunshine—and the highway was packed with cars heading for the island. They stopped in town to buy groceries at the local supermarket, roaming up and down the aisles together, quibbling about this and that like an old married couple. Then they drove on to Pirate's Beach.

As they pulled up to the house, Tess saw that the storm shutters had been raised. With the sun glinting off the windows, the place looked even more charming than she remembered.

"Julie must have called ahead and had the caretaker get the house ready for us," Will said as they climbed the steps.

With the air conditioner humming away, the interior was already deliciously cool and inviting. Stepping through the French doors that opened off the first-floor deck, Tess smiled with pleasure as she eyed the old-fashioned white wicker furniture with green-and-white-striped cushions filling the living room. The house was as lovely inside as outside, and Tess had no doubt they'd have a wonderful time there together. Or at least she didn't until Will led her over to the second-floor staircase.

"You can have the master bedroom," he said. "There's an adjoining bath and a balcony with a couple of chaise longues. Since I'll be using one of the guest rooms downstairs, you'll have lots of privacy, too."

The room was lovely, and the view from the sliding glass doors truly breathtaking. Yet Tess felt nothing but dismay. She'd thought…

What? That he'd be sharing a room with her? But only lovers shared a room, and they *weren't* lovers. They were *friends,* and that's obviously how Will intended them to remain.

She shouldn't be surprised. He'd slept on the sofa last night, hadn't he? That should have been her first clue that he was merely looking after her again, just as he had at the hospital. And no wonder, after the way he'd found her yesterday. He'd probably brought her here only because he was afraid to leave her alone. And all the time she'd been thinking… Nothing more than a lot of romantic nonsense, she chided herself.

What a fool she'd been! What a silly, silly fool. While she'd been daydreaming about making love with him, all he'd really had in mind was a little…baby-sitting.

She ought to demand that he take her back to San Antonio. Better yet, she ought to call a taxi and get out of there on her own. But if she acted like a woman scorned, then he'd realize what *she'd* had in mind, wouldn't he? And she'd feel like even more of a ninny than she did already.

Overcome by an almost overwhelming sense of weariness, she sat on the edge of the bed and stared out the glass doors.

"Hey, what's wrong?" Will asked, setting her overnight bag on the floor, then coming to stand beside her. "Don't you like the room?"

"I love it. But I'm kind of…sleepy all of a sudden." Tess felt his hand on her hair, but she didn't look at him, afraid that he'd realize she was lying.

"Why don't you rest while I put the groceries away?"

"I think I will."

"Then, maybe later, when it cools off a bit, we can take a walk on the beach."

"Maybe..."

After he'd gone, she got up and closed the bedroom door. Then she returned to the bed, kicked off her moccasins and lay down atop the comforter.

As she again stared out the glass doors at the gently rolling waves, she thought about crying, then caught herself up short. If she'd learned anything the past few weeks, it was that crying did no good at all.

Back at Will's apartment, she'd vowed to savor every moment and allow what would be to be. And just because some of her desires weren't going to be fulfilled didn't mean she couldn't make the most of those that would. She'd always wanted to spend a couple of weeks at the beach, lazing in the sun and splashing in the surf. And that was exactly what she was going to do. As for Will...

As far as she was concerned, he could do whatever he wanted. She wasn't about to force herself on him in any way. She was perfectly capable of fending for herself, and it was past time she got back to doing just that.

When she went back to San Antonio two weeks from now, she intended to be as strong and independent as she'd ever been. She'd gotten along fine without Will Landon before, and she could do it again. She could and she *would*.

Chapter Nine

Will stood at the foot of the second-floor staircase, hands tucked in the back pockets of his cutoffs, gazing into the semi-darkness above. Two days had passed since he and Tess had arrived at the beach house, and so far, their time together hadn't gone exactly as he'd thought it would. Rather than spending one long, lazy hour after another with each other, they seemed to meet only at dinnertime. And then Tess couldn't seem to get away from him fast enough.

But why? When he'd mentioned going to the beach house Sunday morning, she'd seemed a bit hesitant at first, but she hadn't voiced any protest at all. Nor had she seemed upset after they'd talked about Julie and Philip. In fact, by the time they'd left his apartment, she'd appeared to be quite happy about the prospect of spending the next couple of weeks with him.

They'd made the drive down to the island without any problems that he could recall. She'd told him about the new classes she was preparing to teach in the fall, and he'd updated her on the Kaminski and Hodges cases. She'd been glad to hear that Eddie was now out of prison while Walter was awaiting trial at the Harris County jail. They'd even had a good time at the grocery store, discovering what each other liked and disliked as they wandered up and down the aisles, loading their cart.

To the best of his knowledge, things had been going really well until they'd arrived at the beach house. But then, between the time they'd walked through the French doors and the time he'd left her alone in the upstairs bedroom, something had happened. And for the life of him, he couldn't figure out what it was.

Nor could he understand why she seemed so intent on avoiding him. Not that she wasn't pleasant when they happened upon each other. But they'd met so infrequently over the past two days that he was finding it harder and harder to believe they were actually staying in the same house.

The past couple of mornings, she'd come down very early and gone out on her own to walk along the beach. By the time he'd pulled on some clothes and caught up with her, however, she'd claimed she was ready to go back in again. And the past couple of evenings, when he'd invited her to join him on the deck after dinner, she'd told him she preferred sitting on the balcony. Then she'd gone upstairs…alone.

He'd told himself that she probably just needed a little time to adjust to their being together in such intimate surroundings. But, damn it, they weren't actually *together* in any noticeable way at all. And if she kept acting as if he had the plague, they weren't going to be.

Keeping in mind what Dr. Wells had said to him, Will didn't want to push her into anything she might not really be ready for. Although he certainly didn't know how walking on the beach with him in the morning or enjoying a glass of wine on the deck with him in the evening would cause her any kind of upset.

Confused and frustrated, Will turned away from the staircase and paced to the French doors. For the past two days, the weather had been beautiful, but since early that morning, thunderheads had been building out over the gulf. According to the weather report he'd heard on the noon news, strong storms were predicted for late that afternoon, and were expected to continue well into tomorrow.

It was only two o'clock, and already dark clouds streaked with lightning roiled across the whitecapped water. The wind had picked up considerably, and the wave heights had doubled in the past hour, as well.

Aware that once the storm began in earnest, he'd be stuck inside for what could be quite a while, Will stepped out onto the deck. It hadn't started raining yet, and the lightning was far enough out not to be a danger. And to be honest, he actually kind of liked watching storms build over the gulf. Not that he was foolhardy. He and Tess would have been long gone if a hurricane had been in the forecast, but the storm heading their way wasn't going to be nearly that intense.

Standing by the railing with the cool wind ruffling his hair, Will wished he could figure out not only where he'd gone wrong with Tess, but how he could make things right between them once again. One thing for sure…they had to start spending some time together soon, or he'd never have a chance to convince her of how much she'd come to mean to him. He wanted her in every way a man could want a woman. But as long as she was determined to stay away from him, how could he let her know that?

Unfortunately he had a feeling the nasty weather wasn't going to help at all. She'd have even more of an excuse to hide out upstairs. Frowning, he glanced over his shoulder at the second-floor balcony. For one long moment, he considered climbing the stairs, cornering her up in her aerie and confronting her once and for all.

Finally, however, he turned back to the wind and the coming rain. If she truly wanted nothing to do with him, he'd rather wait a while longer to find out. For the time being, he'd prefer to hang on to his hope that they'd have a future together. That was why he'd brought her here in the first place and why he'd done his damnedest to be patient thus far.

He realized that he was going to have to tell her how he felt sooner or later. But he wasn't about to do it until he was ready for the worst. And since that wasn't the case yet, he might as well let it ride.

There would be time enough to talk to Tess tomorrow or the next day or the next. For now, however, he was going to stay where he was. Alone on the deck with the darkening sky lit by lightning and the rumble of thunder all around him, he was going to stand with the wind in his face and wait for the storm to break.

Arms crossed at her waist, Tess stood a few feet from the sliding glass doors in the bedroom, eyeing the dark clouds swirling over the water, her anxiety mounting steadily. As a streak of lightning flashed across the sky, followed by the mutter of distant thunder, she flinched and took a step back.

The storm heading inland was going to be a bad one, and that didn't bode well for her. Although she didn't mind run-of-the-mill rain showers, the addition of high winds, lightning and thunder had terrified her ever since her mother had—

Hugging herself tighter, she shook her head, refusing to let that particular thought take shape. She had to get ahold of herself, and she had to do it now. It had been years since she'd been so rattled by the mere threat of bad weather. But then it had also been years since she'd been caught in the midst of so much emotional turmoil.

Her vow to give Will a wide berth had been easier made than kept. Though she'd tried to be subtle, she knew her intentional avoidance had been all too obvious to him. She'd seen the hurt look in his eyes each time she'd made a lame excuse then run away.

Yet what else could she do? Tell him she was in love with him, then beg him to have his way with her and risk having him laugh in her face? Not that he'd be *that* cruel. But rejection was rejection, and she wasn't up to getting another dose of it just yet.

Lightning sizzled through the ominously blackening clouds, followed even more closely by now-booming thunder that sent a shiver racing up Tess's spine. Maybe if she closed the drapes she wouldn't feel quite so afraid. But somehow she couldn't seem to make herself move any closer to the glass doors. What if they flew open and she was sucked out into the maelstrom? Just like…just like—

"*No,*" she sobbed, squeezing her eyes shut as she tried desperately to block out the awful memories.

She'd never expected to be haunted by them again. In fact, for years now, through the worst weather, she'd always managed to hold them at bay. But today…

She couldn't make herself go anywhere near the glass doors. Nor could she stay up here alone any longer and hang on to her sanity. She had to go downstairs and she had to find Will. He would calm her fears and keep her safe just as he'd done at the hospital. She knew he would. She *did*…

Whirling around, she crossed the room and ran down the stairs, her bare feet gliding through the thick carpet. Pausing in the living room, she looked around wildly, suddenly aware that there weren't any lights on anywhere downstairs. What if he'd gone off somewhere without telling her?

"Oh, Will…" she murmured.

Her heart pounding, she raced into the little kitchen, then the back bedroom she knew he'd been using, but both rooms were empty.

He wasn't there, she thought as she returned to the living room. He *wasn't*—

Outside, lightning lit up the growing darkness again, and for just an instant, Tess saw him through the French doors. He was standing on the deck, arms braced against the railing, the wind ruffling his hair as he stared out across the open water. He hadn't left her after all. But what was he doing out there? Didn't he know…?

Her fingers clenched into fists, she forced herself to move toward the French doors. She had to tell him to come in before…before… She reached for the doorknob, but her hand trembled so badly she couldn't get a grip on it.

Oh, Will, please…

Seeming to sense her silent plea, he turned and met her gaze, then quickly crossed the deck. As she backed away, he flung the door open, then let it slam shut as he took her in his arms and held her close.

"Tess, what's wrong?" he murmured into her hair. "You look like you've seen a ghost."

She clung to him, shivering violently, unable to say a word. But he was there with her, and in a minute or two she'd be all right. Already the worst of her fear had begun to abate, though the awful memories still lingered.

"Tess, sweetheart, tell me what's wrong," Will insisted as he stroked her back soothingly.

"The storm..." She pressed her face against his shoulder, suddenly embarrassed by her childish behavior, yet unwilling to relinquish the shelter she'd found in his embrace. "It kind of scared me."

"*Kind of* scared you?" He scooped her into his arms and carried her over to the wicker sofa. Then, sitting down, he settled her on his lap. "You were downright *terrified* when I walked through that door, and you're still shaking like a leaf. And it's not *that* bad out there, at least not as storms go around here."

"I know," she admitted. "But I had sort of a bad experience once when I was a kid. And being alone in a strange place..." She curled closer to him as he tightened his hold on her. "I came downstairs, but I couldn't find you. Then I saw you standing outside and I just...panicked."

"Why?"

Tess shrugged and shook her head. She'd spent years putting the past behind her. But thanks to a few dark clouds and a little lightning and thunder, it had definitely caught up with her today. But still...

"Sometimes talking about what makes you afraid helps to put it into perspective," Will urged softly. "Trust me, Tess. It does." He bent his head and kissed her cheek, his lips brushing against her skin lightly yet lingeringly. "So what happened to make you so afraid of storms?"

She'd never trusted anyone more, Tess thought as she nestled even closer to him. And she knew if anyone could help her overcome her demons, it would be Will.

"My mother was an alcoholic," she began at last. Baring her soul had never come easily, but there were some things she couldn't keep bottled up inside her any longer. "I didn't realize it until I was older. For a long time, I just thought everybody's mother slept all afternoon, the same way I thought everybody's father cooked dinner, washed clothes and cleaned the house after going to work all day.

"When I started school, though, and went to my friends' houses, I began to understand that my mother was...different. I also found out that it was wiser not to invite anyone home with me, because I never knew how she'd act. Still it wasn't too bad. At least not when my father was there.

"But then, one night just after I'd had my tenth birthday, he didn't come home from work. By the time I realized something was wrong, my mother was already passed out cold, so she was no help. I waited up most of the night for him, then called his office in the morning. The receptionist put me through to him. I was so relieved..." she murmured.

"But not for long," Will said, resting his cheek against her hair.

"No, not for long. He told me that he couldn't live with my mother anymore, that he'd filed for divorce, and when he got settled somewhere, he'd come and get me. I waited and waited for him to call me, but he never did. Finally I called his office again. When the receptionist told me he'd gone to work for a company in Oklahoma, I realized I wasn't ever going to see him again."

"Oh, Tess—"

"My mother had been getting worse and worse," Tess continued. She appreciated Will's obvious sympathy, but more than anything, she wanted to be done with her story once and for all. "The more she drank, the more abusive she was, and she'd started going to bars and bringing men home with her. Anyway, the day I found out my father had left town without me, I went a little crazy.

"I told her it was her fault that he'd left, and she told me I could leave, too, if I didn't like it. She literally kicked me out of the house and locked the door. And she did it during a terrible storm...lightning and thunder, high winds and torrential rains. I pounded on the door, begging her to let me in, but she refused. I was too afraid to try to get to a friend's house. So I curled up under the bushes as close to the house as I could.

"She let me in the next morning, and I never mentioned her drinking to her again after that. In fact, I stayed out of her way as much as I could. She eventually had to sell our house. We moved into an apartment, and by the time I was in high school, we were living on welfare and food stamps. I worked part-time and took college prep courses. I thought that if I could save a little money, then win a college scholarship, I'd finally be able to get away from her.

"But then I met Bryan Harper..."

"Jonathan's father?" Will asked quietly, still soothing her with his gentle stroking.

"We worked on a science project together during our junior year in high school, and started dating after that. He didn't seem to mind that I was from the wrong side of the tracks. By the time we started our senior year, we were talking about getting married after graduation and going off to college together. I was madly in love with him, and I think he loved me, too.

"However, to make a long story short, I ended up pregnant. He wanted to marry me right away, but his parents had other ideas. They sent him out to California to live with relatives, then offered to pay me if I'd have an abortion. I told them to keep their money, and went to the Amberton Home instead.

"I knew I couldn't take care of a baby on my own. And I certainly couldn't have gone back home with him. So..." She sighed softly, sadly, then finished quietly. "I finished high school at Amberton, then worked two, sometimes three jobs to put myself through college. Three years ago I completed my Ph.D. and joined the faculty at St. Scholastica."

Outside, lightning flashed time and time again, thunder rolled continuously, and the wind lashed rain against the windows. But sitting there in Will's arms, Tess realized that she'd never be bothered by storms again. Confession truly had been good for her soul.

"I'm sorry, Tess," Will muttered at last, his voice husky. "So sorry you had to go through all that alone."

"Granted, I would have preferred a more normal home life, but some good did come out of the bad...like Jonathan. And I think I turned out all right, too. Didn't I?" she asked lightly, refusing to allow Will to feel sorry for her.

She'd had her fair share of hard knocks, and she'd made some mistakes, as well, but life went on. And all along, she'd done the best she could with what she'd had.

"As far as I'm concerned, Professor, you're one of the kindest, most courageous women I've ever met. You're also smart and funny, and damned pretty to boot," he added, sliding a finger under her chin and tilting her face up so that she met his gaze.

"Oh, Will," she murmured. Reaching up, she rested her hand along the curve of his cheek, and before she realized what she was doing, spoke her thoughts aloud. "I really *do* love you. I just wish—"

Suddenly aware of what she'd done, she started to draw her hand away, but he caught it in his, then turned and pressed his lips against her palm.

"Sometimes that's all it takes for wishes to come true," he said. "Especially if the feeling is mutual."

"Mutual?" She eyed him with confusion, her pulse fluttering.

"You don't know, do you?"

"Know what?"

"That I love you, too." He took her mouth in a long, slow, deep kiss. "But I have a really good idea how to remedy that," he added, his breath whispering against her skin as he nuzzled her neck, then nibbled at her earlobe.

"Oh, you do, do you?" Tess queried, slipping her arms around his neck as he raised his head and gazed at her again.

"Mmm, yes. I'd say a little show along with the tell ought to leave no doubt in your mind about how much you mean to me."

Smiling wickedly, he slid his hand under her T-shirt and brushed his thumb over her nipple ever so gently, sending a shaft of desire shooting through her. With a sigh of unutterable pleasure, Tess arched against him, glad that she hadn't bothered with a bra that morning.

"Oh, Will, that feels so…so good."

Not only good, but *right.* They'd been meant to love each other. Maybe not for always, but for now. And for Tess, *now* was all that mattered.

"*You* feel good, Tess," Will growled, taking her mouth again, a little more urgently than he had the first time.

Tilting her head to give him easier access, Tess opened her mouth for him, welcoming the rhythmic glide of his tongue against hers as she threaded her fingers through his shaggy hair.

Beyond the French doors, the storm continued to build, but she had no thought for anything other then the passion they shared. She wanted Will. She wanted him in the worst way. And as she shifted on his lap, she realized that he wanted her, too.

As if reading her mind, he raised his head again and eyed her with an intensity that sent a shiver of anticipation racing up her spine. A moment later, he stood, still holding her in his arms, and strode toward the back bedroom.

He set her on the bed he'd left unmade that morning, then crossed to the dresser and lit the small lamp atop it.

"All right?" he asked as he returned to the bed.

Smiling, she nodded.

"Good. Now, let's get you out of those clothes."

"What a wonderful idea." Standing, she tugged her T-shirt over her head as he unzipped her shorts, then slid them down her legs along with her panties.

"You, too," she added, wanting to feel his naked body close to hers.

But as she reached for the hem of his T-shirt, he caught her hands in his and held her arms wide, his eyes on the long, narrow scar slashing across her right side just below her breast.

"Oh, Tess…" he muttered, his voice oddly hoarse. "Sweetheart…"

"We can turn off the light if…if…" She'd gotten used to the scar, but maybe he found it unappealing.

"No," he said as he knelt in front of her, still holding her hands in his. "I want to see you when I make love to you." Ever so gently, he feathered his lips along the mark left by the surgery she'd had. "But I don't want to hurt you."

"Believe me, you're...not," she sighed as his shaggy hair brushed against her breast.

Letting go of her hands to grasp her hips, he trailed his lips over her body. As he moved lower, then lower still, she trembled with the need building deep within her.

"Will, please..." she begged softly, and felt him smile as he pressed his mouth against the most intimate part of her.

She cried out in surprise, bracing her hands on his shoulders as she melted under the heat of his soft, wet caress. Just as she was sure her legs would buckle under her, Will stood, then lifted her into his arms and laid her on the bed. Holding her gaze, he stripped out of his shorts and T-shirt, then stretched out beside her and gathered her into his arms.

"Tell me if I do anything to hurt you," he said, nuzzling her neck as his clever hands roved over her body, tantalizing her first here, then there, until he finally, gently teased her legs apart.

"You won't. I'm all healed...." she whispered, twisting under him as she slid her arms around his neck. "But I'm not...not using anything..." Much as she would have loved having Will's baby, she couldn't be anything less than honest with him.

"Not to worry." He kissed her briefly yet so thoroughly that he took her breath away. Then he rolled over, opened the drawer of the nightstand and took out several foil packets. After opening one, he turned back to her and held her close once again. "I'll protect you, Tess. Always," he vowed.

Wordlessly she threaded her fingers through his hair, pulled his head down and kissed him as he settled between her legs.

"I love you," he muttered, holding her gaze as he slowly, gently entered her.

"I love you...too." Lifting her hips, she welcomed him with a soft cry of delight. Then, wrapping her legs around him, she moved with him toward the fulfillment she craved from the bottom of her soul.

Sliding an arm under her, Will deepened his thrusts, taking her higher and higher, until she felt herself spinning out of control, her body convulsing in one shudder of ecstasy after another. A moment later, Will, too, found his release, calling her name as he arched back and sheathed himself in her one final time.

As they lay together afterward, Tess realized that she'd never been so well and truly loved in her life. Luxuriating in the afterglow of the intimacy she'd shared with Will, she listened to the storm raging on outside without experiencing even the slightest flicker of fear. As long as she was with Will, she knew she'd be all right. They had more than ten days of their two weeks together to share, and for the time being, she wasn't going to think any further ahead than that.

"Doing okay?" he asked, tangling his fingers in her hair and tipping her face up so that she met his gaze.

"Better than okay," she murmured, kissing the tip of his chin, then the side of his neck and the hollow at the base of his throat as she rubbed her palm against his chest, savoring the smoothness of his skin. "What about you?"

"You tell me." He took her hand in his and moved it down his body.

"Mmm, I think we're going to need another of those little foil packets real soon," she replied as she trailed her fingertips along the length of him, delighting in the strength of his renewed desire.

"I think you're right." Putting his hands on her hips, he lifted her up and settled her atop him. "But you tell me exactly when," he added, his eyes full of mischief as he gazed up at her.

Bending over him, she brushed her lips over him ever so lightly, starting with his mouth and slowly, *slowly* working her way down until *he* said *when.* Growling with frustration, he tumbled her onto her back again and claimed her with a possessiveness that left no doubt in her mind that she would always be his, whether they were together or…not.

* * *

They spent the rest of their two weeks together just as Will had hoped they would, getting to know each other a little better every day. And the more Will knew of Tess, the more his respect and admiration, as well as his love for her grew. She was one in a million, and he had no intention of ever letting her go. Not when he knew that she loved him, too.

Yet as the days passed, he couldn't help but sense that she was holding back a small part of herself. She'd trusted him with the most intimate details of her past, and on a day-to-day basis, she gladly accepted all the love he had to offer her. But as for the future...

Considering her past experiences with men, he couldn't really blame her for shying away from planning too far ahead. First her father, then Bryan Harper had abandoned her when the going got tough. And he had a feeling that somewhere deep inside her, Tess was already bracing herself for the moment when she expected him to do the same.

While she continued to willingly share bits and pieces of her past with him, honestly admitting to the hardships she'd endured as she fought to make a decent life for herself, each time he tried to talk about the future, she immediately changed the subject. He could have forced the issue, but he hadn't. They'd seemed to have time on their side, and rather than spending hour after hour arguing with her, he'd preferred to work on building a solid foundation upon which their relationship could grow.

But tomorrow he was taking her back to San Antonio, and there were some things he wanted to be sure she understood before then. Like the fact that he intended to spend the rest of his life with her, come hell or high water.

Since today was their last day at the beach house, Tess had insisted that they set the place to rights before they did anything else. So together they'd mopped and vacuumed and dusted, washed towels and changed the linens on the bed in the master bedroom.

Of course, they'd somehow ended up rolling around on the bed, laughing and making love with half the sheets on the floor. But then they'd done a lot of that over the past couple of weeks, which only reinforced Will's belief that he'd never get enough of her no matter how long he lived.

They had splashed in the surf for a while in the afternoon, took a long, leisurely shower together, then grilled chicken for dinner. And now, with the sun sinking into the far horizon, they were taking a last walk along the beach, the breeze ruffling their hair, the hard-packed sand cool and wet beneath their bare feet.

As he glanced at Tess, she looked up at him and smiled so sweetly yet so sadly that he wanted to pull her into his arms and hold her close. But they had to talk tonight, and now was as good a time as any. If he allowed himself to get sidetracked, he knew he'd be sorry in the long run.

"Did you have a good time here?" he asked, threading his fingers through hers as he nonchalantly gazed off into the distance.

"The time of my life." She leaned close to him and rested her head against his shoulder for an instant as they continued walking, then straightened again. "Thanks, Will. I'll...I'll never forget it."

"Some good memories to replace the bad, huh?"

"Yes..."

"And just the first of many, many more," he added, watching her out of the corner of his eye.

She didn't say anything, but he saw her frown as she turned her face away.

"I've been doing some thinking...." he added, bracing himself for the resistance he knew would be forthcoming.

"Always a bad sign," she replied lightly, the too-bright smile dragging at the corners of her mouth not quite making it all the way to her pale eyes.

"Hey, this is important. So cut me a little slack," he said, only half-teasingly. "I made a few calls earlier in the week. The Bexar County district attorney's office is looking for an experienced investigator, and I'd like to apply for the job. But first I want to know if I'm correct in assuming that you'd like to stay in San Antonio. From what you've said, I know you enjoy teaching at St. Scholastica. And I just—"

"What *are* you talking about?" Tess demanded, stopping short, then turning to face him, something very akin to fear in her eyes. "Of course I want to stay in San Antonio and continue teaching at St. Scholastica. But that's no reason for you to consider quitting your job and moving away from Houston."

"It is if we're going to get married and have a family." He reached out and trailed his fingertips along the curve of her cheek. "After the past couple of weeks, you've got to know how much I love you, Tess. And while long-distance relationships may work for some couples, that's not what I want for us."

"But the past couple of weeks were just a...just a...respite. You have a job, an apartment, and...and responsibilities to your family...." She whirled away from him and headed back to the house, obviously as determined as ever to avoid discussing the possibility of their having any kind of future together.

"I can get another job, the lease on my apartment will be up in October anyway, and while I enjoy seeing Julie, Philip and Jonathan on a regular basis, I don't consider that a good-enough reason to stay in Houston. Not when you're in San Antonio," he replied, falling into step beside her.

"You say that now, but what about—" She shrugged and shook her head, refusing to look at him as she all but ran along the beach.

"What?" Will asked, catching her hand and pulling her around to face him.

"Your sister," Tess shot back, anguish in her eyes. "You told me that she was afraid I'd try to go after Jonathan in some way. She'll think—" Again she shook her head. "I know how much she means to you, Will. And I just don't want to come between you."

"Believe me, you *won't.* Sooner or later Julie's going to come to her senses. You've always had Jonathan's best interests at heart, and if she'd just set aside her fear for a moment, I think she'd finally realize that you've never been any threat to her and never will be."

"But what if she doesn't?"

"Then *she'll* be the loser." Aware of how desperately Tess needed his reassurance, Will pulled her into his arms and held her close as the twilight deepened around them. "I love you, Tess. I want to spend the rest of my life with you."

"Oh, Will..." She clung to him, her face pressed against his shoulder.

"I'm not saying it's going to be easy, even if Julie is on our side," he added. "One way or another, we're all going to have to deal with the fact that you're Jonathan's birth mother. As he gets older and wiser, he's going to start asking questions about you, whether you're a part of his life on a regular basis or not. But I'd like to believe that because we love each other as much as we do, we'll be able to make it through the rough spots together."

Leaning back in his arms, Tess gazed up at him, the slightest hint of hope evident in her eyes. Still she resisted. "I don't know, Will. I wish I could be as sure as you are, but..."

"Do you love me?"

"You know that I do."

"Then trust me, too. I'm not going to let you down. Not now and not ever."

Taking her hand, he led her up the steps of the beach house. Inside, he turned to her again and kissed her with a hunger that seemed only to intensify with each passing day.

Within moments they were lying naked on the bed in the guest room. After pausing just long enough to protect her, Will settled himself between her thighs. Then, threading his fingers through her hair, he held her gaze as he entered her with one long, slow, infinitely sweet caress. With a soft cry of delight, she opened herself to him, arching into his thrusts with a need that sent his spirits soaring.

They belonged to each other, and nothing would ever keep them apart. Not even her lingering doubts...

On the drive back to San Antonio the next day, Tess tried desperately to distance herself from Will. She didn't want to do it, but despite all that he'd said to her the night before, she knew that she should. He was so determined to believe that their love would be enough to keep them together. But hadn't she learned otherwise long ago? She'd loved her father, and she'd loved Bryan Harper, and both of them had said they loved *her.* Yet neither of them had come back to her. And she was afraid Will wouldn't come back to her, either.

Unfortunately, however, Will had other ideas. Each time she withdrew from him, he said or did something to remind her that he was there for her now and would be for always because of how much she meant to him. After a while, Tess gave up. She finally stopped fighting him and allowed herself to enjoy his company for the rest of the time they had left together.

When they arrived at her house, he brought in her overnight bag for her. Then he closed and locked her front door, lifted her into his arms and carried her back to her bedroom. Ignoring her halfhearted protests, he made dangerously delicious love to her until her senses reeled. And when he finally, reluctantly left her to return to Houston, he did so with the promise that he would not only call her every evening during the week, but would return again on the following Friday night.

Tess wanted to believe him. Really she did. But while she didn't doubt that he'd call her, she knew in her heart that she wouldn't see him over the weekend. He'd obviously forgotten that Saturday was Jonathan's tenth birthday. But she hadn't. With that in mind, she simply couldn't allow herself to think that Will would be anywhere but with his nephew on that very special day. And after staying away one weekend, Will would find it even easier to stay away the next and then the next.

As for her... She'd spend Saturday as she'd done for the past ten years, alone with her memories. At least, she'd have lots of good ones this year, she thought, holding the little silver-framed photograph up to the light as she sat on the edge of her wildly rumpled bed.

Smiling sadly, she set the photograph aside and switched off the lamp. Her summer hadn't turned out to be anything at all as she'd planned, but it had certainly been one she'd never forget. She'd shared a few precious moments with the child she had thought she would never see again. And she'd spent a few precious weeks with a kind and decent man who'd made her feel alive again. She couldn't have asked for more. And she wouldn't.

Lying down on the bed, she buried her face in her pillow and breathed in the scent of him. She would always love him, regardless. And she would miss him deeply in the long, lonely days ahead. But she had no regrets. No regrets at all.

The first few weeks were going to be hard. She had no doubt of that. But she absolutely refused to wallow in self-pity. Instead, she intended to get by as she always had, putting one foot in front of the other without looking back.

Chapter Ten

"Will, what are you doing here?" Julie asked, smiling with obvious pleasure as she opened the front door and gestured for him to come in. "I didn't think we'd see you until the party tomorrow."

Since he'd returned from Galveston, Will had talked to his sister just once to let her know that he was home again. He'd also thanked her for the use of the beach house, but other than that, he hadn't said too much to her, even when she'd asked about Tess. He'd gotten the feeling that all she'd really wanted was his reassurance that Tess was safely back in San Antonio, and that was all he'd told her.

The rest he'd preferred to say face-to-face, and that was exactly what he planned to do right now. Then he was going to hop in his Blazer and head for San Antonio to spend the weekend with Tess, just as he'd promised her.

"Where's Jonathan?" he asked, following Julie into the living room.

"Up in his room with a couple of friends. He's getting an early start on the festivities by having a sleep-over." Frowning, she eyed the shopping bag he was carrying as she sat on the sofa. "What's that?"

"According to your son, it's the absolutely, positively *best* video game in the whole world. And considering what I paid for it, I can only hope he's right," Will replied, smiling wryly as he set the bag on the coffee table, then wandered over to the front window.

"Don't you want to wait and give it to him at the party tomorrow?"

Unsure how the sister he'd loved for as long as he could remember would take what he had to say next, Will hesitated for several moments. But then he thought of Tess, waiting for him in San Antonio and, unless he was mistaken, wondering if he'd show up.

She'd sounded a little more tentative each evening when he'd talked to her. And he'd known that she would believe he'd come back to her only when she opened her front door and saw him standing there. But before he could go to her, he had to deal with Julie, and he had to do so as gently yet as firmly as he could. She meant a lot to him, and he didn't want her to be hurt. But from now on, Tess was going to come first with him, in the way a woman should with a man who truly loved her.

"I won't be at Jonathan's party tomorrow," he answered at last, turning to face her. "When I leave here, I'm driving to San Antonio to spend the weekend with Tess."

"But you were just with her for two weeks," Julie protested, fear evident in her eyes. "Do you *have* to see her again *this* weekend? It's Jonathan's birthday...." Her voice trailed off as she met his gaze, and suddenly she seemed to put two and two together. "That's why you're going over there, isn't it? *Because* it's his birthday."

"That's one of the reasons. To my knowledge, she's spent every August 17 alone, but that's not going to be the case tomorrow. In fact, if it's up to me, that won't be the case ever again. Which brings me to the other reason why I'm going to San Antonio. I'm planning on asking her to marry me."

"But you hardly know her." Julie stood and crossed the

room, turning her back on him as she paused in front of a table filled with family photographs. "Wouldn't it be better to wait until you're really sure that's what you want?"

"I know Tess as well as I know you, Julie. She's a wonderful person, strong and smart, as well as kind and generous. She doesn't have a spiteful bone in her body. And whether you want to believe it or not, she'd die before she'd ever do anything to hurt anyone, including you, your husband or your son," he replied, willing his sister to believe him. "As for waiting, why should I when I've never been more sure of anything than I am that I want her to be my wife?"

Still standing with her back to him, Julie fiddled with the framed photographs for a minute or two without saying anything. Yet Will knew better than to think he'd won her over. No matter what, that was going to take a while.

Still she wasn't arguing with what he'd said about Tess, and he couldn't help but feel that was a good sign. She knew that Tess had never asked for any concessions at all where the boy was concerned. And after already seeing how Tess had behaved with Jonathan on the two occasions when they'd met at the hospital, Julie also had to have begun to realize that she'd never say or do anything to upset him. Yet Will sensed that she still had grave reservations about what he intended to do.

"So...have you thought about where you'll...live?" she asked, glancing over her shoulder at him, her eyes bright with unshed tears. "Or will you have one of those modern commuter marriages, with Tess living in San Antonio and you living here in Houston?"

She said the last with such obvious hope that Will's heart ached for her. She didn't like what he was doing, but she wasn't trying to stand in his way. In fact, she actually seemed to be trying to understand.

"Tess should be offered tenure at St. Scholastica within the next couple of years, so she'd be foolish to give up her position on the faculty there, especially when so many other colleges and universities are cutting back. Since I want to be with her more than just weekends, I'll be moving to San Antonio at the end of the month."

"But what about *your* job?"

"I've already given my two weeks' notice at the D.A.'s office here," he admitted. "But I doubt I'll be out of work long. There's an opening for an investigator in the Bexar County D.A.'s office. I'm interviewing for it on Monday. If I get it, great. If not, I can always try to get on the San Antonio police force. Or maybe I'll go out on my own as a private investigator. I like the kind of work I do, and luckily I can do it just about anywhere."

"You're really serious about all this, aren't you?"

"More serious than I've ever been about anything."

"But...when will we see you?"

"You can see *us* whenever you want. San Antonio's just a three-hour drive from Houston. We can come here for a weekend, or vice versa. Or we can all meet at the beach house in Galveston. I'm not moving to the end of the earth, you know." He crossed to her and rested his hands on her shoulders. "I want us to be a family, Julie. *All* of us. We've been so blessed to have each other all these years. And you've been lucky enough to have Philip and Jonathan in your life, too. Now I'm going to have Tess. Be happy for me, for *us.* Please..." he murmured as he turned her to face him.

"I want to be, Will. Really I do. But what about Jonathan? What do we tell him a few years from now when he starts asking questions? I don't want him to be hurt. And I don't want him to end up hating...any of us."

"If he asks, we tell him the truth and hope that he understands. Tess didn't give him up for adoption because she didn't love him or want him. And she certainly didn't risk her life for him on a whim. I think Jonathan's going to be smart enough to realize that down the line.

"As I told Tess last week, we're all going to have to deal with her relationship to Jonathan both now and in the future. But we've got so much love going for us that I can't help but believe everything will work out just fine in the end."

"I hope so."

"Trust me, it will." Drawing her into his arms, he hugged her. "I'll call you when I get back Monday night, all right?"

"All right." She hesitated, then asked quietly, "What about the party tomorrow? Jonathan's going to wonder why you aren't there. What do you want me to tell him?"

"If we're going to avoid problems in the future, I think we're going to have to tell him the truth."

"Which is?"

"That I'm sorry I had to miss his party, but I just couldn't wait any longer to ask Tess to marry me."

"I don't think he'll mind, then. In fact, considering how often he's asked about her, I think he'll actually be glad," Julie admitted rather ruefully.

"If that doesn't bode well for the future, then nothing does," he replied, offering her an encouraging smile.

When she smiled back, his heart lightened considerably. With the love they shared, they *did* have a lot going for them. Now all he had to do was convince Tess of it, too.

"Give Jonathan a hug for me. Oh, and give this to Philip," Will added, pulling the check his brother-in-law had sent Tess from his wallet and handing it to Julie.

"But after all she did—" Julie began.

"What she did for Jonathan, she did out of love."

As if finally realizing that all Will had said about Tess was true, Julie nodded slowly as she took the check from him. "Tell her...tell her I'm looking forward to seeing her again...soon."

"I'll do that, Julie. With pleasure..."

He said goodbye to his sister, then climbed into his Blazer and headed for the freeway. In three hours max he'd be with Tess once more, and he could hardly wait. The five days they'd been apart had been five days too many, especially considering how determined she seemed to be to believe that she wasn't going to see him again.

Tonight, however, he was going to prove her wrong once and for all. Smiling, he slid his hand into his jacket pocket and fingered the small, black velvet jewelry box as he'd done off and on all day. Tonight he wasn't going to just talk about marriage. He was going to propose to her with all the formality that she deserved.

They probably wouldn't be able to get married for a couple

of weeks, and he'd have to spend most of that time in Houston. But he hoped that as long as she was wearing the ring he'd bought just for her, she'd no longer doubt how serious he was about their being together forever.

Like most married couples, they were going to have their fair share of problems, but he wanted her to know in her heart that he'd always be there for her. Always...

She should have called a friend and gone out to dinner and a movie, Tess chided herself as she gathered up her gardening tools, then lugged a plastic bag full of weeds over to the trash can. The yard work she'd insisted on doing could have easily been put off until tomorrow. And she wouldn't have suffered the anxiety of waiting for Will to call and say he wasn't coming.

But she hadn't been able to let go of that last little kernel of hope that had somehow lodged itself deep in her heart. In her head, she was prepared for the excuses he'd make, but in her heart, in her foolish, foolish heart, she still insisted on believing she might not have to hear them after all. And for the life her, she didn't know why.

She'd spent the entire week doing exactly what she'd vowed to do last Sunday night. For the most part, she'd gone on with her life as if the past nine weeks hadn't happened. With single-minded determination, she'd gotten up early each morning, dressed and gone into her office on campus. There she'd busied herself preparing for the start of the fall semester just after Labor Day, catching up on her reading and starting on her lesson plans for the two new classes she'd be teaching.

She'd also made the hour's drive to Austin one day to have lunch with Richard and do what she could to smooth his still slightly ruffled feathers. She never did tell him exactly what had happened while she was in Houston. But once she'd gotten him started on what he'd seen and done in Ireland, he no longer seemed to care enough to press her about it.

She'd also taken time to either write or call Lydia, Ina and Harry. All three had been good friends to her while she'd been in the hospital, and she had every intention of keeping in touch with them, too.

Evenings she'd spent at home, working on her flower beds, slowly but surely getting them back in shape after the neglect they'd suffered. She'd stayed outside as long as she could, but eventually she'd been forced to go into the house again. And then, in spite of her best intentions, she'd found herself waiting for Will to call.

Which he did, every night, just after nine o'clock as he'd promised. Just the sound of his voice sent her spirits soaring in a dangerous way. And as he'd told her about his day and she'd told him about hers, more often than not he'd managed to make her laugh.

Still each night she'd also found herself waiting for the moment when he would tell her that he'd changed his mind about the weekend. Only he never did. When she'd talked to him last night, she'd almost broached the subject herself, but she couldn't seem to find the right words to begin. In the end, she'd let it go, merely murmuring a halfhearted agreement when he told he'd see her tonight.

He'd said he would try to be there by nine, but Tess fully expected him to call before then. Yet she couldn't completely ignore the little shiver of anticipation that raced through her when she finally walked into her kitchen and glanced at the clock. It was already after eight o'clock, and she still had to take a shower. Although why she suddenly felt as if she had to hurry she had no idea. What difference would her state of personal hygiene make when all she planned to do was answer the telephone?

Still she showered in record time, pulled on a clean pair of shorts and a T-shirt and left her hair curling loosely around her shoulders, the whole time mentally chastising herself for her foolishness.

Hadn't she learned the hard way that men—

The peal of the doorbell echoed through her quiet house, startling her out of her reverie. Eyeing the little alarm clock on her nightstand, she saw that it was just past eight-thirty. Must be Susan, she told herself as she padded barefoot down the hallway, her pulse pounding. Just Susan…

Her hand trembling just a little, she opened the door, then uttered a soft, wordless cry.

"Well, Professor, aren't you going to invite me in?" Will asked, his voice full of teasing laughter.

For several long moments, Tess could do nothing but stare at him. He was dressed almost exactly as he'd been the first time she'd seen him, only his tie was slightly askew. He'd obviously come straight from work, and even then he must have broken the speed limit or he'd never have arrived so early.

Despite all her doubts, he'd kept his promise to her. He'd not only chosen to be with her, but he'd done so at a time when she wasn't the only one who needed him. And looking back, she realized that tonight wasn't the first time he'd done that. She remembered all the hours he'd spent with her at the hospital and the days they'd been together in Galveston, and she knew that the only foolish thing she'd done was to doubt him. But that was something she'd never do again.

All along he'd believed that their love for each other was enough to see them through, and finally she was ready to believe it, too. They could share each other's successes and soothe each other's hurts. They could have a future together and, if he wanted, a family.

"Will, I'm so glad you're here," she murmured as she stepped into his arms.

He kissed her as if they'd been apart for years instead of days, then swept her into his arms and headed back to her bedroom.

"I swore I was going to behave myself," he growled as he tossed her on the bed and tore off his jacket.

"Why on earth would you want to do that?" she asked, smiling seductively as she wriggled out of her shorts.

"I thought it might be nice for a change."

"Mmm, *this* is what's nice," she cooed, bending over him as he stretched out beside her and feathering her lips down his body.

"Ah, Tess, keep that up and I'm going to turn you every which way but loose."

"I do declare, you make the most wonderful promises, Mr. Landon...."

"And I keep them, too," he muttered, hauling her up so that he could look her in the eye. "Every last one of them."

"I know," Tess replied, smiling as she put her arms around his neck and pulled him closer for a kiss. "I know...."

Sometime later, as they nestled together on the bed, their bodies slowly cooling, Will smoothed a hand over her hair.

"You didn't think I would be here this weekend, did you?" he asked.

"No."

"Why not?"

"Tomorrow's Jonathan's birthday. I just assumed you'd want to be with him and...his parents."

"You thought I'd leave you alone, knowing how you felt about him?"

"I didn't know what to think. I've been alone so long, I guess I just took for granted that's the way it would always end up being for me."

"Well, I've got news for you, sweetheart. You're never going to be alone again on Jonathan's birthday or any other day. I'm going to be right here with you." Rolling away from her for a moment, he picked his jacket up off the floor and took a small, square box from one of the pockets.

"I meant to do this right—you sitting in a chair and me on one knee in front of you..."

"Sounds interesting..."

"And here I used to think you were shy." He bent his head and kissed her, then took her left hand in his. "Anyway, I'm not getting out of this bed, at least not for a while yet, so..." He slipped the diamond solitaire onto her ring finger. "Will you marry me, Tess?"

She gazed at the dazzling, emerald-cut diamond and thought of all that had happened in her reasonably short life, balancing the pain and humiliation she'd suffered in the past with the hope and joy she'd found with Will. And she knew that with a little trust added to her love for him, happiness would be hers forever.

"Oh, yes…I will…."

Three weeks later, on the first Saturday in September, Will stood beside Tess in the vestibule of the chapel on the grounds of the St. Scholastica campus. Hands tucked in the pockets of his suit pants, he stared out the open doorway at the long driveway curving down to the street as he barely restrained the urge to pace.

Behind them, the interior of the chapel glowed with candlelight. Fresh flowers decorated the small altar, and almost all the pews were filled with their assorted friends. Ina was there along with Lydia and Harry, who were now a couple. So was Susan Wylie and her family, several of Tess's friends on the faculty and her graduate assistants. Some of Will's friends from HPD and the D.A.'s office were there, as well. But the three people he'd most wanted to be at his wedding—aside from Tess, of course—hadn't arrived yet. And there was no guarantee that they would.

"They'll be here. I know they will," Tess murmured, resting a hand on his arm.

"How can you be so sure?" he asked, gazing down at her, his heart aching with love.

She looked so very beautiful. Her old-fashioned cream silk dress, with its high neck, short sleeves, fitted bodice and long, pleated skirt just skimming her ankles suited her perfectly, as did the tiny pearls she'd braided into her hair in lieu of a veil. Soon, very soon she was going to be his wife, and more than anything, he wanted her to be happy.

"You've made a believer out of me," she said, smiling up at him in a way that never failed to make his pulse pound.

"But we can't keep our guests waiting much longer," he reminded her, returning her smile as he covered her hand with his.

They'd delayed almost ten minutes already, and off to one side, her friend Richard, who was supposed to give her away, and the minister who was supposed to officiate at the ceremony eyed them with growing concern.

"We'll wait," Tess insisted.

"She never actually said they'd come...."

"But she never actually said they wouldn't, either. She loves you, Will, and she's going to be here."

"But—"

"We'll wait," she said.

"I never knew you were such a bossy little thing," he mused softly.

"And you thought I was shy, too. Remember?" she teased, reminding him of the night he'd proposed in such a way that he felt himself blushing. "So, want to call the whole thing off?"

"Not on your—"

"There they are," she interrupted, her hand tightening on his arm.

The dark blue BMW roared up the drive, then screeched to a halt just behind Will's Blazer. A moment later, Julie, Philip and Jonathan hurried up the steps and through the open doorway, pausing only when they saw Tess and Will standing off to one side.

"I'm sorry we're late...so sorry," Julie said, her eyes glittering with tears. "There was a bad accident on the freeway, and then we got lost, and I thought...I thought..."

"We'd never have started without you," Tess assured her, closing the distance between them and hugging her soon-to-be sister-in-law.

"Thank you," Julie murmured as she stepped back and met Tess's gaze. "You look lovely." She glanced at her brother. "You're a lucky man, Will, a very lucky man."

"Can I call you Aunt Tess now?" Jonathan asked, moving to stand beside his mother.

"I'd be honored if you did," Tess replied, blinking back tears of her own. He looked just as healthy and happy as she'd hoped he would.

"What about a hug? Can I have one, too?"

"Oh, yes..." She held the boy close for several joyful moments, then released him and turned back to Julie and Philip. "There's a special place reserved for all of you up front."

"We're on our way," Philip replied, taking Julie and Jonathan by the hand and heading up the aisle.

As the minister followed them, Richard nodded to Tess, letting her know he was ready whenever she was, then moved just inside the chapel to give her and Will a last moment or two of privacy.

Smiling, Tess reached for her bouquet as she met Will's gaze.

"Don't say it," he warned, a hint of laughter in his husky voice.

"Say what?" she asked innocently.

"I told you so."

"I won't if you won't," she vowed.

"Fair enough." He curved his palm against her cheek. "Now, what do you say we get this show on the road, Professor?"

"I'd say you have the most wonderful ideas, Mr. Landon. Which is only one of the many reasons why I love you."

* * * * *